GUARDIAN IN THE KEYS
A LOGAN DODGE ADVENTURE

FLORIDA KEYS
ADVENTURE SERIES
VOLUME 16

Copyright © 2022 by Matthew Rief
All rights reserved.

No part of this book may be reproduced in any form or by any electronic or mechanical means, including information storage and retrieval systems, without written permission from the author, except for the use of brief quotations in a book review.

This book is a work of fiction. Names, characters, businesses, places, events and incidents are either the products of the author's imagination or used in a fictitious manner. Any resemblance to actual persons, living or dead, or actual events is purely coincidental.

Edited by Eliza Dee, Clio Editing Services
Proofread by Donna Rich and Nancy Brown (Redline Proofreading and Editing)

LOGAN DODGE ADVENTURES

Gold in the Keys
Hunted in the Keys
Revenge in the Keys
Betrayed in the Keys
Redemption in the Keys
Corruption in the Keys
Predator in the Keys
Legend in the Keys
Abducted in the Keys
Showdown in the Keys
Avenged in the Keys
Broken in the Keys
Payback in the Keys
Condemned in the Keys
Voyage in the Keys
Guardian in the Keys
Menace in the Keys

JASON WAKE NOVELS

Caribbean Wake
Surging Wake
Relentless Wake
Turbulent Wake
Furious Wake
Perilous Wake

Join the Adventure!

Sign up for my newsletter to receive updates on upcoming books on my website:

matthewrief.com

ONE

Manhattan
Winter 2012

Lily Cohen didn't realize that something was wrong when she climbed into bed and turned off the lights. The twenty-two-year-old supermodel felt safe in her 26th floor apartment. The door was locked and deadbolted. The unit quiet and empty and dark.

But when her eyes snapped open just after 2 a.m., a chilling realization washed over her.

She wasn't alone.

Someone was there.

She sat up slightly, then froze as her eyes made out a dark figure standing at the foot of her bed. She became paralyzed with fear. Terror-struck. Her heart pounding harder than she knew it could.

Then the figure moved. A slow raise of an arm, and a hand gripping a suppressed pistol aimed right at her.

"Good morning," the man said. He had a hard,

rough, terrifying voice. Cold and calm. Borderline casual. The man swiveled his weapon. "On your feet, Miss Cohen."

Lily swallowed hard. She couldn't move. Nothing but a tremble in her hands.

He ordered her up again while stepping closer.

She brushed aside the covers and slid out. Nearly six feet tall and stunningly beautiful, Lily wore pajama pants and a tank top, and had her blond hair tied back.

"Into the living room," the man said, gesturing with his handgun again.

He followed her out, the pistol aimed at her head. City lights bled in through big windows, illuminating a couch and table and chairs. She glanced back and got a good look at the terrifying intruder for the first time. He was dressed all in black. Wore coverings over his shoes. Gloves over his hands. And a ski mask.

"The kitchen," he said.

Lily nearly had a heart attack as she spotted another dark, tall figure standing stoically behind her dining table. The second man had a shoulder bag open and was positioning a plastic bag full of pills onto the glass surface. He slid back a chair, then disappeared into her bedroom.

The first man prodded her around a countertop and into the kitchen.

"Grab that bottle of Grey Goose from the cupboard," he said. "And a tumbler."

She swallowed and did as he said, moving in a daze as she opened a cabinet, then grabbed and set both items on the counter.

"Fill the glass and drink it."

Lily unscrewed the cap with shaky hands and spilled as she topped off the glass. Breathing fast, she eyed the masked man once more. He kept his weapon steady, aimed two feet in front of her nose. She raised the spirit and splashed it all down her throat. Made a face as it burned in her stomach.

"Again," the man said.

She continued filling and chugging until she'd downed four glasses in all. Then the man gestured her toward the nearby dining table and the seat that was already pulled back.

"Good. Now, leave the glass and bottle on the counter and have a seat."

Her terror heightened, but the rapid, intense jolt of alcohol had made her dizzy and distant. She paused, so the man gave her a soft prod with the barrel of his weapon. Lily stepped forward like a zombie. She felt halfway into a dream as she lumbered toward the chair and plopped into it.

The man moved in front of her. Tapped his weapon against the thick glass beside the bag of round light blue pills. "Now, you're gonna chew and swallow three of these."

She lost her breath, then shook faster.

"I… I won't," she said, uttering words for the first time since she'd awoken into the worst nightmare of her life.

The man stood silent, then stepped closer, keeping his weapon aimed right at her.

"You have two choices, Miss Cohen," he said, his voice still eerily casual. "Either do as I say, or after my colleague and I are finished with you, we'll drive up north to Hartford. Pay a visit to your parents at forty-three Providence Street." She gasped, bowing her head from the weight of the man's words. "Then we'll head to Cincinnati. Visit your brother Caleb's home and introduce ourselves to him and his family."

Lily gasped again and nearly fell out of her chair. Tears welled up and streaked down her face.

"Decide, Miss Cohen," the man said, tapping the barrel of his weapon against the side of her head. "I don't have all night."

With a trembling hand, Lily did as she was ordered.

She grabbed the plastic bag and removed three of the pills. Cupped them in her right hand and stared at the little tablets. Then she closed her eyes and threw them into her mouth, chomping and swallowing them.

The effects were nearly instant.

She leaned back and looked skyward. Her pupils shrunk. Her breathing slowed. And her head rotated lazily.

Then she faded out of consciousness. Her mouth opened and her eyes closed, and she sank back into her chair. Her head fell forward as she went limp, and her breathing slowed even more.

The killer stood perfectly still, watching until it was over. Then he surveyed Lily's lifeless body before casually sliding out his phone. He checked the time, then made a call. It was answered on the first ring and the masked man spoke first. Just two words.

"It's done."

There was a short pause, then a confident, middle-aged voice said. "One more."

The line went dead. The man dropped the phone

back into his pocket, then he and his partner for the evening made sure the scene was spotless of their presence before heading for the door.

One more.

But the next target was different.

The final hit required deeper planning, more careful execution, and a completely different approach. There were more variables involved and things needed to be buttoned up. Perfect and precise. There was no room for error.

And failure was out of the question.

There were reputations at stake. Careers. Powerful people and lots of money. Everything needed to be perfect, and it would be. Their boss always ensured it. He'd been keeping their operation untarnished for nearly thirty years and he'd do it again.

The hitman stopped at the door. Turned and took one more long gaze at Lily's dead body.

Then a confident smile formed on his lips as he reached for the handle.

TWO

Florida Keys
Three Weeks Later

Dawn burned gloriously on the blue horizon, blooming in vibrant hues of orange and red and casting radiant sparkles across the sea.

I stepped barefoot to the edge of the swim platform of *Dodging Bullets II*, my forty-eight-foot Baia Flash, mug of freshly brewed coffee in hand as I watched Mother Nature's display. Taking a sip, I relished the warm caffeinated beverage, then set the mug on the edge of the sunbed.

I reached high overhead, stretching all of my six-foot-two frame. Leaning back, I performed a series of slow shoulder rotations. I was in for a long day.

A momentous day.

I heard footsteps at my back and turned as my best friend, Jack, emerged from below deck. He wore only boardshorts, and his curly blond hair was its usual unkempt mess.

He stopped at the top step, gazing out over the tropical paradise his ancestors had called home for generations.

"Good day for a duel," he said in a slow, epic voice.

I nodded confidently. "It's not too late to back out, you know. Save yourself the embarrassment."

"We'll see who's embarrassed come nightfall. I'd start doing some vocal exercises if I were you. Might as well strive to at least lose with some dignity."

My beach bum friend was usually the most laid-back guy in any port. But every year, on the fateful last day of March, Jack's habitual smile lost steam. March 31 marks the last day of lobster season in the Florida Keys, and the beginning of what Jack often dubs "four months of conchs wandering the desert, on the verge of an identity crisis." Most islanders aren't quite as dramatic about it as Jack.

But he and I had developed a source of solace in the heartbreak. A lobster hangover remedy in the form of a little friendly competition, the rules of which were simple. Three dive sites. Six lobsters apiece. The man with the greatest total weight by sundown was crowned Lord of the Hunt.

In addition to having to buy rounds of drinks for patrons at our favorite local watering hole, Salty Pete's, the loser also had to get on stage and sing a karaoke song of the winner's choosing. And then there was the year of bragging rights, and when it comes to two competitive best friends going head to head, the stakes don't get any higher than that.

The three sites were chosen from Jack's fabled "Key to the Keys," a treasure trove of knowledge

Jack's family had assembled over the years. One that had been passed down from generation to generation and polished and amended as new locations were discovered and new technologies made their way into the fray.

In essence, it was a map of all the best sites in the Middle and Lower Keys to catch lobster. They were ranked on quality and degree of secrecy, and we often started out the season at the most popular and well-known lobster honey holes and worked our way to the more secret ones as the year progressed and bug inventory dwindled.

And on the final day of the year, Jack and I held the competition, continuing the tradition. Freediving the three most secretive and abundant spots in the lower islands. Locations few people, even conchs, knew about.

After a light breakfast, we grabbed our masks, snorkels, fins, and weight belts, along with gloves, nets, and tickle sticks. Tools of the trade.

Gazing out over the miles of turquoise waters surrounding us, I sucked a deep breath of fresh morning air into my lungs. It was a near-perfect day to be out on the water. Barely a breath of wind, and visibility nearing a hundred feet.

Our first site of the day was a place we called the Lobster's Garden, an abundant section of reef near Pelican Shoal, roughly six miles southeast of Boca Chica Key, the only of the three legendary honey holes located on the Atlantic side of the archipelago.

We sat on the edge of the swim platform and donned our masks and fins.

"You gonna fight clean this year?" I said, referring

to the previous year, when Jack had put a cricket in my snorkel while my head had been down scouring the seafloor.

He chuckled. "Hey, that's part of the fun."

He patted me on the back, then slipped into the water. I grinned and looked around one more time before following him. All jokes aside, I couldn't think of a better way to spend a day.

Stepping off a boat and into warm, translucent water is one of my favorite sensations on Earth. A swift awakening of the senses. The sounds of the surface vanish in an instant, replaced by the churning of bubbles, and then a soothing stillness—the underwater world appearing through the dancing froth in a vibrant array of colors and shapes and life.

I relaxed and let my body rise gently back to the surface. Keeping my eyes trained down, I blew a strong gust of air, blasting the water from my snorkel, then took slow, rhythmic breaths.

From the surface, it was nearly impossible to spot the lines of crevices intermixed amongst the coral twenty feet below us. That was what made the Garden such a great spot.

I sucked in a breath and dove down with smooth strokes, gliding over the rocks and coral heads and peeking under the ledges. I spotted a nice tucked-away cave up ahead with a good dozen antennae barely poking out of it. I finned closer to engage, but Jack beat me to it, the wiry conch sweeping in out of nowhere and cutting me off as he kicked straight for the little assemblage of crustaceans.

And the hunt begins.

I chuckled a few bubbles and hung back, letting

him have it. Deciding to survey more of the site before pulling the trigger.

I regretted conceding the spot less than a minute later when I spotted Jack kicking for the surface with a whopper of a lobster firm in his grasp. His eyes were locked onto me. And his grin was broad as the horizon. The look sent a clear message.

Game on.

It wasn't long before I spotted another lobster lair. Taking a deep breath, I descended with big cycles of my freediving fins, then grabbed a jagged algae-coated rock, approaching the den slowly and peeking inside.

I picked out the biggest of the bunch. Positioning my net near the opening, I reached in with my tickle stick and gave the bug's backside a little nudge. The crustacean turned and rocketed out of the grotto in a blur, flashing into rays of sunlight and whooshing right into the cross-connecting fibers of my net.

I reached in with a gloved hand, grabbed hold of his spine, then stuffed him into my catch bag. He wasn't a monster by any means, but clearly well above legal size. After diving down and catching another one, I deposited them in the Baia's livewell, then went right back at it.

After two hours of scouring the reefs and crevices, flying over the lively seafloor, and taking intermittent breaks, we each had our two biggest.

"Looks like the rightful king's about to reclaim his throne," Jack said after adding up the weights. "Beat you by a cool four ounces. What can I say, it's my lucky day."

I laughed as I snagged a towel and dried off. "It's

always your lucky day."

He spread his arms out wide. "Yeah. This is our backyard. We're the two luckiest men alive."

I eyed our catch, then shielded the sun as I gazed to the north. "The day is still young."

"Yes, it is. And I'm just getting warmed up, compadre."

We weighed anchor, fired up the Baia's twin 600-horsepower engines, and rocketed toward the second site. This one was twenty miles to the northeast, in an area just west of the Content Keys. The group of small, mostly uninhabited islands situated in the shallow waters of the Great White Heron National Wildlife Refuge were some of the most notorious for finding an abundance of large bugs. But our next destination was located in a tough-to-reach spot, with strong currents and sporadic sandbars.

The area was a secret among conchs, and over the years, Jack and his family had found the perfect spots among the waterways and nearby encroaching mangroves. The result was his second favorite honey hole in the Lower or Middle Keys.

The waters of the Atlantic side were calm, but they paled in comparison to the smoothness of the Gulf side. It was like cruising over glass.

Lobster were far more abundant in general on the Gulf side, but the surplus of crustaceans came with a cost. Navigating the extensive and ever-shifting network of shoals, cuts, islands, and reefs was not for the faint of heart or inexperienced sailors. Many a seasoned mariner had found themselves beached on a sandbar or their hulls scraped to pieces by shallow coral heads.

My luck shifted at the second site. In the shallows of the backcountry, gliding over clusters of cuts and thick patches of turtle grass, I managed to haul in some of the largest bugs I'd ever found. And though Jack had captured some impressive specimens as well, I edged him by a hair.

"Looks like it's all gonna come down to Cornucopia," Jack said as the time ran out on the second site.

I smiled. Our third and final site of the day, Cornucopia was a place that even most of the saltiest conchs believed to be a myth. Our own little tropical fish tank with more resident lobster per square foot of underwater real estate than anywhere I'd ever been.

I pulled myself out of the water and sat on the swim platform. Stretched my arms and grabbed the tips of my fins to stretch out my legs. We'd been at it for just over five hours. Diving, stalking, surfacing, repeat. While stretching, I felt a weird soreness near the back of my right shoulder.

"You doin' all right there, old-timer?" Jack laughed.

Just over a month earlier, I'd turned thirty-five. I still felt young, and I stuck to a vigorous workout regimen religiously, keeping my strength up to par and my body fat in single digits. But years of dangerous adventures, and the passage of time, were beginning to be noticeable. And not just in the numerous scars I'd collected throughout my life.

"I'm only three months older than you," I said as I came to my feet and toweled off.

"Yeah. And you always will be."

We relaxed for a bit, grilling up some freshly

fileted grouper along with shrimp kabobs and potatoes, blanketing everything in Southernmost Blend, a favorite seasoning of ours conjured up by the Key West Spice Company. Then we relaxed around the dinette, downing coconut water and savoring the succulent food while taking in the sights and catching our breath.

My phone buzzed on the table. I checked the screen and saw that I had an incoming call from my wife's sat phone.

"Hey, there's Lewis and Clark," I said, perking up. "How are my two favorite explorers?"

"We're just on a trail, Dad," my daughter, Scarlett, said.

"And I don't think Lewis and Clark ever explored Arizona," my wife added. "But we're good. Having lunch at Phantom Ranch."

I smiled, slightly envious. Most people's idea of a mother-daughter date probably involves a trip to the spa, dinner, and maybe a movie. But Angelina was a unique breed, and she and Scarlett had been planning a rim-to-rim hike of the Grand Canyon for months. With Scarlett on spring break, and with it being a great time of the year to make the long desert hike, they'd left the previous day and had hit the trail earlier that morning.

"This place is so beautiful," our enthusiastic daughter said, her voice full of life. "We're looking at part of the Colorado River right now while we eat. I can't believe how big this canyon is."

"I hope you're taking a lot of pictures. And I expect some epic stories when you return."

"Oh, we are," Scarlett said. "And we'll have

plenty." Before I could ask another question, she swiftly changed the subject. "You guys seen Jasmine Cruz? She's supposedly in Key West right now. I hope we make it back in time to see her."

"Who?" I said.

She laughed. "Of course you've never heard of her, Dad. She's only an international socialite, model, and movie star. She's like the most famous woman on the planet."

"Even I've heard of her, bro," Jack said with a chuckle. "Haven't you ever glanced at the magazines while in line at the grocery store?"

I shrugged. "I guess not."

"Well, get her autograph for me if you see her, all right, Uncle Jack?" Scarlett said.

"About a hundred thousand people visit Key West for spring break, so I wouldn't get your hopes up for us spotting her," Jack said. "But if we do, I'll be sure to."

"You surviving without us, babe?" Ange asked.

"Barely," I said.

"Today's the duel, right?" she said. "You guys playing fair this year?"

"So far," I said. "But we all know Jack's a pirate in disguise, so who knows."

He and my wife both laughed.

"You know what the best thing is about your little annual competition?" Ange said. "I win either way. I already talked to Pete, and he's got some new tracks to choose from for karaoke this year."

Jack and I exchanged glances. As if the stakes hadn't been high enough already.

We talked a couple minutes more, then said our I-love-yous and agreed to talk again that evening.

Setting my phone back on the table, I downed another shrimp, then leaned back and nursed my beer. I missed my family a lot, but it was nice having some time just us guys.

"Ange bringing up Pete reminds me," Jack said. "He invited us to go fishing tomorrow. Said it's been too long since the three of us went out and cast lines."

I laughed. "We went fishing with Pete last week."

"I guess that's too long in his book," he said with a chuckle. "Pete's been living on island time for sixty-something years."

Our conversation drifted aimlessly as it often did, then I brought up Jack's nephew, Isaac. The seventeen-year-old was a genuine brainiac. A real wunderkind when it came to computer coding. He'd been in college for a while, accepted early into an accelerated online program. But after that year, he was heading to the campus up north. Turning eighteen and moving out.

Jack leaned back. "It's weird. When my brother died years ago and his widow asked me if I could take Isaac in, I was scared as could be. I mean, you know me. I can barely take care of myself. So, I wasn't sure how I was going to take care of another human being. And Isaac and I couldn't be more different. We've had our fair share of headbutting over the years. But now… now I can't imagine the house without him." He tossed a potato wedge down the hatch, then added, "It's gonna be weird living alone again."

I leaned back, took a slow slip, then said, "You don't have to live alone." Before he could ask what I meant, I added, "You know, you and I were sitting in this exact spot a couple years ago when you asked me when I was gonna man up. Now it's my turn."

Jack laughed. "What do you mean?"

"Lauren's an amazing woman," I said, referring to Lauren Sweetin, his girlfriend of nearly two years.

"A fact if there ever was one," he said, smiling and leaning back and downing a swig of coconut water. I watched my old friend closely as his gaze drifted along the horizon, then came back to me. His eyes widened. "Oh. That's what you mean." He laughed. "Boy, I've been out in the sun too much today. Took me over a minute to hop onto that conga line of thought."

I chuckled, then said, "I'm sure you've thought about it."

"Of course I have. A woman like Sweetie? She's the whole package."

"But?" I said, figuring there had to be one in there somewhere.

"But I just... I just don't know if I'm cut out for marriage. I'm a pretty free spirit. Always have been. And I like that. I'm not sure I could anchor down."

I took a moment to think that one over. I pictured Ange, then geared up to get all sentimental. "The right person won't be an anchor. The right person will be an engine. And fuel. And a rudder and everything else. The right person will make you better—they'll make everything better."

He pressed his lips together, then nodded while gazing out over the island-riddled waters.

"A Navy SEAL and a philosopher?" he said.

I checked the time, then said, "And reigning Lord of the Hunt."

He laughed, then rose. Planted a foot on the transom and gazed out over our tropical playground. "Not for long. Let's get to Cornucopia. I've got a title to reclaim."

THREE

After the late lunch, we motored to the third and final site for the day. After a year of friendly trash talking, it would all come down to this.

We navigated twenty miles west, out of the Contents, past our island home hanging onto the end of US-1, and into a group of scattered uninhabited islands. Jack cranked up the stereo, blasting Bob Marley's "Bad Boys" as we closed in on the site in an act that had also become part of the long-standing tradition.

The area isn't particularly known for stellar lobstering, but we had an ace up our sleeve that stretched back nearly a hundred years.

It was Jack's great-great-grandfather who'd first stumbled upon the honey hole by accident. And as Jack often said, the coordinates of the trove were as valuable as anything his ancestors had ever passed down in their wills.

Cornucopia was tucked away between clusters of mangrove-infested islands, so navigating the narrow cuts and channels was nearly impossible if you hadn't done it before. And you needed to time the tides just right. From the outside, the cove was impossible to spot. And it was far too small for any pilot to attempt a water landing in a seaplane.

But the views inside were spectacular. Lively reefs swarming with all sorts of marine life. Beautiful shorelines. The place was especially beautiful around sunset, rays shining through the thick tangles of branches and leaves. It was a truly unique place in an island chain that offers some of the most spectacular scenery found anywhere in the world.

And a tucked-away corner on one side of the cove offered the best supply of lobster we'd found anywhere, not just in the Keys but in the world. It was the perfect location to wrap up a lobster season, and to wrap up the competition every year. And we'd always had it all to ourselves.

But as we weaved around the islands surrounding our secret little paradise, we got our first glimpse of the shallow, narrow channel that led into it and spotted a boat anchored right at the mouth.

"No way," Jack said, noticing the vessel the moment I did.

He grabbed a pair of binoculars from the dashboard as I eased our speed back to fifteen knots.

"It's Cali," Jack said. He let out a big breath and brushed back his hair. "Thank Neptune it's one of us. I thought this whole thing was blown."

I brought us down to an idle as we approached the familiar dive operator who ran charters out of Marathon. We often ran into Calihan Brooks during our trips out on the water, or at restaurants up and down the islands, but this was the first time we'd ever seen him near the mouth of Cornucopia.

Jack stood on the bow and waved at the friendly face.

"What brings you this far west, Cali?" Jack said. "You don't have enough honey holes in your neck of the islands?"

The short, round-bellied man wore a long-sleeve rash guard, a ball cap, and sunglasses. He stepped to the railing of his charter boat, then paused a beat, biting his lip.

"What's going on?" I said, his body language anything but normal.

Cali sighed. "I'm sorry, guys."

"Sorry for what?" Jack said.

He paused again, then looked toward the winding channel that led into the secret cove.

Jack planted his hands on his hips. "What did you do, man?"

"I'm sorry. It's just for a couple of hours. Then we'll all be out of here."

"What's going on, Cali?" I asked again. "Who's with you?"

"Just a teeny, tiny group of… out-of-towners."

Jack threw his hands in the air, acting like someone had just stabbed him in the back.

"They offered me a lot for this," Cali explained. "I mean a lot. More than I usually make in a month and just for one little afternoon gig."

"But why here?" I said, raising an eyebrow at him. "There's not exactly a shortage of scenic locales in the islands."

"They needed somewhere beautiful but also

completely private with no one else around for an important photo shoot."

Jack grunted. "So, you took them to one of the best kept local secrets in all the Keys?"

Cali shrugged. "This was the best place I could think of. Like I said, it's just for a couple of hours. Then we'll be gone. It's my wife's birthday and I made reservations at Chef Michael's so I'm crossing my fingers it'll be even sooner."

"We're in the middle of the March thirty-first duel, Cali," Jack said. "This is sacred stuff you're messing with."

"Again, I'm sorry."

Jack flared his nostrils. "You sold out, man. Now everyone's going to know about this place. You've single-handedly ruined a hundred-year-old secret. How do you feel about that?"

Cali chuckled and held up his hands. "It's not like that. These are West Coasters. Hollywood types. They don't know where we are or how to tell others to find it. And even if they did, they don't care."

Jack held his angry stare at the charter captain, then looked back at me. I just leaned against the gunwale, then took a swig of coconut water.

"Please, guys," Cali said. "This is a big deal for me. Huge. You have no idea how much these guys shelled out for this thing."

Jack shivered and muttered, "Judas."

I laughed. "Jack's just being dramatic."

"Of course I am," Jack said, trying hard not to crack a smile as well. "But that's not the point. It's the principle. I wouldn't give up this site for a million bucks."

I looked around, seeing only Cali on the boat, but his Zodiac was gone. "Why aren't you with them if it's a charter?"

"That's the best part. All they needed was a ride here and to borrow my RHIB. I'm basically just a chauffeur today. They've got their own divers and equipment. It's just their people inside the cove on my Zodiac."

"What time did you get here, Cali?" I said.

"'Bout twenty minutes ago."

"That's cutting it awful close to sundown if you're gonna be here a few hours," Jack said, staring at the deck.

I thought a moment, then said, "We'll paddle in slowly and head over to the west side. I'm guessing they'll be on the other side, near the pretty reef sections, right?"

Cali nodded. "I told them where the most scenic parts are."

"Great. We should be able to stay out of their view over there. Win-win."

"What if they see you?" Cali said. "I assured them they wouldn't be bothered in there."

Jack snickered. "Well, it's a good thing, then, that no one owns the sea, isn't it?"

"They won't see us, Cali," I said. "Or hear us. You have my word on that. So long as they're on the eastern side, they'll never know we're there."

Cali smiled. "Thanks, Logan. I owe you both. Next dinner at Pete's is on me."

"Next three are on you," Jack said.

"You got it."

We dropped anchor about fifty yards from Cali on

the opposite side of the opening. Unlatching a twelve-foot two-person sit-atop kayak from the starboard gunwale, we loaded our gear, then locked up the Baia. Then Cali threw us another wave as we paddled into the channel.

"He's lucky his residency status doesn't get revoked," Jack said as I waved back. "Some conch he is."

"All right, all right," I said. "You don't want to get too riled up. You're gonna need all two of your wits and your notorious conch focus if you're going to beat me."

We paddled through the winding waterway, popping out into the cove a couple minutes later. As we entered, we could hear faint chatter around the sharp bend but saw nothing.

"Come on," I said, pointing an end of my paddle toward the left alcove. "We'll have the whole Cornucopia to ourselves. Let's just keep quiet."

"I can't believe I'm sneaking into my own honey hole," Jack said. "My ancestors are rolling over in their sandy graves right now."

We paddled across a stretch of perfectly calm water that deepened gradually. Soon it was ten feet down, and slathered with turtle grass and clusters of jutting rocks and coral heads.

"How's it look?" I said to Jack as he leaned over and stared toward the bottom.

He smiled. "There're enough antennas down there to get a signal from Mars."

My heart rate ticked up a bit, excitement taking over. Diving for lobster is a rush. Diving for lobster in the Keys is nirvana. But diving for lobster at the best honey hole I'd ever experienced was the closest thing to being a kid on Christmas morning.

Jack tied off the kayak to a thick mangrove branch and we both donned our gear.

"You ready, bro?" Jack said, his eyes all focus under curly strands of hair.

I nodded, then chuckled. "It'll be just like last year," I said, reminiscing about how I'd claimed victory by an ounce on the final site.

"Last year was a fluke. Like the Miracle on Ice, or Valvano's NC State. You besting me is right up there with those."

"We'll see about that," I said, spitting onto the lenses of my mask and rinsing them off lightly to keep them from fogging up.

"Care to make it more interesting this year, then?" Jack said.

"A case of Paradise Sunsets?"

"How about a bottle from the chest?"

I fell silent. "You sure?"

He shrugged. "It's been a while since we hauled it up. Over ten years now. I think it's time to enjoy one of them."

Lobster honey holes weren't the only things identified on the famous Rubio charts. There was also a treasure chest. Not one of the gold-and-rubies variety, but filled with old spirits and sealed up and buried in a hundred feet of water at a hidden location. The chest had been another tradition started by Jack's great-great-grandfather and had been submerged in secret for nearly a hundred years, only uncovered and hauled up a couple times since.

"May the best man win," I said, then we gave each

other a fist bump and slid into the cove.

Things got off to a rocky start for me. I quickly nabbed two biggies, but in less than an hour at the site, Jack rounded up a couple of behemoths. The two largest lobsters of the day.

"I'm telling you, bro," he said, his face beaming brighter than the sun as he loaded the bugs into the livewell, "I know this cove as well as my own backyard. It's like a part of me."

I went back at it, needing to score big if I was going to stand a chance. I finned all over the site, under the ledges, around the bright coral, and into every nook and cranny. The cove was spectacular, and this was the less beautiful but more bountiful side.

I spotted dozens of nice keepers, but none were big enough to win the day. I kept at it, but soon, time was winding down. The sun was descending to the west, sinking beneath the walls of thick foliage and shooting intense beams through the tangled branches. The view was breathtaking, reminding me yet again just how special the site was.

Forced to ignore the wondrous display, I dove back down, circling around the farther edges of the site, working my way out, and needing a miracle. Jack was already out of the water, lounging on the kayak, a celebratory beer in hand as he kicked back and watched the sunset and my desperate last-ditch effort to retain my title.

Just when I thought all hope was officially lost, a beam of light shot through the water in an intense pillar, illuminating a small section of rocky seafloor. There, sticking out from an alcove, I spotted two of the largest antennae I'd ever seen on a bug. It was like the heavens were sending me a sign and showing me the way to victory.

I kicked ahead a good ten yards, nearly rounding the sharp bend in the encroaching mangroves, then sucked in a breath and duck dove toward my last hope. I swept down and around, then blinked, hardly believing what I was seeing. Right in front of me, its body tucked under an overhang, was the largest spiny lobster I'd ever seen.

My mouth dropped open as I gazed at the marvelous creature—the sort of lobster that legends are made of.

I closed in on the leviathan, but it was old and wise and saw me coming. It slipped right out of its hiding place and took off in a blur for a thick tangle of swaying seagrass.

I flattened my body and rocketed forward, kicking with everything I had. The monster made it into the grass, but I closed in and spooked him out the other side. The crustacean made a final dash, racing for a deep crevice in the rock. I gave chase with a vigorous kick of my fins.

With my net and tickle stick clutched in my left hand, I had no choice but to reach with my right. Hooking around the ledge moments after the lobster entered, I contorted my upper body and reached inside as far as I could. The lobster noticed me, but it was too late. The fabric hugging my outstretched fingers clamped down over its hard, prickly carapace.

I grabbed hold and squeezed tight. Feeling its jagged shell in my flexed gloved hand, I fought for a better hold as the massive lobster struggled to wriggle free and pin itself against the rock. I dragged him out, my arm muscles burning as he popped free, and grinned as I adjusted my grip and pinned the creature against a slab of brain coral.

Victory was mine.

My eyes lit up even bigger when I saw my catch up close. There was no way my old conch friend was beating this one. Not only was it going to ensure another year as Lord of the Hunt, it would also score me a picture framed on the wall at Pete's. Probably on the first floor. Right near the entrance.

As I shifted around, preparing to net my catch and seal the deal, a flash of movement in my peripherals hijacked my attention. Maintaining my hold on the lobster, I snapped my head toward the movement.

In my tunnel-vision, heat-of-the-moment chase, I'd finned to within thirty yards of the out-of-towners and their photo shoot. My eyes locked onto a camera guy in full scuba gear, his reticle trained on a beautiful woman in a pink bikini. Donning just a mask and fins, the woman was fifteen feet down and gliding in a smooth fluid motion over a picturesque spread of colorful coral. Just as she arched toward the surface, a second diver swooped in from behind her. The diver grabbed the woman by an ankle and vented air from his BCD.

I watched in horror and borderline disbelief as the woman struggled, her thrashing body pulled deeper.

FOUR

I've seen death before.

The aftermath. The events leading up to it. And the act itself.

Again and again I've seen it, and this woman was full-on panicking—right on the brink of death. And the diver gripping her tight was severe and sure in his movements. Attempting cold-blooded murder.

There was no time to think things through—no time to fully take in what I was witnessing and formulate a proper course of action.

I let go of the lobster.

It scurried away as I released my net and tickle stick, unclipped my catch bag, and threw myself away from the rock, kicking with big, strong cycles over the painted seafloor.

My eyes remained locked on the act before me—the woman fighting and thrashing to escape the diver's grasp while the camera guy just watched, his lens angled away from the action. Bubbles fluttered from the frantic woman's mouth, sparkling as they caught the late-afternoon rays on their trip to the surface.

She was on the verge of blacking out and turned motionless just as I reached them. Arriving at the attacker's back, I snatched the strap of his mask and yanked it off, letting it sink to the bottom. At the same time I grabbed his air hose and jerked his regulator free.

He loosened his grip on the woman and spun around. I slugged him in the nose and shoved him away from his victim. With the diver panicking and a cloud of blood pluming from his nostrils, I looped an arm around the woman and kicked for the surface. It only took three cycles to cover the distance and break out into the open air.

I gasped and sucked in rapid lungfuls while keeping the woman's head above water. She wasn't breathing and was limp in my arms, her raven-black hair draped over her smooth olive skin.

I turned and swam for Cali's Zodiac. Racing right up to the starboard pontoon, I kicked hard with my fins, launching up high enough from the water to rest the woman's body on the fiberglass deck. Then I swiftly slipped off my fins and mask and splashed up beside her.

"Who the hell are you?" a high-pitched voice said as I picked her up again.

A young man wearing a vibrant white-and-gold shirt and purple sunglasses stood with his hands on his hips as I pushed forward and adjusted her into a more natural position.

"What the hell's going on?" he said.

I ignored him and went to work, angling her chin

back to open her airway. Hovering an ear over her mouth, I detected no air flowing in or out, and her chest was still.

"Hey," the young guy barked, "I said—"

"She needs CPR, now!"

The guy stomped over and grabbed me by an arm.

Big mistake.

With no time or desire to reason with the fool, I rose and hurled an elbow into his jaw. His lights went out in a blink, and he crumpled to the deck.

I turned my attention back to the woman, hyperawareness taking over as I positioned my hands and went right into thirty chest compressions. My heart pounded harder with every passing second, the woman lying motionless beneath me.

Once done with the cycle, I leaned over and gave two quick rescue breaths, then went back into it.

"Come on, come on," I said, trying to will the woman back to life.

She was ravishing—like an angel resting peacefully beneath me, and she was right on death's doorstep.

When I hit the eighteenth compression, she coughed up water and shook. I sighed in relief as her hazel eyes sprang wide. She coughed again and gasped, tilting her head left and right.

"It's okay," I said softly, holding a hand over her. "Just breathe. Breathe."

A series of splashes caught my attention. The camera guy and the diver whose gear I'd torn free were both on the surface, heading for the boat. The guy hadn't found his mask and was wheezing and wiping the saltwater from his eyes as blood streamed from his broken nose.

I stood, unsheathed my dive knife, and held it up. "Either of you so much as touch this boat and I'll bury this in your skull."

They both froze.

Then the one I'd attacked glared at me and said, "You have no idea what you're doing, man. No idea who you're messing with."

"Yeah, I get that a lot. By the way, your nose is bleeding."

It was an understatement. There was a substantial river of crimson flowing through both nostrils, down his lips and chin, and splattering into the water.

Before letting him continue our little chat, I stood tall and faced to the south. Positioning my right thumb and index finger in my mouth, I was about to whistle to Jack, but my friend was already on his way over, seated on the kayak and paddling swiftly across the cove.

I returned my attention to the woman. She was still on her back, still fending off the panic and confusion that'd taken over her.

"Everything's going to be all right," I said, kneeling beside her and helping her sit up. "What's your name?"

She blinked and looked around, her mouth still hanging open. She looked almost confused by the question, and I worried that maybe she was experiencing memory loss due to oxygen deprivation.

Eventually, though, she got a name out.

"Jasmine," she said.

Her voice was soft and feminine.

"Good to meet you, Jasmine," I said. "I'm Owen.

And as I said, you're safe now."

I gave her my middle name, not wanting her or the guys she was with to know who I was.

"Who the hell do you think you are?" a voice barked from the water.

Jasmine took one look at the diver who'd attacked her, then burst into tears, throwing her face into her hands and shaking. She looked broken, like her entire world was crumbling to pieces.

"You're safe now," I repeated, then I leaned over and patted her softly on the shoulder. "Sit tight and relax. I'll be right back."

I rose and turned and stomped to the transom. The diver who'd tried to commit murder was kicking toward me, his eyes big and his face red with rage. He closed in on the stern just as Jack arrived, gliding to a stop right beside the RHIB.

"Look, I don't know who the hell any of you are," I said, planting my hands on my hips as I addressed the two divers, "but this is what's going to happen. First, you're both going to remove your gear. Everything down to your trunks. Then you're gonna climb aboard and we're gonna hand you over to the police."

"No!" Jasmine shouted, looking up from her hands. Her face was coated in tears, her eyes soaked and red. "Don't call the police."

I eyed the woman curiously, then turned as the diver who'd attempted murder removed his BCD and fins and grabbed hold of the ladder attached to the port pontoon. He climbed up onto the boat, then wiped a layer of blood from his chin and glared at me. He was nearly my height and looked like he hit the gym at least a couple times a week.

Seeing that he was unarmed, I let him step closer. Let him bend his knees and prepare to engage me. I decided that whichever limb he threw my way was going to be the one I'd break. It would be his decision. A choose your own adventure kind of thing.

He went with his dominant right arm. A tight fist, a lunge, and a laughable excuse for a punch. It was polished crystal clear why this guy had tried to kill the helpless woman while she was vulnerable, unawares, and underwater. I doubted he could take anyone in an even fight.

The punch hit nothing but air. And he slipped and nearly fell in the process. I caught him by the arm, stabilizing him for a fraction of a second before driving my momentum the opposite way as his. His arm whirled back behind him and cracked, the radius and the ulna both snapping like tree branches.

His cry was high-pitched and overly dramatic, like a side character in a cheesy horror film. An easy front kick hurled him and his two hundred pounds of designer muscles back into the water, where he thrashed and cried and cursed some more.

"Little harder to swim with a broken arm, huh?" I said. "I promise it's even harder with two, so I'd recommend that you both shut up and stay in the water for now."

Jack had his compact Desert Eagle gripped with both hands and aimed at the two guys. "You two better sit tight and do as my friend says. I've seen him beat down guys far harder than you punks."

I helped tie the kayak to the Zodiac's starboard gunwale, then Jack climbed aboard and kept his aim locked on the two guys in the water.

"I got these two," he said. Then he turned to look at Jasmine up close for the first time and added, "You make sure she's all—" He paused, his mouth hung open, and he lowered his sunglasses. Leaning over to me, he lowered his voice and said, "Dude, you realize that's Jasmine Cruz, right?"

I thought back to the phone conversation with Ange and Scarlett earlier that day and the celebrity my daughter had mentioned. Then I looked back at the two divers. The camera guy treading water silently, and the guy who'd attacked me wincing and crying, and blood still pouring out through his nose.

Then I peered back at Jasmine. She was sitting on the deck with her back against the gunwale, her legs bent and her body draped over them. Her eyes were teary as they met mine, and she was still shaking a little.

I stepped over and knelt back beside her. "It's going to be all right," I said again in a calm voice. "You're safe now."

She sobbed and fought to catch her breath and calm her rapidly beating heart.

"I really think you should reconsider getting law enforcement involved," I said. "I'm good friends with the local chief of police, and these two should really be put in jail."

"You can't!" she exclaimed. "No, you can't call the police. Please."

I had no idea what was going on here, but one thing was evident. This woman was terrified. Deeply. Through to her core. And she was begging me not to get the law involved, something I preferred not to do anyway under usual circumstances.

"All right, you don't want us to call the police," I said. "What would you have us do?"

She fell silent. "I... I don't know. I just know I can't be around these monsters. And I can't let anyone else know where I am. It's... it's too important. Not until I figure things out."

I looked up to my best friend, and he just shrugged, unsure of what to do as well.

I thought a moment, then I patted Jasmine on the shoulder, rose again, and stepped aft to address the guys in the water.

"Well, it looks like today is you morons' lucky day," I said in as demeaning a tone as I could muster. "Because attempted first-degree murder would win you both a lifetime behind bars. But here's how you're not so lucky. You're all on my bad side now. That means you have one option if you want to continue leading your pathetic little lives." I stepped to the edge, stood taller, and stared right at the two divers while stabbing a finger at them. "You get the hell out of my islands. Immediately. And if I see your ugly mugs again, I won't be so lenient."

Then I told them that for every word any of them spoke, I'd break another bone. That shut them both up. The camera guy removed his gear, and Jack and I helped both of them up onto the deck. We sat them at the stern next to their unconscious friend and tied all three of them up at the wrists, the big guy squealing from his broken bones.

Before setting off, I hailed Cali on the radio, letting him know we were heading out with his boat and he was off the hook for babysitter duty.

"Why? What's going on?" he said.

"We had a bit of an altercation."

"Is everyone all right?"

"Yeah, we're fine. We'll take care of escorting these landlubbers back to Hueso. Looks like you'll make it to dinner after all."

"You guys sure?"

"Yeah. And we'll give you the full story at Pete's sometime, but for now that's all I can say."

"Understood, brother. And I owe you one. Like I said, it's Maggie's birthday and we've been looking forward to this dinner for months."

Ending the call, we raised the anchor and I powered up the engine, accelerating us across the cove. Jasmine scooted up to the seat beside me, her hands sliding off her tear-coated face so she could look at me. I noticed she was shivering, so I grabbed a big towel from a gear locker and draped it over her.

"Thank you," she said, the words barely reaching my ears over the sounds of the engine.

"You're welcome."

"No," she gasped, then swallowed, still overcome with emotion. "Not just for the towel."

I gave her a quick nod, then cut the rest of the way to the opening out through the narrow channel. It was slow going, and the encroaching mangrove branches scraped against the sides at a couple of the narrowest points.

"Where are we going?" Jasmine said.

"Back to Key West. I hope you don't have a problem with that too. 'Cause there aren't exactly a lot of options."

She thought for a moment, then shook her head. "I

can't go to Key West. Not in this boat. People will recognize me."

"Well, then, rest assured, we're not taking this little guy."

She looked at me confused until a few seconds later when we rounded the final sharp mangrove-lined bend and the Baia came into view just a hundred yards ahead. I slowed as we approached.

"This is your guys' boat?" she said.

"It's his," Jack said, gesturing toward me. "And shift over to the left side, Miss Cruz."

She did so, then grabbed a small backpack from the deck and said, "Just Jasmine."

We redistributed our weight so I could climb aboard the Baia without causing the Zodiac to teeter too much. Then Jack killed the engine and I helped Jasmine aboard.

Cali stared at us from across the opening of the waterway. After we heaved the two divers and the young punk I'd knocked unconscious onto the deck, along with the kayak, the Marathon dive operator arrived to retrieve his RHIB.

"They already paid you, right?" I said to Cali.

He nodded.

"Good. I'm guessing you met them in Marathon?"

Cali shook his head. "Knight Pier in Key Weird, actually."

I nodded. "Thanks for not asking questions."

Cali rubbed the back of his neck. "I've learned it's often best not to with you. Though I'll want the full story someday."

We waved as he motored off, heading east toward the Atlantic side of the Keys. After huddling the three guys up under the topside dinette and securing them to the deck, I walked Jasmine down into the saloon.

"You can relax and take some time to yourself down here," I said, motioning to the half-moon cushioned seat.

She sat down and I grabbed a thin blanket and draped it over her. Then I stepped to the galley and pulled a Mexican Coke from the fridge along with a coconut water.

"To take the edge off," I said, popping the top of the glass bottle and handing her the Coke. "And you're probably dehydrated," I added, setting the coconut water beside her.

"Thank you," she muttered.

"Jack and I will be right up there if you need anything. We've got a half-hour trip back to Key West to drop these three off. Then maybe you can tell us what's going on and we can try to help."

She replied only with a slight but grateful nod, and I headed back topside.

I fired up the Baia's engines and rocketed us east while Jack sat behind me and kept an eye on our three new friends. Five minutes into the journey, he motioned to the livewell, then said, "I guess this means I'm the winner this year."

I sighed, having completely forgotten about the colossal lobster I'd relinquished back in the cove. Before I could say anything, he said, "Or we'll just have to call it a draw on account of a technicality."

FIVE

After giving Jasmine ten minutes alone, and with another six miles to our destination, I stepped back down into the saloon. She was still sitting in the same spot, but her posture was better and the tears had stopped.

She looked toward me as I came down, slightly spooked at first, then relaxing when she realized it was me.

"Sorry," I said, then stepped across to the galley. "Just getting some coffee." I filled a mug, took a slow sip, then offered some to her.

She shook her head, then stared at her bare feet a moment.

"Thank you again," she said, uttering her first words since we'd left the channel. "For saving my life."

I took another sip, then leaned against the counter. "How are you feeling?"

She let out a deep breath, then looked up and brushed her hair back. "A little better."

I nodded. That was clear by the color in her features. And she was no longer shaking and breathing fast.

"How are you okay?" she said, blinking rapidly. "After what happened?"

"I didn't almost die."

"No. But you were attacked. And you're acting like nothing happened."

"I guess like anything, you get more accustomed to things the more you experience them."

She shot me a bewildered look. "If you don't mind my asking, what do you do for a living, Owen?"

I rubbed the back of my neck. "First off, Owen's actually my middle name. My first name's Logan. I just didn't want those three idiots to know it. And I don't have a job. Not anymore. I used to work as a private contractor. Before that I served in the Navy."

"Doing what?" she said. "In the Navy?"

"I was Special Forces."

She paused. Bit her lip. "So that explains the whole… everything you did back there."

Then she fell into deep thought.

"You sure you're okay?" I said. "You're not feeling dizzy at all?" I stepped closer and eyed her carefully, paying particular attention to her pupils. "Earlier on the boat, just after you came to—I asked your name, and you looked confused."

"I guess I'm a little dizzy, but that's… I was just taken aback. I can't remember the last time someone asked me my name. You didn't recognize me?"

I shook my head. "Didn't even know your name until I spoke to my daughter earlier today and she mentioned you were visiting the islands. But I'm not exactly up to date on pop culture."

She fell silent, and I sat down beside her. "Jasmine, I wanted to wait until the intensity had worn off. To let you calm down a little. But if we're going to continue helping you, you'll have to tell us what's going on. Everything."

She swallowed hard. Bowed her head again. Then tears returned, welling up. "I don't know where to begin."

"Who wants you dead?" I asked, figuring that would be a good place to start. "'Cause those three seem too incompetent to be doing something like this all on their own. And the fact that you don't want us to contact the authorities tells me there's something bigger going on here."

She took a series of breaths, calming herself. "You're right. It's not them. They're just… caught up in it, I guess. Friends of mine. Or at least, I thought they were." She buried her face in her hands another moment, then said. "The person behind it all is—" She paused a couple seconds, then opened her mouth to speak again. Just as she did Jack stepped down from the topside deck.

"We're about a mile from Higgs, bro," he said.

I strode over to him and poked my head up for a view of the waters surrounding us. Seeing the area was relatively clear of boat traffic and the current was slow, I shut off the engine and said, "Let's drift for a bit."

Then I switched on the stereo to Pirate Radio, keeping the volume just high enough for the three guys topside to not hear our conversation below deck.

I pocketed my keys, then Jack followed me back

down into the saloon.

"Miss Cruz was just about to tell us who's trying to kill her," I said, giving her the floor once again.

She cleared her throat. "I'm hesitant to tell you. Even with your background, Logan. He's dangerous. And very powerful."

I held her gaze, unflinching and undeterred. Someone being dangerous and powerful had never scared me before, and that wasn't about to change.

She threw her hands up in defeat. "Okay. His name is… Lucius Xavier. You've heard of him, I'm sure?"

Jack and I looked at each other blankly, then shook our heads in unison.

"He's a rich and prominent business mogul," she explained. "One of the most powerful men in Hollywood."

I rubbed my chin. "Okay. Why does this guy want you dead?"

She let out a deep breath. "Because I discovered the truth about him. I'd heard rumors about him, of course. There are rumors about everyone, though. I mean, it's Hollywood, right? That's what the life of a celebrity is. A sea of rumors, and it's what drives so many people crazy.

"But then I found out he was into bad stuff. Like really bad stuff. Twisted, evil things. Many of them involving underage girls."

A powerful chill crawled up my spine. There were few topics that riled me up faster.

"What did you do when you found out?"

"After puking my brains out? I picked up my phone to call 9-1-1, but I couldn't. I didn't have hard evidence. Hell, I didn't have any evidence other than my own testimony of what I'd witnessed and the things other women have told me."

"What have you seen and heard?" I said.

"He's forced himself on women. Most are young aspiring models and actresses. If they don't comply willingly, he drugs and rapes them. Then he forges signatures on legal documents and extorts them. Threatens to kill them if they speak out. Threatens their families. And they aren't empty threats. Remember Cassandra Song, the model who died a few months ago? The supposed car accident? Or even more recently Lily Cohen, who supposedly died from an accidental drug overdose in her New York City apartment?"

"But you haven't brought any of this to light?" Jack said.

"That's the problem," she said. "I don't have any hard evidence. After discovering the truth about Lucius, I knew I had to do something. I decided to make a documentary. I had several of his victims who were prepared to speak out publicly."

"Let me guess," I said, "Cassandra Song and Lily Cohen?"

She nodded gravely. "There were more victims willing to step forward, but after the two of them died I was terrified. So, I put the plan aside for the time being. Hoping Lucius would never find out I was involved. But apparently he did."

"And now he wants you dead," I said.

She nodded. "Yes."

"What are you going to do?"

She sighed. "I don't know. I'm still trying to

process everything, you know? I hoped to have more time to build a case against him. But I guess I don't. And I never imagined he'd get my friends to turn on me. Timo has been my assistant for years."

"Extortion is a powerful weapon. It can turn even those closest against you."

The room went silent, me and Jack just observing the woman as another wave of anguish washed over her. It was tough to watch. Her life had been ripped apart. And now she was supposedly at the mercy of a rich and powerful man who wanted her dead.

"Please help me," she said. "I… I'm in big trouble. I don't know what to do."

"What can we do?" Jack said.

"I need somewhere to stay and hide while I figure this whole mess out." She looked up at me, intensity in her honey-brown eyes. "I don't know who else to turn to. Please help me."

"We're just a couple of beach bums," I said. "You'd be better off with a real security firm."

"Yeah, right. After the moves you just pulled back there?" She shook her head. "Normal people can't do that. And besides, I'm not asking for charity. I can pay you. I can pay you a lot."

"I don't want anything."

"I'm worth a lot of money. I can give you—"

"I don't want your money, Miss Cruz."

"Then why did you save me?"

The fact that she'd even asked the question struck me as sad. "Because you were in trouble. Because it was the right thing to do."

It was like I'd uttered words that were completely foreign to her. "I'm sorry, I just… that's not something you hear very often. Not in my circle anyway."

"Sounds like you need a new circle."

She teared up again at that, my words striking a chord I hadn't intended them to. Part of her inner circle had evidently just tried to murder her.

Her body shook and she broke down again, head buried in her hands once more. "Please help me, Logan. Please. I don't know what I can offer you, other than I need it and I hope it's also the right thing to do." She fought to control her breathing, then said, "This guy's a monster. I need to bring him down. If it's the last thing I do, I need to put a stop to his cruelty."

I watched her a moment—looked into her watery, sincere eyes. Then I glanced at my best friend as he let out a deep breath and shot me a knowing look.

"All right, Miss Cruz," I said, kneeling beside her. "We'll help you. But if I'm going to do this, you need to agree to do what I say, all right?"

She thanked me and agreed, then I motioned to Jack. "Let's drop off our unwanted guests."

Jack and I returned topside. I fired up the engines and motored us the short distance northeast to a dock near Higgs Beach. Then we untied the three. The guy I'd knocked out had slowly come to his senses, but he was still out of it when we forced them to their feet, then prodded them off my boat and onto the end of a dock.

"We parked our car at Smathers Beach," the young guy grunted.

"I know," I said. "So you guys have a nice long walk down the beach to think about everything you've done. Then you're gonna get into your car, drive up out of the islands, and never come back here again, understood?"

I grabbed the big guy whose arm I'd broken, fiddling with the fractured bones until he cried and nearly collapsed.

"Understood," he squealed. "Understood."

We watched them a moment as they stumbled down the planks.

Jack chuckled. "If the Three Stooges are smart, we won't see them again. I'm guessing they'll need a restroom given you just scared the shit out of them."

I fired up the engines and motored us away from the dock, cruising southwest.

"Just hope we're making the right decision letting them go," I said, looking back over my shoulder at them.

Jack shrugged. "What are they going to tell whoever put them up to the murder? That they were bested by two tanned guys in boardshorts? That wouldn't exactly narrow it down in South Florida."

I nodded, but I knew that a skilled, smart contract killer could probably figure out who Jack and I were even based on the little the three guys had seen and heard. They'd at least be able to narrow it down a whole lot.

"The good news is that karma is about to hit those three like a freight train," I said.

When Jack eyed me curiously, I explained that if what Jasmine said was true, then they were the recruited and extorted tip of a long spear. And the tip always gets mangled. Whoever was running things would likely take care of them. They were loose ends, after all. And if what Jasmine said was untrue and the three tried something against me again, I'd simply follow through on my warning. It wouldn't be difficult. They were as amateur as it gets.

"So if it's all true," Jack said, "if those three were the tip of the spear, who's going to be sent next?"

SIX

Grand Canyon
Earlier That Morning

Angelina and Scarlett stood along the South Rim, gazing out over the colossal expanse before them. The sight took both their breaths away, and they stood frozen, staring at the broad, intricately sculpted chasm for over a minute.

After their over-two-thousand-mile flight from Key West International, they'd taken a helicopter from Las Vegas to Grand Canyon National Airport. Then they'd spent the night in Grand Canyon Village, rising early for a five a.m. start on the trail.

Dawn had yet to break, but they could see clear across to the northern edge.

Their destination.

"You ready, kiddo?" Ange said, patting her daughter on the back.

Scarlett beamed. Tightened the straps of her backpack. Then turned to face the first length of trail.

"This will be a trip for the ages. Let's do it."

The mother-daughter team trekked confidently, eager to embark on an adventure they'd been planning for months. Both wore leggings, breathable long-sleeve shirts, hiking boots, and sun hats. Their backpacks were packed tight, stuffed with everything they'd need for two nights in the world-renowned backcountry.

Their planned route was one of the most difficult and notorious hikes in the country. The twenty-one-mile hike began with nearly a mile descent into the earth, followed by an ascent of over a mile on the other side. But Ange had never been one to shy away from a challenge. In fact, she preferred to face them head-on—to stare them in the eye and smile confidently. And then to get to work.

And the first step of the endeavor had been preparation.

She and Scarlett had spent the past few months reading guidebooks, watching YouTube videos, and perusing online forums. They'd also, in addition to their usual workout routines, spent three days a week at a local gym in Key West, toiling for hours on StairMasters. Every item they wore and packed had been chosen carefully. In Ange's experience, being prepared was the most important aspect of a battle, no matter what it was.

The early-morning hike down the canyon was nothing short of remarkable. Every corner they rounded offered new angles—different glimpses of the magnificent natural wonder. Each stratum of the canyon walls featured distinctive hues of red. Light brownish yellow. Gray. Delicate green and pink. And in its depths, brown, slate-gray, and violet.

And the natural beauty around them only intensified as the sun crept up over the distant desert, setting the western sky ablaze with glowing strokes of red.

Ange loved her Key West sunrises, but there was something about a desert sunrise that was unlike anything else. And the spectacular array of colors, combined with the towering stretches of steep rockfaces and the distant growling Colorado River below, left them both in awe. Scarlett especially couldn't get over the sheer vastness of the wide, chasmic landscape littered with imposing peaks, buttes, gorges, and ravines.

Three and a half hours and seven miles of carved trails and switchbacks later, they reached the bottom. Trekking through a tunnel, they stepped onto the Black Bridge, a narrow four-hundred-foot suspension number that'd been offering easy passage across the tumultuous waterway since 1928.

The ancient Colorado flowed below them, its smooth waters a healthy shade of green, and clear at its edges. A trio of rafts rounded a bend to the east, packed with fortunate wide-eyed visitors soaking up the surroundings from below.

Ange and Scarlett refilled their water bottles just past the bridge, then pressed onward to Phantom Ranch, a historic oasis nestled along Bright Angel Creek. Picking up a couple pack lunches, lemonades, and iced teas from the Canteen, they trekked back and up to a shaded picnic table with views of the rust-colored walls of rock, Phantom Stream, and peekaboo glimpses of the Colorado a half mile back.

"This place has a cool vibe," Scarlett said, looking around at all the hikers.

Ange smiled. "Not everyone's idea of a fun spring break is to hike the Grand Canyon. And tough-to-reach natural places like this attract a special crowd."

Many of their fellow trekkers were in their late teens and early twenties. College kids, mostly, from Arizona and California, but some coming from all over the country, no doubt.

Ange eyed her daughter with admiration. The adventurous sixteen-year-old had needed no convincing to fly across the country to a place she'd only read about and undertake one of the most rewarding but grueling popular hikes in the country. She wanted to cherish these moments, knowing that soon her daughter would be off taking on the world.

Scarlett checked her watch. "Just after ten here. That means twelve o'clock back home, right?"

"Actually one," Ange said. "Arizona doesn't observe daylight saving time."

Scarlett thought for a moment, then nodded and added, "We should call Dad and Jack and let them know we made it down safe."

Ange chuckled. "Sure, but remember it's March thirty-first. It might be tough to catch them while they're not in the water."

Ange finished off the rest of her bagel, then took a long pull of her electrolyte-infused water and unzipped her backpack. Reaching into an inner compartment, she pulled out a sat phone and flipped up its antennae. After a quick chat with Logan and Jack, she put it back into her pack and they downed the rest of their lunch.

"He sounds happy," Ange said. "I wonder who's going to win their little duel this year."

"I wonder how many clean dishes will be left in the kitchen when we get home."

Ange laughed. "Hey, he's not that much of a slob."

Scarlett threw her hands in the air. "Care to wager on it, then? I got ten bucks says we won't be able to fit a bowl in the sink."

Ange looked down. "I can't take that bet."

"See!" Scarlett said, nearly losing it.

Ange rounded up their trash, then downed more of her water.

"All right," she said, rising and reaching high over her head, arching her back and stretching. "We've got the hardest sections still ahead of us."

Scarlett kindly asked another hiker to take their picture, then the two of them set off, navigating through the underbelly of the natural wonder of the World.

After covering another six miles on the trail, they watched as a lean silver-haired man appeared from an adjoining trail. He was walking with light steps and had a massive smile on his face as he scanned through pictures on his big digital camera.

"Sure hope you don't pass up Ribbon," he said in a cheery voice while bounding past them toward Phantom. "Been coming here for thirty years. Never seen the falls so pretty as today. Nearly as pretty as you two."

The man continued onward, and the two stopped to catch their breath while staring down the path the guy had appeared on, in the direction of a distant thundering waterfall.

"Can we check it out, Mom?" Scarlett said.

Ange eyed the distant falls, then unfolded and looked down at her map. "It'll add a good hour of hiking to our trip. And like I said, the trail's about to—"

"But look at it," Scarlett exclaimed, pointing at the distant wall of water cascading down from the parched, vermilion landscape. "We could always add another night if we need to. You heard the ranger back at Phantom. Some of the reservations got canceled last minute." She clasped her hands together. "Please, Mom. I'll even switch packs with you since yours is a bit heavier."

Ange checked the map again, then thought over the long route still ahead of them.

"You booked a one-way flight to Vegas just in case something came up, right?" Scarlett said. "Well, something just came up."

The truth was, Ange had booked a one-way flight because she wanted to surprise her daughter with two days of shows and spas in Vegas following their adventures in the canyon. But she figured an extra hour of hiking couldn't hurt.

Besides, there was no arguing with her opiniated, witty daughter. After all, the falls did look amazing, even from afar. And the afternoon heat was getting intense, heating the mercury to over eighty degrees. A nice cooling off under a big natural showerhead was a good idea.

Scarlett's smile took over her face as Ange agreed, and the two exchanged bags, then turned and headed down the less-traveled path. With every step, the rumbling waterfall grew louder up ahead. Winding through thick green vegetation, they reached the base of the falls twenty minutes later.

The roar was booming. A bubbly deluge gushing out from a smooth rockface and soaring a hundred feet down the sheer canyon walls before splashing into a towering dome of travertine.

"Guidebook says that big spire is caused by minerals in the water," Ange said, glancing down at the pocket-sized book.

There was a small handful of trekkers spread around and behind the wonder. Snapping photos, dipping their heads into the cool cascade, and gazing up in awe.

Ange and Scarlett stepped closer, closing their eyes in unison as a whoosh of warm desert wind tossed plumes of cool mist into their faces. Up close, the sound was deafening, the thunderous roar amplified by the surrounding cliffs like the inside of a drum. A small rainbow formed in the constant haze of moisture emanating around its base.

After a quick dip in the ice-cold pool at the bottom, they climbed along the rockface to the top of the moss-covered tower, gazing out over the landscape from a perched position at the back of the waterfall.

"Excuse me," Scarlett said, approaching a college-aged guy wearing a cutoff shirt and a Seattle Mariners ball cap. "Could you take a picture of us?"

It was already the third time that day the outgoing teenager had asked a stranger for a photograph.

The young man nodded and grabbed her phone, then Ange and Scarlett slid off their backpacks and moved into position. Boots just up from the moss line on the smooth, damp rock. Their backs to the wall of water, the top edge of the unique dome, and distant canyons.

He snapped a couple, then handed the device back over.

"Good?" he said as Scarlett swiped through the images.

Scarlett smiled and thanked him, then grabbed her bag.

"You think you could take ours as well?"

"Of course."

He rounded up his two buddies, then they posed in the same spot, though closer to the edge. Their boots right on top of the moss and dripping rock.

Scarlett slid her bag over her right shoulder and took a couple shots. They changed up their poses, and she giggled, then gave a thumbs-up. Ange stepped back and rested her right boot on a crag to tighten her laces.

The three guys marched toward Scarlett, the guy with the Mariners hat taking up the rear. He slipped as they joked around, his back boot sliding over the smooth, wet rockface. He flailed backward in a blink, then his upper body whipped over the edge.

There was no time for Scarlett to do anything but react. Being closest to the guy as he slid uncontrollably toward the steep drop, she lunged and dove forward.

Scarlett landed hard on the slick stone. She glided, catching herself in a crook with her left hand and reaching as far ahead as she could with her right. She gripped tight to the strap of her backpack as it jumbled off her shoulder and dangled over the edge into the waterfall.

In the heat of the intense moment, the guy fought hopelessly to catch and slow himself. Scarlett flung the backpack toward him just as all hope seemed lost and his devastating fall to the rocks below appeared imminent. With water splashing toward him, Scarlett watched as the frantic young man reached up and grabbed for anything he could in a last-ditch effort. His left hand gripped the other strap of her backpack, then his right dug into the moss, his fingers fighting for grip.

His momentum stopped, and he held on motionless for a second in the torrent. Scarlett grunted, her body shaking as she fought to keep him steady while supporting them along the top edge of the rockface.

Ange appeared behind her. Fast and agile and strong, she grabbed her daughter by the legs and pulled until the young man was high enough to climb back up onto the edge. When he reached skyward, Scarlett released the backpack and clasped him by the wrist. The guy was pulled up, but Scarlett's backpack tumbled over the edge, disappearing from her view.

The moment the guy had himself under control, Ange pulled back, sliding her daughter to safety. Scarlett rolled onto her back and caught her breath. It was rushed and loud, even with the water grumbling beside them.

"Are you all right?" Ange said, kneeling down and inspecting her daughter from head to toe.

Scarlett gave a thumbs-up. "Fully adrenalized. If that's a word." She turned to gaze at the water. "Plus, I got that refreshing shower I was hoping for."

The two other guys had climbed over to help their

friend, and the young man crawled to the dry ground, gasping for air. He was drenched and covered in dirt and had cuts along his arms, hands, and left leg. But he was alive.

Once he caught his breath, he thanked Scarlett again and again. Then a park ranger, who'd apparently witnessed the incident from afar, commended Scarlett on her bravery and chastised the young men for being reckless and disrespectful toward what was a sacred site for the native Zuni people.

While they talked, Ange and Scarlett slipped away and climbed back down to the bottom. They found Ange's backpack wedged against a rock in the shallow pool, then heaved it over to a shady spot to inspect it. It was dirty, slightly cut up, and soaked, but still structurally sound. It wasn't until they opened the main compartment that they realized the extent of the damage.

"Looks like we won't be making any calls anytime soon," Ange said, pulling out the sat phone, which had a broken antenna and a big crack across its screen.

SEVEN

I motored us past the southernmost tip, then cut north beside Fort Zachary Taylor. Keeping a good distance from downtown Key West off the starboard side, we wrapped around Sunset Key and tied to a mooring buoy among a hundred other sailboats on the windward side of Wisteria Island. We needed a place to sit tight for a bit and formulate a course of action before cruising to my slip at the Conch Harbor Marina.

"First things first," I said to Jasmine after tying us off and stepping down into the saloon. "You need to lose your smartphone."

"What?" she said, looking like I'd just told her to chop off one of her hands.

"Get rid of it. Or at least shut it off for the time being."

"Then how am I supposed to—"

I handed her a burner flip phone I'd already snagged from a locker in the guest cabin. "No data or Wi-Fi, and no Bluetooth. No apps whatsoever. This thing's a glorified walkie-talkie and that's just what you need right now."

She pulled out her smartphone and handed it to me. I instantly shut it off, then stowed it in the safe in the main cabin's closet.

"How am I supposed to use it?" Jasmine said, eyeing the device like a relic from the Stone Age. "I think I know maybe three numbers by heart."

"Let's start there," I said. "Whose numbers do you know?"

"The number for my mom's nursing home in Malibu. She has severe dementia."

"And the other two?"

"My agent and business manager. But she works for Lucius."

"That rules her out. The third?"

"My fiancé."

I shot a look toward Jack. "You're engaged?"

She nodded. "To Wyatt Cash. Boy, you guys weren't kidding about being out of the pop culture loop."

Jack shrugged. "We boat, we dive, we fish, and for entertainment we have some of the best live music at our disposal nearly every night of the week. Then there's movies if we're desperate. What more do we need?"

I fell silent a moment, then said, "Okay. I don't want this to come across the wrong way, and it should be a stupid question, but do you trust your fiancé? With your life?"

She bit her lip and hesitated, which really answered the question better than words could.

"How can you be engaged to someone you don't

even trust?" Jack said.

"I do trust him. And, well, we aren't *really* engaged. I mean we are, but we aren't, you know what I mean?"

Jack and I both stared at her with equal parts amazement and confusion.

"No," I said. "I don't know what you mean."

"Like, it's more of a business move," she explained. "To help us get more exposure in the media. It's a clout tactic."

I shook my head in bewilderment. Being a celebrity was truly a strange animal that I would never understand.

We formulated a quick plan. For the upcoming night, Jasmine just needed a place to stay hidden until she could figure out what to do next.

"I'm parked close to the marina," I said. "We'll load into my truck and head over to Jack's place. You can wear a disguise or something so no one recognizes you, and I can do a couple triple turns to make sure we don't have a tail."

In addition to a house inland being the best option to keep her hidden, I also didn't relish the idea of sleeping on a boat alone with a beautiful woman who wasn't my wife.

"You'll be safe there, Miss Cruz," Jack said.

"You don't have a house?" she asked me.

"At the moment, you're standing in it. My family's home on the land part of Earth is being rebuilt at the moment."

She paused at that a second, then blinked her mind back into the conversation. "Rebuilt?"

"Long story."

Jack and I headed back topside, then untied from the mooring buoy, and I piloted us around Wisteria, across the basin, and into Key West Bight. The waters were packed, spring breakers in full swing. Speedboats, sailboats, jet skis, paddleboarders, and hydrocycles, all mixing together on the calm waterway as the distant sun arched toward the ocean.

The lines of people along the shore seemed denser than usual as I snugged into slip twenty-four, the same little slice of dock space I'd moored in ever since buying the first *Dodging Bullets* four years earlier.

Once in position, I shut off the engines and Jack and I tied us off. I headed below deck, while Jack took a quick look around.

I passed Jasmine and entered the master stateroom. Rummaging through my closet, I found a big sweatshirt. Then I grabbed a ball cap and sunglasses.

"Here," I said, handing her the clothes.

She'd donned a thin, colorful sundress over her bikini—the kind of outfit that would make her stand out like a sore thumb to a group of vigilant paparazzi.

She removed the dress, bunched it up into her bag, then slid into the sweatshirt. It was huge on her, the grungy fabric reaching down well past her hips. She was putting her hair in a ponytail when Jack's head poked down.

"We've got a little problem," he said, then swung himself down the steps.

He pointed toward the shore and handed me a pair of binoculars. I climbed up just enough to get a clear view of the marina, then gazed through the magnifying lenses.

"Focus near the entrance to the marina," Jack said.

I did so and instantly spotted three people standing idly and holding big cameras with long telephoto lenses.

"Paparazzi," I said.

Jasmine rose up beside us. "Seriously? How could they possibly know I'm here?"

I scanned along the shore, stopping occasionally to adjust the focus. "Looks like there are patches of them hanging out at the base of all the downtown marinas. They're figuring you'd be using one of the charters out of Key West. It was smart to go with a Marathon charter, but it won't exactly be easy for you to lay low here."

"There's no way we're making it to your truck without one of those guys spotting her," Jack said.

"And they're like seagulls," Jasmine said. "One shows up, then all of a sudden there's twenty more." She stepped back down into the saloon. "I can't let them see me. It'll be online in minutes, and Lucius will know who I'm with. What vehicle I rode in. Everything."

I lowered the binos and dropped back down as well. Under normal circumstances, we could've just loaded up into my nearby tied-off Zodiac, motored around the island, and cut right into the channel that Jack and my properties are situated on. But all boat traffic through the little canal was halted for the next couple days until a team wrapped up a dredging job to deepen shallow portions of the opening.

I took a moment to think everything through, then said, "All right. Here's what we're gonna do. Jack, you head to your place. We'll hide out here until late tonight, then sneak into my truck and drive over to meet you there. Then we'll reevaluate, but you'll be much safer inland and in a local's house than here at the waterfront, so I think the move will be worth the risk. Hopefully these paparazzi disperse eventually."

Jack nodded. "For now, let's move the Baia around and tuck it in bed with the other long-termers. Just as an extra precaution."

"Good idea," I said.

"It's all right to just take whatever slip you want?" Jasmine said. "Don't you need to talk to the marina manager or something first?"

Jack grinned at her as he climbed back topside. "I don't think he'll mind."

We moved the Baia to an adjacent dock, cozying up between two big pleasure vessels that were both covered in big canvases. Hauling a cover from a storage locker, we unfurled it over the Baia, leaving only a small unzipped space for us to navigate in and out. It would get hot, but I had a little air conditioner aboard, and with the connection to shore power we could run it all night if need be.

After the Baia was completely covered, I said, "All right, Jack. We'll wait for the coast to be clear later tonight, then cruise over to your place."

"Keep your wits sharp," he said. "I'll see you later."

"Thanks, brother. And congrats on reclaiming your title."

He made a face like he'd eaten something sour. "Doesn't taste as sweet when it's by default. Like I said before, I think we gotta call it a draw this year. On account of the... extenuating circumstances." I chuckled, and he turned to Jasmine, giving her a short bow. "Miss Cruz."

"Thank you, Jack. For everything." She wrapped her arms around him and squeezed tight. When he got free, Jack climbed up the steps, leapt to the dock, and flip-flopped down the planks.

"He's a good friend," Jasmine said.

"Good as they come. And a great man."

"You are too," she said. "A great man, that is. I'm thinking it was fate that you spotted what was happening today."

I checked the time. It was just after eight, which meant we had at least four hours to kill before I'd consider moving Jasmine to Jack's place. Opening the fridge, I grabbed a bottle of mango juice, then took a long swig of the delicious liquid. I offered her some, but she waved me off.

"What did Jack mean earlier when he said the marina manager wouldn't mind?"

I smiled. "Jack owns the marina."

She laughed, then removed her ball cap and set it on the table. "You two are just full of surprises." She grabbed the collar of her shirt and stretched it out a little. "Is it okay to take this off for now? It's pretty hot under here."

"Yeah, of course," I said, not having registered that she was still wearing her disguise.

She slowly pulled the extra-large sweater over the top of her head, revealing her bikini-clad body that was coated in a thin layer of sweat. Then she pulled out her hair tie and let the long strands fall gently, fanning out behind her.

Jasmine eyed me and shrugged. "Well, now

what?"

I plucked my wedding ring from a nearby drawer, having removed the gold band early that morning to prevent losing it, then slid it back into place over my finger.

Then I grabbed Jasmine's bag off the deck and handed it to her. "First, you need to put some clothes on."

As she slid back into her sundress, I stepped over to the coffeemaker and set it up with an extra scoop of grounds. Then I grabbed my laptop, sat at the saloon dinette, and cracked it open.

"Now, we get to work, Jasmine." When the screen booted up, I added, "To begin, I need you to tell me everything you know about Lucius Xavier."

EIGHT

"Where the hell is this guy?" Timo spat, his hand shaking as he cupped three more extra-strength Tylenol into his mouth, chewing and dry-swallowing the pills while wincing from the pain of his broken arm.

The three men were packed into a silver Mercedes sedan. Timo in the passenger seat, Rodney behind the wheel, and the camera guy in back. They were parked seemingly in the middle of nowhere—idling alongside a dirt-and-gravel road three miles from the nearest stretch of pavement on the outskirts of Homestead. They'd been waiting for nearly two hours, and the late-afternoon sun was still relentless. There was no shade. The tallest shrubs for miles barely bigger than their vehicle.

Timo winced again. His busted arm was throbbing. He'd yet to make it to a doctor.

Closing his eyes and clenching his teeth, he fought hard to ignore it, then checked the time again.

"What the hell?" he grunted.

"He'd better show soon," Rodney said. "We're running low on gas, and the engine's probably gonna overheat before that. Then we'll lose our AC."

They were miles from anyone or anything. They had their phones, but who were they going to call? The only ones who could help them had assured them that backup was on the way.

Another fifteen minutes passed. Timo wanted to call up their boss, but they weren't exactly in a good position to be getting upset and making demands.

They'd had one job, and they'd failed.

And now their mission was clear. They needed to disappear. To lie low for a while until the whole Jasmine Cruz situation was handled properly. They didn't care what they had to do. They were still getting paid, and the prospect kept them parked out there until long after the sun set.

Rodney swatted a mosquito. "How the hell did he get in here?" he said, wiping the dead bug off the dashboard.

They were tired. And thirsty. And hungry.

Just when Rodney was about to say to hell with it and drive to the nearest dive for some sustenance, they spotted headlights in the rearview. They were distant at first. A faint pair of blurry, glowing orbs that cut through the strands of grass surrounding them like fireflies. They remained small for what felt like an eternity, then swiftly grew, blossoming until the beams were glaring into the mirror.

The headlights belonged to a black Range Rover. It flew across the desolate road, braking to a stop right beside the sedan.

The SUV idled for a moment, then its tinted

passenger window whirred down. Rodney lowered his window as well. In the driver's seat of the SUV sat a Hispanic guy with short jet-black hair. He wore sunglasses and a black ball cap set low over his face as he stared straight at them.

"You three," he grunted, "in the back. Now."

He jammed a thumb toward the back seat of his vehicle.

Rodney swallowed hard, then rolled up his window, shut off the engine, and killed the lights. The two others followed Timo's lead as he stepped out into the humid evening. The sounds of crickets echoed across the wide-open space. Shuffling quickly to avoid the mosquitoes, they squished into the back seat of the Range Rover and slammed the doors.

Without looking back, the driver reached behind him, handing the three a tablet. The screen displayed a cluster of photographs in rows of four. Headshots.

"Run your eyes over the images," the guy said calmly. "Then tell me which one attacked you."

Timo and the others had sent over everything they could remember about the guy. Height over six feet, but not six four. Lean, but muscular. Caucasian, but with a tan. Dark brown hair and eyes. Maybe midthirties. Had a big boat, so most likely resided in the Keys. Most likely in or near Key West.

But the biggest clue was the incident itself. The three of them had relayed the whole thing as best they could. The mystery man had been efficient, to say the least. Fast and skilled and fearless. He was evidently a man who possessed impressive combat training. Not your average joe.

So they narrowed down their list of potential

names the most by searching only for veterans. They couldn't get into the military records to see specific duties, levels of training, or ranks people had held, but they could see veteran status and branch.

That still left a decent-sized list of potential names. But it was manageable.

The three guys ran through the pictures one by one. Halfway through the nearly five dozen photos, they stopped and looked at each other.

"What is it?" the driver grunted.

Timo clicked on a face shot to make it bigger, then passed it forward. "This is him."

The driver examined it a moment. "You sure?"

"Certain. That's him."

The driver scrolled down silently, then whispered, "Logan Dodge."

He ran his eyes over the basic information served up by the database. Birth date. Previous occupations. And a home address.

The driver clicked the screen black, then set it on the passenger seat. "All right."

"Now what?" Timo said, agitated. "Where's the money? Where's the helicopter?"

The driver sat still, breathing slow and stretching his neck. Then he cracked his knuckles. "I can't believe you're still getting paid."

He shook his head, then reached beside him and pulled up a Browning Hi-Power pistol. The three men in the back seat shuddered as he held up the weapon.

"If it were up to me," the mysterious man said, turning back and staring at the three in turn with dark, soulless eyes, "I'd just bury lead in your skulls one at a time, then make some alligator's night."

Timo swallowed hard. "Well, it's not up to you. Lucius assured us we'd still get paid."

The man narrowed his gaze, the barrel of his pistol aimed at the roof. His finger tight on the trigger.

He sighed and jerked his hand. Swung it around and faced forward. Timo let out a breath he'd been holding for half a minute.

"Your boss is much more lenient than I, that's for sure. But he's in charge."

The man set his pistol down, leaned forward, and grabbed a metal briefcase from the passenger floormat. He handed it back, and the three men relaxed as Timo grabbed it. He set it on Rodney's lap, nearly smiling as he reached for the latches. But they wouldn't open. He turned it up, allowing the moonlight washing into the interior to let him see a lock with a series of six numbered dials.

"What's the code?" Timo said.

The driver shrugged. "Hell if I know."

"Then how are we supposed to—"

"I was told you'd receive it once you're airborne. The helicopter's on the way. Landing site is at the end of this road. Two miles ahead." He adjusted his rearview mirror. "Now, get the hell out of my car."

Timo and the others froze, then he reached for the handle.

As they slid out, the driver added, "Oh, and be expecting a call from Lucius when you get there. I guess he wants to do the honors himself."

The three stepped out and slammed the doors. The stranger hit the gas the moment they were gone, peeling out and spitting back rocks before flying ahead fifty yards, turning around, and blasting past them, heading in the direction he'd come.

Timo carried the briefcase back into their Mercedes.

"Not exactly a people person, is he?" Rodney said.

"I'm guessing it's not a valued trait for a cold-blooded killer."

Rodney drove the two miles. The road got worse with every passing minute. Big potholes. Roots sprouting up everywhere. It was mostly rocks and shrubs by the time they reached a circle of partly barren dirt that marked the end. There was nothing there aside from scattered old and rusted appliances and a pile of pallets surrounded by big tin cans that were riddled with bullets. Someone had used the area for target practice.

They kept the engine running and the AC blasting and waited again. This time, it only took ten minutes before Timo's phone rang. The man himself was calling him.

"Hello, sir," Timo said.

"You met with the asset?" Lucius said in his smooth, elegant voice.

"We did. And he figured out who attacked us. It will all be taken care of soon. This whole mess."

"I know it will."

The line fell silent, the man's words hanging in the air.

Timo wiped a layer of sweat from his brow. "We've received our payment."

"Good."

More silence. Stretched out long and eerie. And unnerving.

"But… but we need the code to open it, sir."

"Ah, that's right."

He gave the code, speaking the numbers slowly one by one, and Timo spun the dials. A beep sounded, and a green light illuminated. The latches unlocked. Timo relaxed again as he flicked them up and hinged open the metal briefcase.

Then he nearly had a heart attack.

"Lucius, you… you said—"

"That you three would get your reward," Lucius said, his voice turning sinister.

Timo's eyes bulged as he stared down at two neatly packed blocks of C-4 explosives. They were secured professionally and rigged to a metal box housing the detonation circuitry and blasting cap.

He began to shake, then the other two leaned over and cursed under their breaths.

"And this, gentlemen," Lucius continued, "is your reward for utter failure."

Timo slid the briefcase off him, the hard body rattling to his feet. He reached frantically for the door, the others doing the same. Gasping and shaking.

Timo managed to shove his door open, then the bombs exploded in a powerful surge of heat and flames. Pieces of the Mercedes blasted apart and flew in all directions as the car was swallowed up by the massive explosion.

NINE

Jasmine told me everything she'd witnessed and heard about Lucius Xavier, and I understood why her first rection to it all had been to fight the urge to hurl.

My stomach churned as well, and my pulse quickened. A couple times my right hand clenched into a tight fist unconsciously. I'd dealt with some vile people in my time—stood toe to toe against some of the worst human beings ever to walk the planet. But the things Jasmine relayed to me sent disconcerting chills up my spine and made my soul swell with anger.

But I fought to keep it together. If I was going to find a way to keep Jasmine out of harm's way and get to the bottom of everything, I'd need all my wits fully intact. All cylinders firing.

I took a moment to collect my thoughts after Jasmine wrapped up, then said, "You mentioned before that you don't have any hard evidence."

She shook her head. "Lucius is good at what he does. No. Other than my account of what he's done to me, and what I've seen him do to others, I don't have any evidence."

I rubbed my chin. "That should be enough to get the ball rolling. At least to cause an investigation to take place. Especially if you can get other women to come forward as well."

"I don't think I could. Everyone I know is scared of him."

I fell silent again, then grabbed my phone. "Okay. I'm gonna make some calls. See if I can find someone who can do some digging into all of this for us."

She gave a smile. "I thought you were just a beach bum?" Before I could reply, she added, "It's okay. Your secret's safe with me."

I started with people I thought would be most likely to be able to get ahold of government intel. Scott Cooper, my former division officer in the Navy, a former senator, and the current leader of a classified group of covert operatives, got my first call. He had access to powerful people and databases. And his team worked with some of the best intel gathering specialists and hackers in the world.

I caught Scott at a busy time, as usual, but he promised to see what he could find and get back to me. My next call was to Darius Maddox, a Homeland Security agent. I'd first met Darius the previous year, when he'd been sent to Key West to track and take down a fugitive and former comrade of mine named Nathan Brier. Working together, we'd developed mutual respect that had eventually turned into friendship. Smart and highly focused, Maddox was a former Army Ranger. Though this wasn't exactly a bread-and-butter case for a Homeland agent, Maddox had a lot of contacts in other federal agencies, and I knew that if there was anyone who could help me get info on a high-profile abuser, it was him.

I couldn't catch Darius on his cell, so I sent him a message via a secure messaging program. He replied within the hour, also letting me know he'd search for whatever he could find and send it my way.

With two of my closest contacts on the job, I delved in deeper myself. Searching for everything I could on Lucius, using info Jasmine gave me to try and paint a picture of the guy and his operation. But despite four hours of focused effort and two big mugs of coffee, I felt like I hadn't made any headway. Everything I found about Lucius Xavier was positive. The guy was painted as a saint in Tinseltown. Beloved and practically worshipped by all. I couldn't find a single negative thing about the guy.

Leaning back, I let out a deep breath, then pinched the bridge of my nose. Checking the time and seeing it was just after eleven, I grabbed my phone and called Ange and Scarlett, smiling in anticipation of hearing my two favorite voices. I was also eager to hear Ange's opinion on everything that had happened that day. Everything Jasmine had told me. Not only was Ange my best friend, she was also my greatest confidant and source of advice.

But the call didn't connect. I pressed call and received nothing but a fast robotic response, letting me know that the number was unreachable.

I tried again and got the same result. Then I tried each of their cellphones but, as expected, they had no service at the bottom of the Grand Canyon.

A hint of worry washed over me. Ange was as

capable a human as I'd ever met. She could take care of herself and others, even in dangerous and hostile environments. But still, this was my wife and daughter, and it was unusual for Ange to go anywhere off the grid and switch her sat phone off. In fact, I couldn't remember her ever doing it in the years we'd been together.

Five minutes later, I received a call from Jack

"Looks like the coast is clear," he said. "I'm not picking up any paparazzi on the marina cams."

"We'll be right over."

"Stay dry. This one's gonna be a real downpour."

We ended the call, and as if my conch friend had summoned the weather himself, a roar of thunder tore across the quiet night.

Jasmine got back into her disguise, just in case a few straggling photographers were still lingering nearby. Then I stowed my laptop in a bag and slid the strap over my shoulder, and we grabbed rain slickers and an umbrella, switched off the lights, and locked up.

I stepped out first, performing a quick sweep of the area around the Baia and walking the length of the dock. The marina was dark and quiet. A stiff breeze had built up, blowing a mountain of solid black clouds straight for us from the sea.

Seeing nothing unusual, I signaled for Jasmine to follow me. Then we zipped up the cover and headed for shore. The downtown streets were still alive and well—a chorus of booming music and lively chatter. Even if it weren't spring break, the noise would continue long into the night. But the waterfront was mostly silent. A couple people walking by, some boaters lounging. Nursing a beer or smoking a cigar. But nothing and no one out of place.

We headed through the gate, across the narrow promenade, and up a set of wooden steps to the parking lot. My black Tacoma 4x4 was parked in the second row, and we made a casual beeline across the dark pavement.

I climbed into the driver's seat and slid my keys into the ignition.

"How far is it to Jack's place?" Jasmine asked after shutting the passenger door and settling in.

"Ten minutes max," I said, then flicked my wrist. "We'll be there in no—"

I paused as an unusual clicking sound filled the air. The dashboard lit up, but the engine didn't power on. Rotating the key back, I paused, then tried it again. It clicked again, even quieter than the first time.

"Sounds like your starter's bad," Jasmine said.

I rotated the key back again, my mouth hanging open in surprise. "Yes. It does."

Tacomas had been my vehicle of choice ever since I'd bought my first one back in high school. Never in all those years had I ever experienced turning a key to anything but a purring engine.

I tried a third time. Same result.

"I just had it serviced last month," I said.

Jasmine looked out her window. "Maybe we can walk inland and hail a cab?"

The moment the words left her lips, thunder resounded again. This time louder, shaking the frame of my truck. Then the heavens opened up, dumping sheets of massive raindrops upon the windshield. And our breath soon steamed the windows.

I sighed, then grabbed an umbrella. "All right. Back to the boat."

We hustled down to the dock and across the planks, unzipping and returning under the cover. We removed our raincoats and collapsed our umbrellas on the deck, then headed back into the lounge.

While Jasmine sat in the galley, I readied the guest cabin, rearranging dive and rebreather gear, sea scooters, and my underwater drone in order to prepare a bed for her. Then I grabbed the portable AC unit and set it up in one of the guest portholes.

By the time I was finished, the rain had stopped. Like the flip of a switch, the world outside had gone from torrential downpour to perfectly silent in a near instant.

There's a common quote tossed around in the island chain. "If you don't like the weather in the Keys, just wait five minutes and it'll change."

And the Keys were living up to that description in spades.

"Who's that?" Jasmine said, pointing a finger toward my security monitor.

I turned and stepped across the room, focusing on the display. There was a dark, shadowy figure on the dock. He was pacing back and forth over by where I usually kept my boat moored on the adjacent dock. And as I tilted my head and focused harder, I saw that the mysterious man was gripping something small and metallic in his right hand.

TEN

"Anyone enters this boat who isn't me, shoot them with this," I said, handing Jasmine a taser.

She eyed the little nonlethal weapon and looked up at me. "Then what?"

"Then get 'em with this," I added, handing her a small can of mace. "Then crawl out the master cabin's hatch and scream out at the top of your lungs that someone's trying to kill you. Wake up everyone within a quarter mile."

She nodded. "You're going out there?"

"Of course I am. Whoever that is, it looks like they're looking for me. It would be rude not to go up there and introduce myself."

"Be careful," she said, giving me an unexpected hug.

I slipped out of it. Looked her dead in the eye. "Be ready with this."

"If anyone comes down here, shoot them. Got it."

"Anyone who isn't me. That's an important distinction."

She cracked a quick smile, then turned serious. "Right. Got it."

I slid my Sig Sauer P226 from my waistband and checked to make sure there was a round already chambered. I knew there was. I kept one ready at all times. But double- and triple-checking came out of force of habit after years of dicey encounters.

With my weapon ready, I quietly unlocked the hatch, then opened it. The mechanism hinged smoothly, and I was instantly grateful for lathering some WD-40 on them just a month prior as part of my routine maintenance schedule.

I stepped out barefoot, shutting and locking the door behind me. Then I unzipped the cover. Nice and slow until I had just enough space to fit through. Once out, I took a look around, then zipped it back shut. Crept down and onto the dock.

I caught a quick glimpse of the distant stranger as I headed to the base of the dock, cut along the shore, then turned and closed in on where he still stood, looking around near slip twenty-four.

I moved in a slight crouch, my feet gliding along, careful not to shift my weight too much or too fast and tilt the dock to give away my approach. The guy was tall and lanky, dressed in dark clothes. He still held the object in his right hand as he stared at the empty space where my boat was usually moored.

He turned when I was twenty yards away, looking around, then placed a hand in his pocket and staggered back toward shore, walking right toward me.

I kept my weapon raised. Ready. The light of the moon broke free of the passing clouds, washing a silver light over the man and allowing me to see clearly the object in his right hand. It was an umbrella.

Then I got a good look at his face.

"Holy crap," I said, relaxing my body, letting out a long sigh and lowering my weapon as I realized that it was the mayor of Key West. "What the hell are you doing here this late, Nix?"

Mayor Nix's mouth was open wide, his chin reaching for the dock. "I... don't you think you're a little paranoid with that gun?"

"I know you're at least somewhat familiar with the law, right? Well, a man has the right to defend his home. This is my home. Now what do you want?"

I shot a quick glance around the marina, making sure the mayor wasn't the only shadowy figure lurking about that evening.

"I'm here to..." He took in a deep breath, then let it out. "I'm here to apologize."

I eyed him skeptically. I wasn't sure what the guy was apologizing for. Truth was, he had a nice long list of things to choose from. Maybe how he'd been a grade-A asshole to me since the first time we'd met over lunch at Moondog Café. Or how he'd fought with all his might to put me behind bars for life for charges that were egregious from the onset. And those were just the tip of the iceberg.

But I didn't care what he was apologizing for since I pegged his chances of being sincere at slim to none.

Instead of giving voice to my thoughts, I simply said, "At midnight? And without calling first?"

He shrugged. "I just happened to be passing by. Been giving things a lot of thought lately. Regarding everything that's happened between you and me. Maybe we got off on the wrong foot."

I couldn't help but laugh. "Well, don't mix up your feet and trip on your way back to shore."

I turned away, and he stepped toward me, trying to cut me off.

"You don't accept my apology?"

I stopped and folded my arms. "I accept the fact that you've either had too much to drink or you've got some kind of ulterior motive."

"Logan, I—"

"Nix, seriously," I said, holding up a hand. "I don't have time for you right now."

"I'm sensing that. Where's your boat anyway? I thought you were at slip twenty-four?"

"Would you get lost?"

His brows furrowed and he swallowed hard.

"Is that any way to talk to your mayor—"

"Nix, seriously. Leave. I don't have time for you right now."

He eventually turned and headed down the dock, exiting through the security gate that he'd somehow managed to get through. I scanned around the marina again. It was quiet as a tomb, aside from a few of the typical night owls reading or smoking a cigar.

I strode back to the Baia.

Mayor Nix apologizing to me? This day just keeps getting weirder and weirder.

ELEVEN

I kept alert during my walk back to the adjoining dock, then climbed back aboard my boat. After zipping through the cover, I slid my key into the door and cracked it open.

"It's me, Jasmine," I said.

Then I pushed it open the rest of the way and climbed down. Jasmine had the light off and was sitting in the shadows, gripping the taser.

I smiled. "Nice job. That's a good position."

"What happened?" she asked as I shut and locked the hatch behind me, then flicked on the lights.

"False alarm."

"Really? Who was that guy, then?"

"Just the local village idiot."

I downed a glass of water, then grabbed and sipped from my mug.

"Oh, you got a call from one of your contacts," Jasmine said. She slid my phone across the table. "Someone named M."

I called Maddox back. As I'd hoped, the guy

provided a trove of intel that poured into my secure email over the next half hour. Names of women connected to Lucius and his modeling agency and production company, all of whom had either died or disappeared from Hollywood over the past twenty years. I'd been agitated already just from the things Jasmine had said, so seeing the evils in black and white made my blood really boil.

Maddox informed me that there were lots of suspicions surrounding Lucius and his group. That a couple investigations had even been initiated by Homeland, FBI, and local law enforcement over the years, but nothing had ever come of it.

"From the looks of the records, it's like the whole thing is a house of cards," Maddox said in his confident baritone. "But it needs that initial prod to a weak point for everything to collapse."

I smiled confidently at that. I liked to think I was pretty good at prodding the weak points of people like Lucius Xavier.

"He's never been taken to court by any of his victims?" I asked, completely baffled by everything I was reading and hearing.

"Some have tried. But nothing's ever made it to court. Everything's been settled outside it. And his name has remained intact due to his power and connections."

"Just out of curiosity, if you were assigned to investigate Lucius Xavier in order to gather hard evidence to bring him down, where would you start?"

He paused. "Just out of curiosity?" I said nothing, and he eventually added, "I'd talk to the police officer who's spearheaded every effort to take Lucius to court. She's a patrol officer with LAPD. Officer Veronica Carter."

"A beat cop leading efforts to take down a powerful mogul?" I said, utterly amazed. "And she's still alive?"

"Far as I know."

"I like her already."

"Me too. But I'm still just scratching the surface here. I'll keep digging, and I'll try to get in touch with Officer Carter."

He sent me over a couple more things, then said, "Look, if you're gonna get involved here..." He paused. "Scratch that. I forgot who I was talking to for a moment there. *When* you get involved here, let me know. I'm between assignments at the moment, so I've got a little spare time."

I told him I would and thanked him for everything, then we ended the call. With my phone still clutched in my hand, I let out a big breath and fell back into the cushioned seat, the weight of everything pushing down on me. A day that had started out on the water, watching the sunrise and eager to get into a friendly competition. And now this.

I grabbed my sat phone and tried calling Ange again. No answer. Not even a stream of rhythmic rings. Just straight to the robotic message, informing me that the device was switched off.

Worry began to set in. Though I'd stumbled into a hell of a predicament myself, the two people I cared most about in the world were at that moment two thousand miles away, and I had no way of getting in touch with them.

I tried not to think about it. It'd only been twelve

hours since we'd spoken, and Ange was… well, Ange. One of the most capable and resourceful human beings I've ever met.

My stomach growled, and I realized I'd only eaten snacks since lunch.

"Are you hungry, Miss Cruz?" I said, stepping to the galley. "I'd planned on a late dinner at Jack's, but I've got enough to whip something up."

She smiled. "Only if you have some good wine to go with it."

I grilled some lobster tails, doused them in melted garlic butter, dripped fresh lime juice onto them, then tucked the succulent meat into warm rolls. Then I opened a bag of potato chips to round out the midnight meal.

"This is incredible," Jasmine said, her eyes growing big after the first bite. "This is the best lobster I've ever had."

"Well, it was swimming around just a couple hours ago. And it pairs well with the Key lime." I opened the fridge and pulled out a chilled bottle of Paradise Sunset beer. "I'm fresh out of wine. Will this do?" I said, holding it up to her.

She nodded and I popped the top and handed it over. I stuck to water, and we leaned back and ate mostly in silence. I couldn't get the images and names out of my head—couldn't wrap my head around how someone could lead such a cruel existence. You get one shot on this Earth. One fast, blink-of-an-eye shot. And that was how this man was choosing to make his mark.

The thought chilled me to the bone.

It wasn't long before our plates were empty.

"That was an incredible dinner," she said. "Thank you, Logan. I can't even remember the last time I had potato chips," she said, closing her eyes as she crunched the fried spud.

"Really?"

"Hey, that's part of the deal. I'm on a strict diet. I need to look my best."

I rose and grabbed her plate, then set them both in the sink.

"Well, I'm guessing you don't eat a lot of sweets, then, either?" I said, opening the tiny freezer and pulling out a carton of Ben & Jerry's cookie dough ice cream.

Her eyes lit up even bigger.

I chuckled. "I'll take that as a no." I removed the top, snagged a spoon, and handed them both to her.

She dug in and savored a bite, and for a moment, I thought she might cry.

"Good, huh?" I said, relaxing into the opposite side of the couch.

She nodded. Downed another bite, then leaned back and sighed. It was nice seeing her loosen up a bit. She'd had a trying day—perhaps the most trying of her entire life. The types of things she'd experienced and had to relate that day were staggering.

"I wish I could live like this," she said while burrowing into the delicious dessert. "Just settle down someplace and lead a laid-back life."

"Why can't you?"

"Fame. Once you have it, there's no going back. Not ever. My privacy is gone, and I'll never have it again."

I thought about that, then a wave of pity washed over me. It was sad. No better word for it. The price you pay for being a celebrity. For a brief moment, I imagined being famous myself. I'd received a small taste of notoriety earlier that year when I'd been accused of murder. Even that had been nearly unbearable, so being a world-renowned celebrity was the kind of what-if scenario that gave a private guy like me shivers.

I rose and stretched. Checked the time again. It was well after one in the morning. I stepped into the galley to do the dishes and clean up a little bit. Grabbing my phone, I played one of my favorite evening playlists, the collection of island music starting out with the Zac Brown Band's "Island Song."

Jasmine finished up, then put the lid back on the ice cream.

"Feel free to finish that if you want," I said.

She laughed. "I'm not feeling quite that crazy."

Then she moved right past me, her hip grazing against me as she put it back in the freezer.

"It's warm in here," she said as I rinsed the plates and set them on the drying rack.

"I can adjust the AC."

"No, it's fine," she said, then disappeared into the guest cabin.

I finished tidying up the place, my mind running through everything that had happened and working hard to chart a course ahead. Then Jasmine stepped back out into the saloon. She'd changed into a thin, dark blue bikini, the swimsuit leaving little to the imagination.

"Well, that beer is amazing," she said, smiling at me. "I think I'll take another one if you got it."

"Help yourself. After you put some clothes on."

She froze, startled at that. "I don't have much in my bag. My luggage is back at our rental house."

"I got you covered," I said, stepping into the master cabin.

I riffled through our closet, then grabbed a thin long-sleeved shirt and some sweatpants. Then I amped up the air conditioning and handed them to her.

"You're kidding, right?" she said, staring at the oversized clothes.

I shook my head. "I agreed to help you on the condition you do as I say. Remember that?"

"Why are you acting like such a prude?"

"Because I'm alone on a boat with a beautiful woman who isn't my wife. I'm sure that's not a big deal where you're from, but for me it is."

"Low blow."

"Is it?"

She paused a beat. "Nothing's going to happen."

"You're right. And I'm glad you agree."

She could call me a prude all she wanted. I didn't care.

Back when I was in the Navy, when we'd return from training exercises or deployments, some of the guys would go out to strip clubs. Scott Cooper, one of the married guys in our platoon, would never come. Not even when some of the guys said he could just be the designated driver.

"Why even put myself in that position?" he'd say. "Why put the temptation there? It's asking for trouble."

I remember spending time thinking about that and finding the logic sound.

"I'll just go to bed, then," Jasmine said, her tone shifting as she stepped toward the guest cabin.

I grabbed the taser, stepped over, and handed it to her.

"Remember," I said, "if—"

"Anyone opens this door, *who isn't you*, shoot them," she said. She gave a nearly imperceptible smile, hesitated, and let out a breath. Then she turned and looked me in the eyes. "Thank you for everything. Really. I owe you my life."

"You're welcome, Jasmine. Now try and get some sleep. I have a feeling we're in for a busy day tomorrow as well."

She nodded. "Good night, Logan."

"Good night."

TWELVE

I rose early the next morning. After another quick sweep of the marina and not seeing anyone or anything suspicious, I brewed coffee, sliced mangoes and bananas, and grabbed a muffin, bringing it all topside.

I curled up part of the cover, needing the fresh air and wanting a good view of the docks. I brought my laptop up and, while eating, decided to perform a quick online search on Jasmine Cruz, wanting to know at least a little about who I was dealing with.

Her name yielded over three hundred million hits on Google. She had hundreds of millions of followers across her various social media platforms. On the first page of the search engine results, there was an article in *Vanity Fair* dubbing her the queen of social media. She'd been named sexiest woman alive. Twice. And one of the ten most influential women alive by *Forbes*. She'd starred in major movies, made appearances on hit TV shows, and had an estimated net worth of nearly half a billion dollars.

A glance at the image results showed a picture of her shaking hands with the pope in one. Meeting our president in another. And one of her nearly completely naked right beside them.

I closed the browser and hinged shut the laptop.

I finished up my food, then tried calling Ange and Scarlett again, but I got the same result. My wife's sat phone was still switched off for some reason.

I began to worry even more and thought about what I could do next. A call to a ranger station at the canyon. Or maybe one to Phantom Ranch, the place where we'd last spoken, to see if there was any news regarding a mother and teenaged daughter.

They were fine. I knew that in my heart. But feeling helpless is the worst feeling in the world, especially when it pertains to the two people I cared most for in the world.

I need to get ahold of them somehow, I told myself.

I checked my watch. It was before six in the morning, which meant three in the morning in Arizona. I decided to wait three more hours, knowing they'd both be up by six. If they didn't answer, I'd begin taking steps to locate them through alternate means.

The hatch opened, and Jasmine appeared, poking her head out. She looked surprisingly happy and well-rested, all things considered.

After I shared my breakfast with her, she eyed my tennis shoes on the deck.

"Are you going for a run?"

"Not this morning. It's just a habit. I always leave them out the night before. Makes it easier to get the motivation ball rolling."

"Why not this morning?"

I raised my eyebrows at her. "You're joking, right? You really want to hang out here by yourself?"

She looked toward shore, then to me, and said, "I could come. I'm not a bad runner, and the exercise would do me good after yesterday. Plus this place looks like a ghost town."

I smiled at that. Key West wasn't exactly known far and wide for its early-morning activities. There was even a common joke that the sunrises are better than the sunsets, but that no one's ever witnessed one while on vacation here.

I scanned the shore, seeing no sign of paparazzi.

"Please?" she said. "I feel like I've been cooped up on this boat forever. Plus I've never seen Key West before."

I wanted to point out that getting a tour of the island shouldn't exactly be high up on our current priority list. But I agreed that the fresh air would do us both good. And I've always found breaking a sweat and getting my heart racing to be the best remedy for overthinking. To clear my head and see the obstacles before me with clarity.

She wore a size eight, and Ange a size nine, but my wife's old sneakers fit well enough with her wearing two pairs of socks.

I did yet another patrol of the marina and nearby lot and road, then returned to find Jasmine wearing my old ball cap along with a pair of sunglasses.

"You sure are cautious," she said as I finished up my survey.

I nodded. "Wouldn't have made it to thirty-five if I

wasn't."

She shot me a surprised look.

"What?" I said.

"Nothing. You just carry yourself like someone much older."

We ambled down the dock, my head on a swivel. As we reached the shore, I spotted Cameron Tyson jogging toward us. The eighteen-year-old star quarterback of the Key West High football team, Cameron had recently accepted a full ride scholarship to play at the University of Florida. He was also Scarlett's boyfriend.

"Can't train today, Cam," I said when he was within earshot, picking up my pace to a brisk walk.

I'd been working out with the teenager every now and then for months and giving him lessons in various martial arts. But given recent events, he'd have to wait for another time.

Cameron slowed to a stop and planted his hands on his hips, breathing heavily. His eyes went from me to Jasmine, then his mouth hung open.

He wiped his mouth and said, "Are you Jas—"

"Yes," I said, moving close to him and looking sternly into his eyes. "But you can't tell anyone she's here. Understand? It's a matter of life and death, Cameron."

He nodded. Swallowed and said, "Have you heard from Scarlett?"

"Not since yesterday afternoon. But I'm sure I will today."

He paused, then I picked up my pace again. Jasmine following step for step.

"Have a good run," I said. "I'll see you later."

Jasmine looked back. "It was good to meet you, Cameron."

She shot a smile his way, then turned forward as we headed down the waterfront.

"He really seems to like your daughter," she said.

"Yeah, he does."

"She must be an awesome girl."

"She is."

Jasmine paused, then added, "Like her father."

"Like her mother," I corrected.

We accelerated into a run, then cut across to Mallory Square. It was as good a place to start as any, the famous waterfront area having been the heartbeat of the island for hundreds of years.

I told her a little about the history of the place as we ran. Jack and Pete were the real experts, but I'd picked up a couple facts here and there. I explained how the shore we were running on had once been a haven for pirates. Then, years after that, the port had been a hub for sponging, salt manufacturing, turtling, and cigar making.

"The island was a huge exporter of all those back in the day," I said between breaths. "But those industries paled in comparison to a uniquely conch occupation that once made Key West the richest city per capita in the United States."

"Leave me in suspense?"

"Wrecking," I said with a smile. "The trade winds run up from Havana, forcing sailing vessels of old to skirt right past our island chain on their voyages back to Europe. Ships have been smashing against the nearby reefs due to storms and negligence for years. Sinking along with their riches. There was a time when you could row out there and free dive twenty feet to a seafloor of gold and silver coins. Locals at the time made fortunes selling off recovered cargo. What a time to be alive, huh?"

We continued past the aquarium, the Mel Fisher Museum, then Truman's Little White House. I started off slow, wanting to gauge how she was doing, before gradually picking up our pace. She stuck with me stride for stride, her form fantastic. By the time we passed the Hemingway House on Whitehead, she was still barely breathing, even with the tropical heat and humidity.

"Ernest Hemingway lived here?" she said as I pointed out the impressive two-story structure surrounded by a wall and tall trees.

I shot her a bewildered look. "You really don't know anything about Key West, do you? He's probably Key West's most famous resident of all time. The legendary author loved it here."

The sun began to rise, sneaking up over the horizon in front of us as we neared the end of Whitehead. It was beautiful, the day rising up and setting fire to the sky.

"Sunsets in Key West are incredible," I said, gesturing toward the seemingly supernatural budding of radiant colors ahead of us. "But sunrises are often even better."

"No kidding," she said, gazing in awe at the sight.

"And I like the early morning. It feels like you have the city to yourself. Take that, for example," I said, pointing toward a twelve-foot-tall concrete buoy painted in red, black, and yellow stripes. "That's the Southernmost Buoy. Marking the southernmost point in the mainland USA. It's not really, since the naval air station extends farther, but the point is that thing usually has a line of people half a football field long standing beside it. People waiting for their turn to snap photos with the famous landmark."

Jasmine chuckled. "Well, then, I should take advantage of this opportunity."

She cut right, skipping over to the four-ton marker. Brushing aside a few loose strands of hair, she leaned against the buoy and shot me an over-the-top smile.

"Would you mind?" she said.

"To commemorate your fun trip?" I said, planting my hands on my hips.

"To find some good in it," she said.

I slid out my phone, dropped to a knee, and lined it up, taking a quick picture that caught the whole buoy along with sunrise-swept skies and glimpses of the sea in the background. She rose and sprang over for a look.

"Hey, that's pretty good," she said as she looked it over. "You're a natural."

"Teenaged daughter. I guess some of her skills rubbed off on me."

"Please send it to me."

"When this is all over," I said, then pocketed my phone and looked around. "Come on."

We continued past Higgs Beach, Martello Tower, and the big fishing pier, running right by where we'd dropped off the three troublemakers the previous day. We'd covered three miles at a decent pace, and she was still sticking with me stride for stride.

"You run very well," I said.

"You seem so surprised."

"I'm just amazed. You don't exactly have a runner's build."

She laughed. "No, I don't. But I do spend hours in the gym every week. Part of the job. Plus it helps me stay sane."

Seeing how well she was doing gave me an idea.

"If you're up for it, I'd like to run to our property. My daughter's car is parked there. It would be nice to have a working vehicle."

"How far?"

"Just over two miles from here."

She picked up her pace. "I'll race you there."

THIRTEEN

The assassin's alarm buzzed him awake. He silenced the device, then sat motionless, his eyes remaining closed. Listening carefully. Then he sat up and blinked and looked around.

A mirror on the wall across from him in the master bedroom suite showed weariness in his rough features and darkness under his eyes.

It'd been a long night.

An explosive night, he thought with a cruel smile.

He slid out of bed, then closed his eyes again and pictured his targets—their faces burned in his mind.

He didn't know much about the mystery man who'd saved Cruz. He was still waiting on the results of the full background check. But he didn't really care. How difficult could the guy be? How much of a threat could he pose?

He followed a strict morning routine, and thirty minutes after rising, the hitman stepped out from the master suite of the waterfront mansion dressed in a button-up shirt tucked into khaki pants.

The luxury house had been rented for Cruz and her posse, but they no longer needed accommodations. And he figured someone might as well use it. He also wanted to be there in case someone showed up in the middle of the night. Maybe Cruz, needing something from her luggage. But no one had.

He slid into his black Range Rover and rocketed out of the driveway. It was a short drive to his destination. Just a couple miles to the east, out of Old Town and into the less touristy part of the island.

He pulled over and idled four houses down from his destination, pulling under the shade of a gumbo-limbo tree in front of a small empty plot of land. Sliding on a pair of rimless sunglasses, he checked himself in the mirror and slicked over his dark, well-trimmed hair.

The assassin glanced at the photo of his target one more time, then checked his equipment. The pistol holstered to his hip, concealed under his waistband. The backup on his ankle. And the boot knife strapped to his other ankle.

Once ready, he put the SUV back into drive and pulled forward, turning right into a seashell driveway.

The property was surrounded by palm and coconut trees and various intermixing tropical bushes. A third of the way across the lot was a residential construction site. The shell of a house being built. Tools and workbenches sat in neat rows. Piles of debris. Stacks of lumber and metal panels for the roof. Two pickup trucks were parked with their tailgates down. And two guys dressed in cargo shorts, cutoff shirts, and faded ball caps stood beside them. They both looked up when the assassin pulled in.

He threw a quick, friendly wave their way, then braked to an easy stop and killed the engine. He slid out with relaxed confidence, then shouldered a bag and strode over to the worksite.

"Good morning," he said in a friendly but businesslike tone. "I'm Chuck Kimble from the Monroe County Building Department, and I'm hoping to take a minute of your time."

"Paul Davis," the crew leader said, stepping over and shaking his hand. "We weren't expecting anyone from the county today."

"I apologize for stopping in like this." He slid out a handful of papers. "It's just a little discrepancy with the permit. Nothing that could halt your progress at the moment. But we'll need these filled out ASAP. Is the owner of the property around?"

Paul shook his head. "He often stops by, though, to lend a hand. If you leave them here, I'll make sure he gets them."

"I'm afraid part of this involves an additional inspection that we need him present for. Is his temporary residence nearby?"

"Look, we've already filled out everything with the county. And the paperwork was filled out correctly, I can assure you."

"If you'll just tell me where I can find him, I'll be out of your hair."

Paul paused a moment. "Logan isn't exactly the most predictable guy. He's always bouncing around. Hard to tell exactly where he'll be."

"Could you call him and ask?"

Paul eyed the guy suspiciously. "No. Now if you'll excuse me, we've got a lot of work to do."

The stranger stood perfectly still as the man turned to resume the start of his workday.

"Maybe I'm not being clear enough," the assassin said, reaching to his hip and sliding out his pistol. He held it out in front of him, just inspecting the weapon casually. Then he leveled it, aiming the barrel right at Paul. "Time to call up Logan."

The man froze a moment. "What the hell's going on here?"

"Just call Logan. Now."

Paul stared at the stranger, then pulled out his phone.

"What do you want me to tell him?"

The assassin smiled. "Don't worry about that." He was simply going to cordially invite Dodge to a little party that was going on at his property. Tell him he needed to come right away, and alone, or the two men would die. "Just hand it over once you've got him on the phone," he added.

Paul did as instructed, locating Logan's number on his phone and pressing the call button. He held the phone up to his ear, listening for the rhythmic sound of the attempted call.

A loud buzzing noise startled the trio. The assassin spun in a flash and took aim toward the sudden sound that'd come from one of the workstations.

He glared as his eyes homed in on a cellphone resting on the table of a chop saw, the little device vibrating like mad.

FOURTEEN

Something was wrong.

The feeling washed over me as we rounded the turn to Palmetto Street, and I eyed my mailbox half a block down. I'm not sure exactly how it works, but after years of experiencing life-or-death situations, the body adapts. It heightens certain senses. Takes minute, seemingly insignificant, details into account subconsciously.

I let off the gas and Jasmine pulled ahead, pumping her arms like mad to win the race.

"Ease up," I said, staring intensely at her.

"What?" she chuckled through gasps for air. "Afraid I'm gonna—"

"Jasmine, stop," I said, putting on the jets again just long enough to grab her hand.

She turned back and looked me in the eyes. Saw the intensity there and stopped.

"What's going on?" she said, looking around frantically.

"I don't know," I said, leading her to the right side

of the road. "But stay behind me."

I scanned up and down the road as we approached my property. Through breaks in the trees and hedges, I saw the frame of our new house, along with the same two pickup trucks I'd seen parked there nearly every day for the past five months. Then I saw a third vehicle. An SUV. Black and big and shiny.

"This way," I whispered, turning into my neighbor's yard.

A fence ran the length of our properties, extending all the way to the channel. Picking a good vantage point, I poked up through the tops of the shrubs and saw Paul Davis, the lead builder for my house, talking to a well-dressed guy wearing sunglasses and carrying a leather bag. I listened carefully but couldn't make anything out. Then I heard my name distinctly.

My gaze tightened.

Something was wrong. Something was off about the guy.

"Stay here," I said, turning to Jasmine. "Keep low and quiet."

Before she could reply, I was off, hustling down the rest of the fence. I peeked into my backyard to make sure there weren't any others, then gripped the end beam tight and flung myself around, over the water, and onto my property. I cut across to the other side, passing my boathouse with my locked-up Robalo center-console inside, then past the fire pit and beach chairs to the opposite hedging.

I crept into the shadows under the stilted structure, then slowed my pace even more as I reached a pile of lumber and sheets of metal roofing beside it. I peeked over for a better view of the interaction.

My jaw dropped. Squinting through the morning rays, I focused on a black pistol in the stranger's right hand. The barrel aimed right at Paul.

I ran through my options. I didn't have a shot. Not from that far off and with both Paul and his partner standing in my way. With no way to achieve a better angle without being spotted, I needed to lure the guy away from them somehow. To create separation.

Listening in on their conversation gave me an idea.

I dropped behind the pile of wood, then crawled slowly toward the nearest workstation. Pulling out my phone, I put it on the loudest vibrate setting, then set it on the metal table of the chop saw. Then I backtracked, cut around the stack, grabbed hold of a two-by-four and waited.

I watched the standoff ensue, taking a small gamble that the guy who was there to kill me wouldn't off Paul unexpectedly.

I watched as Paul grabbed his phone, pressed call, and held it up to his ear. He waited, then my phone vibrated like mad, shattering the stillness. The stranger froze, then turned and stared at my phone. The device buzzing away and creeping along the sawdust-coated surface.

"On your knees," the stranger snapped, his eyes still locked on my phone.

Both builders did as ordered.

"What the hell kind of game are you playing?" he grunted. "You think I'm a fool?"

"It's Logan's number. I swear—"

"Hand it over," he said, holding out a hand.

Paul extended the phone, and the man checked the

screen. His face tightened with anger, then he tossed it aside. He shifted his aim back to my phone as it continued to buzz, and stepped toward it.

I waited. Calm and ready.

The stranger closed in, treading slowly. He kept his weapon aimed at the phone and swept his eyes back and forth over the nearby area.

I kept low, just out of his line of sight around the sharp corner until he moved within striking distance.

Gripping the hardwood tight, I drove up from my hiding place and spun as fast as I could, bashing the end of the beam into the side of the stranger's upper body. He spotted me in his peripherals but was too late to avoid the blow. The solid wood struck him hard, and he grunted and lurched forward but retained control of his weapon.

I lunged forward and dove, crashing into him just as he turned to aim his weapon my way. Catching his wrists, I tackled him to the dirty grass and we rolled once before I pinned his hands to the ground. A solid strike to his hands did the trick, knocking his pistol free, but also left me exposed. The man retaliated with a head butt to my cheek, then an elbow to my shoulder. Then he drove his knees up and kicked me off him.

He snapped to his feet in a blink, removed a knife, and came at me just as I caught my balance. With a fraction of a second to arm myself, I reached for the workstation and grabbed hold of the nearest loose tool—a DeWalt cordless drill with a spade bit locked in its chuck.

The guy lunged and swung his knife at me. His movements were smooth and powerful, and he had good footwork. I knocked away his first strike with the drill and barely avoided the second. He sliced a shallow gash in my arm with a third before I rammed my shoulder into his gut and thrust the sharpened drill bit into his left thigh.

He yelled as he turned and came at me with another quick stab. It nearly burrowed into my abdomen, but I redirected his momentum, slammed his face into the table, and pinned him down. Holding his arm back tight, I squeezed the trigger to power up the drill, hovering the whirling steel tip inches above his face.

"How many more are there?" I said, looking around, expecting more adversaries to appear any moment. "Where are the others?"

"It's just me," the man spat. "I was sent alone. I work alone. I'm all it takes."

He grunted and snarled. Gnashing his teeth, he landed a desperate kick to the inside of my right ankle. Then he relinquished his knife, heaved himself free, and spun hard away from me. The drill jerked downward, the razor tip nearly colliding with the side of his head before jamming into the tabletop.

As I let go of the drill and turned to grab hold of the fleeing killer, he caught me off guard by whipping back toward me. I threw a punch into his chest while he hurled himself into me like a madman. Pushing through the blow I'd landed, he hooked an arm around the back of my neck and put all his weight on top of me, shoving me backward and muscling my face toward the chop saw.

As I struggled to move, he tightened his grip around my neck and fired up the blade with a screeching roar, the razor-sharp serrated edges blurring to the motor's scorching full speed.

My eyes grew big and I pushed with all my strength into his arm as the saw blade spun ferociously over my face. Yanking my other arm free, I threw a palm into the guy's chin and his head snapped back. Then I forced myself down, pulling the killer with me, and manhandled his arm into the blade.

He cried out maniacally as the jagged edges slashed clear through the middle of his hand, taking off three fingers and sending sprays of blood and fragments of bone across the workstation.

His wails intensified as he collapsed to the ground. Shaking, he rolled away from me, then desperately reached toward his ankle with the only good hand he had left.

I grabbed a nearby hammer and stepped toward him, too enraged to ask any more questions. I reared back the heavy tool, and just as his backup weapon saw the light of day, I smashed the steel head into his skull, ending the fight.

Letting go of the hammer, I eyed my lifeless opponent and caught my breath. My heart throbbing fast.

"Holy crap, Logan," Paul said, startling me.

I looked back and saw the carpenter standing just ten paces behind me. He was gripping the assassin's fallen pistol, and staring at the mangled corpse with his mouth agape.

"Are you all right?" he added.

I let out a long exhale, motioning toward my dead assailant. "Better than him."

I calmed myself as I patted down the hitman's body. All he had on him was the keys to his SUV and a burner phone. I took both, then rose, grunting as I placed a hand to the cut across my left bicep.

"What the hell's going on?" Paul's partner said as he rushed over, gazing in awe at the bloodied body. "Why was he after you?"

Jasmine appeared, striding down the driveway with her mouth open.

"We'll need to discuss that one later," I said. "You guys got trash bags?"

Paul nodded as I stepped over to meet Jasmine. Still holding the dead guy's keys, I started up the black SUV.

"I need you to wait inside," I told her, then blasted the AC.

After she climbed into the driver's seat, I shut the door behind me. Paul met me on the way back to the workstation, a box of trash bags in his hands.

In addition to the industrial-grade jumbo black trash bags, they also had a bundle of large sacks in the waste pile that'd been used to haul in sand. I had the attacker, along with his pistol and knife, triple-bagged and sealed in one of the sacks five minutes later, severed fingers and all. Then I removed the tarp over Scarlett's Bronco and hauled the corpse into the back.

"For the time being, I need you both to keep this incident between us," I said to the builders. "There's no time to explain and too much at stake."

Paul nodded. "You just saved our lives. Keeping quiet is the least we can do."

"Thank you. You both take a week off. Paid. I'll let you know when it's safe to get back to the build."

They both nodded, still clearly in shock from what had just happened. After retrieving my phone, I strode back to the Range Rover, motioning for Jasmine to roll down the window.

"Follow me," was all I said.

I fired up the Bronco and rumbled out onto Palmetto. Jasmine backed out, then followed right behind me, and we cut across town. We drove onto US-1, then headed east for five minutes before turning south on Stock Island. A couple turns later, we reached the straightaway of Shrimp Road, then cut left into a long parking lot beside Stock Island Marina. The establishment had long docks reaching out into the largest deepwater harbor in all of the Florida Keys and offered nearly three hundred slips.

Easing into the section of pavement adjacent to A dock, also known as charter boat row, I backed up to a trio of dumpsters tucked into a shaded corner. Seeing that there was no one else nearby, I left the Bronco's engine running, then slid out and threw open the top of the nearest dumpster. A rancid stench wafted out, and I held my breath while peeking inside. The dumpster was three-quarters of the way filled, mostly with bags of fish guts. Just as I'd hoped.

I took one more quick look around to make sure the coast was clear, then threw open the back door. Grabbing the assassin's bagged-up corpse, I heaved it over my shoulder and quickly flung it in with the other trash. Then I closed the lid back up, jumped back into the driver's seat, and cruised out of the lot.

The following day was trash day. And I pegged the chances of anyone rifling through the mountains of fish guts from the nearby charters and discovering the sealed-up body at less than one in a million.

With the corpse dealt with, we switched vehicles. Jasmine followed me in the Bronco back to Key West, cruising another ten minutes to the southeast corner of the island, then I pulled into the long-term parking lot at Key West International Airport. After a quick wipe-down of the interior and a check for loose hairs, I locked the Range Rover with its keys inside and walked the short distance off the grounds back to South Roosevelt Boulevard.

Jasmine was waiting for me with the Bronco's engine idling. I climbed into the driver's seat and hit the gas, my mind and attention still focused.

I thought about the guy I'd just faced off against. He'd been highly skilled. A trained, experienced, and competent killer. A couple of close associates being coerced into attempting the murder of a rich, famous socialite was one thing. But a skilled assassin hired to do the job was another level entirely, and it revealed just how serious the situation had become.

"Logan, you should pull over," Jasmine said.

I barely heard her words, let alone attempted to formulate a response, my attention dominated by the task at hand and the next course of action.

"Logan," Jasmine said again, raising her voice and placing a hand on my shoulder.

I snapped my head over to look at her. She wore a worried expression, then eyed the cut to my arm. Blood was still dripping out, having already soaked most of my shirtsleeve.

"Pull over so I can take a look at that."

In addition to bleeding from the fresh knife wound, I was also still in hyperfocus mode. And I knew that my mind and body likely needed a moment to take a proper breather to relax and think things through.

I performed a quick U-turn, then parked between the road and the running path. Just up from the seawall, the spot offered quintessential views of the Key West horizon. It was one of my favorite paths to run on in the island chain.

I leaned over the center console and plucked a first aid kit from under the back seat.

"Your daughter has a first aid kit in her car? She must be smart."

"She is. But my wife put it here."

Jasmine stopped me as I cracked open the plastic case. "Here," she said, grabbing it from my hands. "Let me."

"You know first aid?"

"I'm not all glitz and glamour. My dad was an EMT. One of the best. He taught me first aid at an early age."

"Sounds like a very smart man," I said, then winced as she doused alcohol on the wound.

"Sorry. He taught me to do that when the injured person is distracted."

I nearly smiled at that. She did a good job, working slow and methodical. Fortunately, the wound hadn't been deep. Basically a minor scrape compared to many of the injuries I've sustained over the years.

She started to speak again, then bit her lip, a wave of emotion washing over her.

"What is it?" I said.

She threaded the needle, then paused and looked out over the water. "I'm just… trying to wrap my head around what I just witnessed." She turned and looked at me with intense eyes. "That guy tried to kill you. You nearly died."

"I wouldn't say nearly. I mean, I never even drew my firearm."

"He had a saw blade roaring inches over your face."

"Okay, so that was sort of close."

She sighed. "I just... I'm so sorry for getting you into this. This is all my fault."

"Don't do that," I said, leaning over and speaking softly. "Don't be sorry. You've done nothing wrong, Jasmine. You hear me? This isn't your fault." I looked away, then let out a deep breath. "This is what people like Lucius Xavier do. They make their victims feel like they're to blame. Like they did something wrong. This is all the work of a conniving murderer. He's the one to blame. Not you."

Her eyes welled up again, then she wiped her face and fought to calm her breathing.

"I've never seen anything like what I just saw."

"I know. Fortunately, most people haven't. The world is full of mostly good people. But some are evil. And dealing with evil is rarely pretty."

I told her two more times that she'd done nothing wrong. That all she'd done was stand up to a vile man even though it wasn't exactly in her best interest. That she was very brave.

She regained her composure, and after she finished stitching me up, I restowed the kit, threw my truck back in gear, then performed another U-turn. I'd spent the time thinking everything over, and I knew what we had to do. The next necessary course of action was clear.

"Where are we going?" Jasmine said.

I floored it back toward the downtown waterfront. "We need to get out of Key West."

FIFTEEN

On the drive to the marina, I shot off a quick message to Jack, then saw that I had a missed call from Maddox. I called him while driving, putting the Homeland agent on speaker.

He led off by quickly saying that he'd managed to uncover more intel pertaining to Lucius and his shady activities. But he'd yet to find anything that could do some serious damage in a case against the mogul. The Homeland agent reiterated that the next course of action should be to meet with Officer Veronica Carter, the LAPD beat cop who'd fought for years to bring Lucius to justice.

"She's viewed as somewhat of an all-around agitator," Maddox explained. "When I called LAPD and spoke to her chief, he informed me that Officer Carter had a knack for rubbing powerful people the wrong way, but that she was one of the best cops they had and always stood up for herself and other officers. Wish I could find more, but if what you say about Lucius Xavier is true, he's doing a hell of a good job of leaving no paper trail."

While Maddox spoke, I noticed Jasmine slip out her burner phone and check the LCD screen. She tapped a few buttons, then perked up and leaned forward.

"One more thing," I said, peeling my eyes away from her. "Any chance that beach shack in the Bahamas has a vacancy?"

He didn't give it a moment's thought. "Homeland would be happy to provide Miss Cruz with accommodations for as long as is needed. I'll see to it. Just give me a couple hours' heads-up before she arrives, and it'll be ready."

Maddox told me he'd sent the additional intel to my email, and we ended the call.

"What is it?" I said the moment the call disconnected.

Jasmine eyed her phone. "I just got a message from Wyatt."

"Your fiancé, right?"

She nodded and whispered to herself as she swiftly read the message. "I told him what happened and he's coming here to the Keys." Then she let out a nearly imperceptible gasp. "And he's bringing Theo."

"Theo?"

She placed fingers over her lips and breathed quickly.

We hit a red light.

"Who's Theo?" I said after bringing us to a stop.

She swallowed. "He's my son."

"You have children?"

She nodded. "I keep forgetting you don't know anything about me. Just one child. He's nine."

I'd never even thought to run my eyes over her family during my search.

Jasmine closed her eyes then turned and stared out her window. "He was with our two nannies in my home in LA which is very well protected. I'm sorry I didn't tell you. I should have. But he was safe there with them."

"Then why is Wyatt bringing him here?"

"He says we all need to get out of the States and go into hiding for a while."

She read the rest of the message. "Their flight lands this evening in Key West and Wyatt wants to meet me at Key West Cemetery. He says the house we rented wouldn't be safe."

I wanted to say "no duh," but I kept that to myself.

Instead of replying, I thought a moment, then shook my head. "The cemetery's a no-go."

"Where should I tell him, then?"

I remembered how Jasmine had reacted when I'd asked if she trusted her fiancé—remembered the hesitation and doubt that had washed across her face.

If we were going to meet them, we'd need to do it someplace more open, with fewer obstructions and access points, and with a means of rapid extraction if need be.

"Logan?" Jasmine said, having yet to receive a reply from me.

"Give me a minute to think that one over. Their flight gets here at what time?"

"He said just after seven."

I thought hard as we cruised over the Palm Avenue Causeway.

Closing my eyes as we hit a line of traffic, I

visualized the island chain. As I was trying to pick an ideal location, something Jack had mentioned the previous day popped into my head.

Yeah, I thought, bobbing my head. *That spot will work nicely.*

I gave Jasmine the very specific meeting spot, and she relayed it to her fiancé. A couple minutes later, I pulled into the parking lot in front of the Conch Harbor Marina. I did a slow lap around the pavement, swiveling my head and keeping a sharp eye out for anything suspicious.

I didn't see anyone who looked out of place aside from a couple paparazzi hunkered down near the gate into the marina. A quick look down the waterfront revealed more photographers along the docks, surveying the harbor in hopes of catching a glimpse of the socialite.

I parked in one of the farthest spots from the water, backing into the space, which was partially shaded by a banana tree. I waited there with the AC gusting, peering across the scene. Then I messaged Jack to see if there was anything he could do about the paparazzi.

He messaged me back a moment later, saying, "I've got an idea."

While waiting, I adjusted my position to face the passenger side. "So, what's the plan now, Jasmine? Your fiancé flies here with your son, and then what?"

She paused. "I don't know. This past twenty-four hours has been a whirlwind. I just don't know." She leaned forward, closing her eyes, then snapped them open and placed a hand on my shoulder. "What should I do, Logan? Tell me what to do?"

I ran my hands through my hair. "From where I sit,

it's simple. Your fiancé's right. You need to get out of here. You and your son. You need to get away. Off the grid and hide until things cool down. And until this Lucius guy gets what's coming to him."

"And if that never happens?"

"Then that would be a first."

"A first?"

"He tried to kill me, Jasmine. Paid someone to kill me. And past experience has proven that the life expectancy for people who do that isn't very long."

"You're going to go after him?"

"Yes. I'm going to go after him."

She fell into deep thought a moment.

"Where will Theo and I hide? There's a small percentage of the global population who wouldn't recognize me."

"My friend I just spoke to works for Homeland. The DHS has a safe house in the Bahamas. It's nice and secluded. And they'll provide protection until things calm down. I'll see to it, Jasmine. You'll be in good hands."

"How can you be certain it's secure?"

"Nothing's perfectly secure. But I know it's damn close because I've stayed there with my own family when we needed a place to lie low for a bit." She raised her eyebrows at me, and I added, "Long story." She bit her lip again, and I said, "You and Theo will be safe."

"How can I ever repay you, Logan?"

"Don't worry about it. And don't say things like that. It's bad luck. We're far from out of the woods yet."

Moments later, the gate to the marina opened and a

skinny, pale young man rushed out with his bicycle. It was Jack's nephew, Isaac, and the seventeen-year-old computer whiz was bounding as fast as he could along the planks.

I quickly shut off the engine and rolled down my window.

"Jasmine Cruz is at Mallory Square!" Isaac exclaimed while hopping onto his bike and pedaling ferociously. "I can't believe it. Jasmine Cruz is at Mallory!"

As if they'd been struck by lightning, the bored-looking trio of photographers jumped to life and raced after the ecstatic bicyclist. The teenager continued to belt out the news as he flew along the waterfront, passing marinas and gaining new followers as he went. By the time he vanished from view, he had a nice crowd of out-of-towners racing after him with their cameras.

I smiled, then scanned over the lot once more. With the coast appearing clear, I rolled up the window to a crack, then we climbed out. Jasmine had her hat and sunglasses on, and I kept my eyes peeled, unsure if the assassin had been telling the truth when he'd said that he'd been sent alone. If I'd learned anything over the years, it was that you can't count on cold-blooded murderers to tell the truth. And that spooked higher-ups in criminal operations like redundancies.

We headed straight for the marina office. Jack met us at the door, ushering us in and shutting it behind us. The curtains were drawn and the small space was empty aside from the three of us.

"Thanks for paving the way," I said. "That was

some good, quick thinking."

"All Isaac's idea," Jack said. "I never knew the kid could act so well. Anyway, I got your other message. The Baia's tanks are full, and the cover's been removed." He looked me over, saw the bandage around my bicep and the intensity on Jasmine's face. "You two all right?"

"Just ran into a little trouble at the house. And it looks like we're gonna be in for another long evening."

"How can I help?"

Jasmine's phone buzzed and she checked the screen. "Wyatt will be there at eight o'clock."

I turned back to my old friend. "Any chance you and Pete would still be up for some fishing this evening?"

"That old seadog? He's always up for it."

I nodded, patted him on the back. "It won't be quite like our typical outings. I'll be in touch with the details, brother."

He nodded. "You two stay safe."

Jasmine and I headed down the dock and boarded the Baia. Within minutes, we had the engines running and the lines cast and we were chugging out of the harbor. Just as we broke free of the bight and I started pressing up our speed, my phone buzzed. I checked the screen and my heart skipped a beat as I saw a number with an Arizona area code.

SIXTEEN

I answered, feeling a wave of relief washing over me at the sound of my wife's voice.

"I can't begin to describe how good it is to hear your voice, Ange," I said after her quick greeting. It was the first thing I'd heard from her in nearly twenty-four hours.

"Sorry for going dark," she said. "We had a little incident at a waterfall. We're both all right, but the sat phone took a nasty fall and didn't make it. We're back at Phantom Ranch now and I'm using a phone they've got here."

I turned to port, skirting us parallel with the waterfront and heading toward the Strait.

"I'm so glad you're both all right," I said, unable to contain my relief.

"Are you okay?" she said. "You sound off. I thought you'd have a little more faith in me after all these years."

"I do. It's not that. It's a… combination of things."

"Let me guess, you're barely managing to survive

without your two favorite people?" She paused, then added, "Wait, is this about your duel with Jack? We're you able to defend your title?"

"No. We actually ran into a bit of a complication while out on the water."

"What happened?"

Where to start? I thought.

"You remember that celebrity Scarlett mentioned yesterday? The one who she said was visiting Key—"

"Jasmine Cruz," Ange said. "You know, your blissful unfamiliarity with mainstream happenings is actually quite impressive."

"I've been hearing that a lot lately."

"I mean, she's like the most famous woman on Earth," Ange added. "What makes you bring her up?"

I paused briefly. "Long story, but she spent the night on the Baia last night."

My wife chuckled, and said, "Yeah, and we ran into Brad Pitt on the trail. And Ryan Gosling." When I didn't respond, her laughing subsided. Then it died off altogether, leaving the line silent. "Wait, you're being serious?"

Now it was my turn to chuckle. "Ange, you know me pretty well. Does this seem like something I'd joke about?"

She laughed some more and gasped. "Jasmine Cruz stayed on our boat? Like the Jasmine Cruz?" She paused, then added, "I can't believe it. What is she like?"

I was speechless, hearing a side of my wife I'd never witnessed before. And it wasn't quite the reaction I'd been expecting. I mean, Ange and I operated on a one hundred percent honesty policy.

And I'd die before I broke my vows to her. But I'd still expected her to be a little upset.

Scarlett, having apparently overheard our conversation, leaned into the microphone, and said, "What's going on? Dad, what—"

Her voice cut off as Ange told her to step away.

"Wait, why did she stay on the Baia?" Ange said once she was over the initial excitement. "You said something about a complication?"

I gave her the gist of it while piloting northeast up along the Lower Keys. Her tone rapidly shifted, especially when I got onto the topic of Lucius Xavier and the things I'd heard and read about the man so far.

She took a moment to digest everything and asked a series of questions, her voice sounding angrier and angrier with each answer.

Then she fell silent for half a minute, and eventually said, "Send me over everything you have on this guy."

I sighed. "Ange, you don't have to do this. I want you and Scarlett to finish your trip."

"You're joking, right?"

"I can handle this."

I could practically feel her fury oozing through the phone.

"You think I'm just gonna continue on with our little hike and ignore everything I just heard? Years of abusing women. Manipulation. Murder. And then he went and made the biggest mistake of his pathetic little life. He attacked my husband." She paused a beat. "Send me over everything you've got. I want to see it all."

"Ange, you—"

"Logan Dodge," she said sternly.

I resigned, knowing there was nothing I could say to keep her from getting involved.

"You're at the bottom of the Grand Canyon. How exactly am I supposed to send everything to you?"

"I saw a fax machine in the main room of the lodge. I'll get you the number."

She handed the phone to Scarlett. I wasn't there to see it, but I didn't need to be. My wife was in full on recon mode.

"Hey, Dad!" Scarlett said.

"Good to hear your voice too, Scar. How's the hike?"

"Never mind that. Did I hear that you met Jasmine Cruz?"

I rubbed the back of my neck while skirting past a line of jet skiers.

"Oh shoot," Scarlett added before I could reply. "Mom's coming back."

"I'll tell you all about it later. You stay safe, all right?"

"We will," she said, then Ange came back over the line and read off a series of numbers.

I agreed to send everything over, and we ended the call after exchanging I-love-yous.

I set my phone on the instrument panel, then gazed out over the turquoise water. Looking skyward, I watched as a C-130 Hercules soared just overhead, coming in for a landing at the naval air station on Boca Chica Key just off our port bow.

I wasn't surprised that Ange wanted to drop everything and get involved. That was her way. It'd always been her way. She wasn't one to notice injustice and turn away from it. I just wished it hadn't come during the middle of their long-awaited mother-daughter trip.

With the water clear ahead of us and no land within half a mile, I stepped away from the cockpit and down the steps. "You have the helm," I said to Jasmine.

She looked at me bug-eyed, then crept over and grabbed the wheel. I snagged my laptop, then returned and cracked it open on the topside dinette.

"Don't do that again," Jasmine said, firing me a worried look. "I've never driven a boat before."

"Piloted," I corrected. Then I shrugged. "You've got it. Just keep her straight, her speed steady, and keep a sharp lookout for anything in front of us."

I sent everything I had on Lucius over to the number Ange had given me, then headed back down to the galley for coffee and hydration. Cracking open a coconut water, I sat at the half-moon cushioned seat and continued constructing a loose plan for the evening in my head.

Once I had a pretty good idea of how I wanted to go about the exchange, and the immediate evacuation of Jasmine and her son from the Keys, I made calls to Jack and Pete, informing them of the roles I hoped they'd play. Being the good friends they were, they both agreed without hesitation, despite the potential risk involved.

When I hung up and returned topside, Jasmine tweaked our course a little, then scratched her temple. "I don't understand why we have to travel to meet Wyatt someplace. Why can't we just meet him at the cemetery in Key West like he asked?"

I polished off my drink, then said, "Do you really want me to answer that?"

"I told you I trust him, Logan."

"You hesitated."

"I…" She let out a heavy sigh. "If Wyatt said he's bringing Theo, that's what he's doing. I can vouch for him. He's not perfect, but I know he cares about me and my son."

"Yesterday morning you could've vouched for your friends too, right?"

She looked away from me and squinted forward.

I stood, moved over, and rested a hand on the dash. "It's just a precaution, Jasmine. If you're right and he's telling the truth and everything goes smoothly, great. But if not, we'll be ready for it."

We fell quiet for a solid minute. She handled herself pretty good at the helm, avoiding a fishing boat and steering clear of paddleboarders.

"Where exactly is this place we're going to?" she eventually said.

"About twenty more miles on this line."

I could see based on her expression that she still thought I was being overly cautious.

But I wasn't.

I didn't want to tell her everything that was on my mind. I'd never met Wyatt Cash. I'd never even heard of the guy, or Lucius, or anyone else she'd mentioned. But I knew there was a good chance that her supposed fiancé was compromised. There were just too many variables that didn't add up, in addition to the fact that, whether I could get Jasmine to admit it or not, she didn't fully trust the guy.

I'd taken down a professional hitman who'd been hired to off us both. And I knew that whoever was sent next would be better. And if Lucius had an ounce of wits, he'd send a whole lot more of them.

SEVENTEEN

Grand Canyon

Angelina watched as sheets of paper fed out from the fax machine. She caught brief glimpses. Headshots of young women. Lines of text. News clippings and investigation reports. There were fifty-three in all by the time the machine stopped feeding and hummed down.

She slid the stack into a manilla folder and stepped up to the cashier. There was a guy wearing slacks and a short-sleeved white button-up talking to the lady behind the counter. His clean clothes and overall level of hygiene made him stand out like a sore thumb, but Ange barely noticed him as she paid.

"How many flights today?" the woman said to the guy.

"Half a dozen. No rest for the weary. Mostly just private couples."

He smiled at Ange as she told the cashier to keep the change. Then she turned on her heel, having barely processed a word of the exchange, and headed back out into the sun.

She trekked a couple hundred yards to the same picnic table she and Scarlett had used the previous day. On the way there, she saw the pilot in the distance, walking along a barely noticeable path toward a distant red-and-black Bell 407 helicopter parked in a small clearing. There was a big picnic blanket sprawled out and a group of four people relaxing and enjoying food and champagne.

Ange reached the picnic table and slid onto one side, setting the folder down in front of her. It was shaded and far enough away from the other tables so no one would hear their conversation.

Scarlett sat on the opposite side, working on a breakfast of scrambled eggs, toast, and sausage. They said nothing as Ange settled in. She took a couple long sips of coffee, then chomped a bite of granola bar as she stared out over the canyon surrounding them. The sun was just peeking up over the western edges, the fiery radiance breaking apart by jagged edges of rock and streaking all around.

After the incident at Ribbon Falls, Ange and Scarlett had returned to the North Kaibab Trail and made the final grueling push up to the North Rim. The landscape had changed dramatically during the ascent, swiftly transitioning from arid desert basins to a spruce fir forest.

They'd reached the top breathless and covered in sweat and had spent two hours taking in the sights from various overlooks before about-facing and heading back down the North Rim. They'd set up their tent at Cottonwood Campground and spent the night under a perfectly clear sky thick with some of the brightest stars they'd ever seen.

In the morning, they'd both risen early and journeyed back to Phantom Ranch for a nice meal and so they could call and check in with Logan.

Ange barely touched her food at first. She went straight for the coffee and the first page in the stack. It contained lines of information about a nineteen-year-old girl from Turkey. She'd modeled for one of Lucius's companies for three years before passing away in a tragic car accident on a San Diego turnpike. She'd been the only casualty, her Lexus flying into the barrier at over a hundred miles per hour. Cause of death was listed as possible mechanical failure, or operator error, but there'd been no traces of drugs or alcohol in her system.

Ange was starving, but she lost her appetite by the third page. One woman had perished in a parasailing accident in Cabo San Lucas. Another had stumbled and fallen off Angel's Landing in Zion National Park. And the most recent was a twenty-one-year-old named Lily Cohen who'd died of a drug overdose in her New York apartment just three weeks earlier.

There were seventeen deaths in all over the past twenty years. All beautiful, promising young women. And all with ties to Lucius Xavier or his companies. The rest of the papers pertained to reported incidents of abuse that had been mysteriously dropped by the victims. Extreme sexual harassment allegations. And even numerous accusations of rape. But none had ever been brought to court.

One of the hardest pages for Ange to stomach was an explanation Jasmine Cruz gave in a faxed-over statement. She explained that the women Lucius had murdered were just the ones he'd been unable to fully control. They were the least cooperative of the bunch. The ones who had stood their ground and threatened to expose his operation.

Most of the women being abused were still alive, having been bought off and silenced by money or threats against their lives or their family members' lives. Or by professional threats. Jasmine spoke of a popular young actress who'd appeared in a couple A-list movies six years back. After refusing Lucius's advances, she'd been blacklisted, her reputation in the community destroyed, and she'd never been able to get a major acting role again.

Ange felt her pulse amp up the more she read. The level of scumbaggery was difficult to comprehend. And the guy was still at it. Still living his life in the lap of luxury and getting away with abuse and extortion and murder.

She stopped halfway through, then stacked the pages and set them aside. Stayed silent for a long moment. Closed her eyes and told herself to breathe. Scarlett let her mom work through it, then clasped her hand.

"Mom, are you all right?"

Ange took two deep breaths, then tried her best not to think about everything she'd just seen, and how sick it made her feel. She checked her watch and was amazed that she'd been poring over the intel for over an hour and a half. Then she closed her eyes, leaned forward, and pinched the bridge of her nose. She opened her eyes and stared at her daughter.

"I know we've both been looking forward to this

trip for a while now," Ange said. "But we might have to cut this thing short and hustle out of here. You all right with that?"

Scarlett took one brief glance at the papers, then said, "Of course." She looked around. "But we're not exactly close to a road down here. It'll take a while to reach the rim."

Ange looked out into the distance. She spotted something small hovering over the canyon to the west. It grew bigger, and she realized it was a helicopter. A black-and-red Bell 407. The same make and model as the one she'd seen on her walk from the lodge.

"Maybe... maybe not."

She grabbed her binos and tracked the helicopter as it soared over the landscape, then swooped in for a soft landing in the same spot it'd taken off from earlier that morning. A return flight back to Las Vegas, she imagined. Then a refuel and a quick turnaround with a different group.

Ange focused through the lenses and watched as the same pilot she'd seen back in the lodge stepped out.

"Come on," she said, gathering the papers.

"Where are we going?"

"Los Angeles."

EIGHTEEN

Ange and Scarlett strapped into seats aboard the helicopter, both gazing out the windows as the rotors picked up speed and lifted them up off the canyon floor. They stared in awe, the sheer walls of various colors blurring past as they cruised up and over the beautiful landscape.

Ange turned and shot a look toward the pilot, who gave her a thumbs-up. A smile and five hundred bucks had convinced him to let her and Scarlett bum a ride to Las Vegas. Then, just over an hour and a hundred and seventy miles of canyon and desert later, another two thousand bucks convinced him to give them a ride to Los Angeles after dropping off the other guests in America's Playground.

While waiting on the tarmac of the helicopter terminal at McCarran Airport, Ange made a call to Logan.

"What else do you know?" Ange said, getting right to her point.

"What do you mean?" Logan replied.

"I mean that, after helping Jasmine and her son go into hiding, you're gonna fly west. Am I right?" She paused, but not long enough to let him answer. "Of course you are. But there's not enough to go on in what you sent me, and I'm guessing your plan isn't to go straight to Lucius and confront him. You'll want ammunition first. Stuff you can use to destroy not just him but his reputation—so what else do you know?"

Logan sighed. "There's a patrol officer with LAPD. Officer Veronica Carter. She's worked with multiple victims to take action against Lucius. But all have been dismissed or settled out of court before they could gain any steam."

"And she's still alive?" Ange said, amazed.

"Far as Maddox knew. After making sure Jasmine and her son are safe, I'm heading there to find and talk to her. See what I can dig up."

They fell silent.

"I gotta do this, Ange."

"I know. We're cut from the same cloth."

"No," Logan said. "I can handle this."

"Nice try. Send me over everything you have on Officer Carter."

"Ange, I—"

"You gonna make me bust out your full name again?" she said sternly. The pilot gave her a thumbs-up, and she and Scarlett strode back toward the helicopter and climbed in through the side door. "Besides, we're already in the air."

"What?"

"We left the canyon an hour ago. We're heading to LA."

"Ange, you—"

"What if it were Scarlett?" she said again. "What if she'd fallen victim to this monster? She was an orphan, Logan. Just like many of these women were. It could have easily been her abused, raped, coerced, and eventually murdered, her death staged to look like a suicide. What would you do then?"

They both knew the answer to that question. Logan would claw through the depths of hell if he had to. He'd stand toe to toe with the devil or whoever else stood in his way. But he'd make it right. He'd settle the score. He'd make it right or he'd die trying.

They both would.

"Just be careful, all right?" Logan said. "That's a long way from home. And it's a different world over there. After I get Jasmine and her son to the safe house in the Bahamas, I'll head straight there and we'll do whatever we have to do to get to the bottom of this. And to make sure no other young women fall victim to this guy."

The pilot fired up the engine and rotors, and they ended the call. The skids lifted off the apron. They rapidly ascended, soaring over the rows of towering hotels and casinos sparkling in the late-morning sun. They tore out of the city and across a seemingly never-ending desert.

Just under two hours later, they closed in on their destination, sweeping over the San Gabriel Mountains. Scarlett gazed through the window in awe as the enormous spread of civilization appeared ahead of them. She'd seen Miami from the air before, but this was a completely different animal and it blew her away. The second most populated metropolitan area in the US, comprised of nearly twenty million people.

A seemingly never-ending spread of housing developments and shopping centers and business parks, running along a wide stretch of sand and surf and continuing long past the outstretched horizon north and south.

The pilot brought them down onto a corner of the LAX airport designated for rotary wing traffic.

"Welcome to the City of Angels," he said. "There are taxis through the terminal there," he added, pointing through the windshield. "And a shuttle to catch domestic or international flights."

When the rotors wound down, Ange and Scarlett grabbed their bags and stepped out onto the tarmac of the bustling airport that was situated less than half a mile from the beach and ten miles from the city center.

After thanking the pilot, they headed inside and toward the taxi area.

"Where are we going?" Scarlett said.

"First, a hotel to drop our stuff off. Then, shopping and a shower. We reek."

Ange booked two nights at a Courtyard Marriot right along Marina Del Ray. The two hopped into a cab, and Scarlett couldn't help staring out the windows as they motored the short trip up the coast. They'd woken up in a tent that morning at a quiet campground in the bottom of the Grand Canyon. Now they were cruising through one of the busiest and most populous cities in the world.

The room had a balcony with a nice view of the marina. Lines of fancy sparkling boats tied off. People lounged by a pool and relaxed under the sun, tipping back cocktails and listening to faint tropical music.

"It's like you found Conch Harbor on the West Coast," Scarlett said as she took in the scene.

They walked to a nearby shopping center and picked out casual outfits. Returning to the room, they rinsed and scrubbed off layers of dirt and sweat, then dressed and headed back out into the California sun.

"Where to now?" Scarlett said, loving being invited to take part in the action for once.

Dangerous, high-stakes activities were nothing new for her parents, but they usually did everything in their power to keep her as far as they could from harm's way. Ange, however, was just biding her time, having booked a flight for Scarlett to head back home that evening. She figured there was no harm in showing her daughter around. Maybe tracking down a local police officer and asking a couple questions while enjoying the California beach vibes.

"Venice Beach," Ange said. "Just a short walk from here."

"And then we're looking for a police officer, right?"

"Officer Veronica Carter." Ange showed a picture of a pretty, serious-faced black woman in her late twenties. "Maddox says she's on bicycle patrol along the promenade."

Ange and Scarlett fit right in walking the wide palm-tree-lined streets of the Golden Coast. They both wore denim shorts, tank tops, and sunglasses. On the short trek to the beach, they passed people on longboards with long flowing hair. People riding bicycles barefoot. And the populace seemed to appear more relaxed and unique the closer they got to their destination.

Scarlett didn't know what to expect from Venice Beach, but when they arrived she was shocked. She gazed upon a vast stretch of fine white sand. Big waves crashing and rumbling and splashing flat in a bubbly haze over the hard-packed pebbles. People playing volleyball. Skateboarders doing tricks. Surfers out riding the swells. A haven for pranksters and tricksters. Artists and musicians.

It reminded Scarlett of Mallory Square back in the Keys, but longer and with far more people.

"Mom," Scarlett said, patting Ange on the shoulder and pointing forward.

There were two cops pedaling toward them, navigating smartly through the throngs of beachgoers. They rolled into view, but both were men.

"Good eye, kiddo," Ange said. "Let's keep looking."

They passed by the quarter-mile-long wooden pier, then a gym with weights right on the beach. The biggest guys Scarlett had ever seen sauntered around shirtless and oiled up and busted out reps of heavy weights, clanking them down and giving each other high fives.

Covering just over a mile of waterfront, keeping their eyes peeled, they reached the heart of the boardwalk.

Far ahead of them was the famous Santa Monica Pier with its renowned Ferris wheel and roller coaster. Then inland were the canals, the buildings of the city far in the distance, and beyond them the Hollywood Hills, though they couldn't see the famous sign from that far away through the veil of smog.

After another twenty minutes of walking and searching, Ange spotted two expensive-looking black bicycles propped onto their stands under a palm tree beside the entrance into a gift shop. The bikes both had black rear rack bags and had LAPD in bold silver letters across their down tubes.

Ange cut across the busy promenade, peeking around racks of colorful towels, postcards, and swimsuits spilling out the store's propped-open front doors. Through the front windows, she could barely make out a female police officer confronting two tall young men. Ange didn't have an angle on the officer's face, but she knew there was a good chance that this was the woman she was looking for.

She continued along the walkway until she could see the side of the structure. There was another officer there. A short, wide-shouldered guy who was watching the back door. Turning back, she stopped again behind one of the display racks and peered back inside. Noticed that there could be trouble brewing.

"You want ice cream, Scar?" Ange said, pointing toward a little stand across the boardwalk as her daughter caught up to her.

Scarlett smiled. Then she noticed the police bikes and the interaction in the store as well and was on to her mother.

"I can help, Mom."

"Move across the path and stay there."

"But, Mom—"

"Now!" she snapped.

Scarlett froze, then swallowed and did as she was told. Weaving through people walking their dogs and a trail of longboarders, she plopped onto a bench in the shade of a cypress tree.

Once Scarlett was out of the picture, Ange moved in closer and observed the interaction carefully. She couldn't tell what it was about, but the two guys were growing heated, and the officer was doing her best to control the situation.

Migrating even closer, Ange got a good look at the officer's face when the woman craned her neck to say something into the radio clipped to her collar. It was Officer Carter. She was sure of it. The picture in her pocket was a perfect match.

The intensity of the scuffle rose even higher. Yells emanated through the walls. Then one of the guys pointed a finger in Officer Carter's face.

That seemed to set her off.

The cop, who'd remained calm and collected throughout the entire encounter, seemed to become a different person entirely. She reached for her hip and withdrew a yellow taser. One of the troublemakers lunged toward her. She stepped back, and with a twitch of her finger, she fired two pointy probes across the six feet between them. The sharp electrodes tore through the fabric of the guy's T-shirt and bit into his chest, delivering a powerful surge of electricity. The man shook and grunted and went down fast, vanishing out of Ange's view.

Before his jolting buddy had even reached the floor, the second guy swiped a bag off the floor and took off. He darted around an aisle and sprinted straight for the propped-open front door, bursting free at a sprint and hurling himself down the set of steps and onto the pavement. Carter appeared a moment later, barking orders to her partner as she pursued, the other guy still out of sight on the shop's floor.

The runner was fast. Lean and young and athletic. And he had a head start. But Carter would get him. Ange had no doubt about that. In less than a hundred yards she'd get to him and pound him to the pavement.

But Ange wasn't about to let him get even that far.

Already in an ideal position to cut the guy off at the corner of the storefront, she jumped forward and rapidly swept her left leg. She struck the guy's shin just as he planted his weight, and he yelled out from the surprise attack and did a near three-sixty before crashing hard onto his back at the base of a trash can.

He rolled and grunted, trying to shake away the daze from the attack. Then he glared up at Ange and reached for his waistband. Ange cut the distance between them in a blur of movement and slammed her heel into the guy's wrist before he could grab the hidden switchblade he'd been reaching for.

"What the hell?" he spat, his body held down.

Officer Carter showed up. Ange grabbed the guy's knife and tossed it onto a nearby patch of grass, then turned and raised her empty hands.

"He's all yours, Officer," she said calmly.

Carter paused a moment, then dropped down and shoved a knee into the guy's back. Ange let off and stepped away as the officer reached for her handcuffs and secured them around the downed man's wrists.

He cursed her out, calling her every name in the book. She ignored it and heaved him to his feet. Ushered him back toward the front of the gift shop, where her partner was just forcing troublemaker number one out onto the boardwalk.

"Thanks for the help," Officer Carter said, keeping a firm grip on the handcuffed man. "But I had him."

Ange nodded. "I know you did. But I couldn't let you have all the fun."

She grinned slightly. "You're a cop?"

Ange shook her head. "No. But I used to be in a... somewhat similar line of work."

The people she'd hunted down in her past life had usually been violent dictators or terrorist leaders, but she didn't mention that.

"Well, you want to swear in?" Carter said. "I'd love having you watching my back." She raised her voice and eyed her partner. "Better than this bozo. Where were you anyway, Jacobs?"

The man laughed as he manhandled the other criminal down the steps. "You said to watch the side door, V."

Carter chuckled, then called in for a squad car with her radio. "Let's get these two into a nice air-conditioned vehicle. How does that sound, boys?"

They both cursed her again, and she took the insults well.

"Thanks again," Carter said, then the two officers ushered the handcuffed men around the shop and into a parking lot.

Less than thirty seconds later, a Dodge Charger police car pulled in and the men were ushered into the back. They continued to berate the officers, hurling insults that were especially directed toward Officer Carter.

One of them called her every name in the book at the top of his lungs, then accused her of being an Uncle Tom as she was about to shut the door.

"You're going away," Carter said in a calm yet authoritative voice. "Why don't you spend that time thinking hard about things you can do to actually make your life better for once? And our community better."

"Why don't you go to hell, Carter. When I get out I'm coming for you."

The officer paused, then nodded briefly and emotionally. "All right. Just know that I'll be praying for you, brother."

The man was stunned speechless as she shut the door. Carter patted the roof, and the driver sped them off. She stood there a moment, just watching in silence as the Charger cut out of sight. Then she composed herself and turned back toward Ange and her partner.

"The air okay up there?" Ange said.

Carter paused a moment, surprised that Ange was still there. "Excuse me?"

"I've just never witnessed someone take such a high road before."

She nearly smiled, then said to her partner, "Hustle back to the bikes, Jacobs. I'll be right there." The guy double-timed it to the boardwalk, and Carter glanced over at Ange, startled a second time that she was still standing there. "Something I can help you with, ma'am? If you're looking for some form of compensation, I'm sorry to say it, but that's not how the whole Good Samaritan thing works."

"I'm not looking for any compensation. Just a minute of your time."

"Uh-oh," she said, then adjusted her sunglasses. "Look, whatever this is about, it'll have to wait. We have a division briefing we're already late for."

She brisked past Ange, heading back toward the promenade and their parked bicycles.

"It's about Lucius Xavier," Ange said, speaking just loud enough for the officer to hear.

Carter froze mid-step. She turned around on her heel then eyed Ange suspiciously. "Okay. You have my attention." Then her gaze veered back and forth between Ange and Scarlett. "Did he hurt either of you? Because if he did, he—"

"No. He didn't do anything to us. Just dozens of other women, it seems."

"And you...?" she said, holding out her palms expectantly.

"I want to talk to you in private." Then she swallowed and added, "Jasmine Cruz is his latest victim. He tried to have her murdered yesterday in Florida and my husband saved her life. Twice. Now he's helping her go into hiding, and I'm here to bring Lucius to his knees."

Carter stared in awe, her mouth agape. She just stood there a long moment. Stunned frozen.

She still hadn't said anything when Officer Jacobs returned, walking both bikes up to them.

"You planning on joining me again anytime soon?" Jacobs said.

Carter held her stare on Ange a second longer, then blinked, closed her mouth, and turned to her partner. "Have lunch at your place, all right? We'll meet back up at the pier at fourteen hundred."

Seeing her serious expression, he gave her a nod while handing over her bicycle. Then he slid onto his seat and pedaled inland.

After he was out of earshot, Carter turned to Ange and Scarlett. "Something about being the arm of law and order really works up my appetite. You two hungry?"

They migrated down the waterfront a short ways, then cut inland for a block to a Mexican restaurant called Tocaya. The place was unassuming from the outside. A simple wooden structure with Spanish music spilling out of it.

Officer Carter picked them out a shady corner spot on the patio that offered privacy from the bulk of the patrons and passersby.

She started them off with orders of chips and salsa, as well as warm plantain chips and freshly made guacamole with pomegranate seeds. On Carter's recommendation, they ordered plates of chicken tinga and fried mahi-mahi tacos, as well as bowls of tortilla soup. Everything was incredible. Some of the best Mexican food that either Ange or Scarlett had ever had.

They dug in and washed everything down with chilled bottles of Mexican Coca-Cola and ice water.

Part way into the tacos, Carter fired Ange the same curious look she'd dished out back in the parking lot. "All right," she said, swallowing a bite, "how can I help you, Angelina?"

Ange splashed some soda down her parched throat. "Just Ange. And I need information on Lucius. Starting with your juiciest. We're gonna build a case against him. Lock him away forever. And given recent events, speed is key. The best testimonies, witnesses, and where we can find him."

Carter smiled. "You sure don't beat around the

bush, do you?"

"I never have."

"I like that," Carter said. Then she leaned forward. "This guy's been on my list for years. I've done everything I can to try and bring his ass to justice. Nothing's worked. He's just got too many people greased. Too many people who will fall along with him if he goes down."

Ange held her intense gaze. Unblinking.

Carter smiled. "I like you, Ange. You've got focus, and a moral compass. We could use more people like you in this city."

"I came to you for answers, not compliments."

Carter chewed another bite and nodded. "Best place to go would be the law offices of Ronald Wessel."

"Go on."

"That's the mother lode. Wessel's been covering Lucius for over twenty years now. Silenced over a hundred witnesses, I'd imagine. Tarnished just as many testimonies. He's the one who handles all the legal loopholes and manipulation and buying off. It all comes from Wessel's office. But the guy's untouchable. A fortification that the law and justice can't break through."

Ange tightened her gaze. "Where can I find him?"

"His main office is in the Aon Center tower. The top floor. It's the third-tallest building in the city. Some of the most expensive office space in the world, so that should tell you something. Business is booming. And Wessel has done well for himself working with Lucius."

The table fell silent as Ange chewed a bite,

mulling everything over. "I gotta ask," she eventually said. "Why has Lucius Xavier been on a patrol officer's list for years?"

Carter held her gaze steady. The officer hesitated a moment, then shrugged. "This is my city. Been living here, walking these streets, all my life. And I don't like scum in my streets."

Ange shook her head. "I'm not buying that answer. There's no shortage of criminal activity around here, so why focus so much on Lucius?"

"Well, you're gonna have to buy it cause that's all I'm saying about it. It's personal."

Ange dropped it, and the conversation turned back to Ronald Wessel. As they finished their food, Ange spent most of the time imagining how the view from the top of the Aon Center would surely be spectacular.

I might just have to swing by and check it out for myself, she thought as she downed the rest of her Coke.

NINETEEN

It was nearly sunset as Jasmine and I stood at the tip of the old railroad bridge extending out from the western corner of Bahia Honda. Originally built by Henry Flagler over a hundred years earlier, the bridge had been constructed to connect what is now Bahia Honda State Park to West Summerland Key. But a section of the now-paved bridge had been removed, and we stood there patiently, watching as the sun sank over the islands.

"How things looking, Jack?" I said into a radio while directing my gaze to the southeast.

We had a nice, perched vantage point, allowing me to see the Baia bobbing just beyond the shallows and buoys.

"No sign of them yet," Jack replied.

While going through the plan I'd cooked up, we'd shown him pictures of Wyatt Cash and Theo Cruz. He was on the lookout for them both, scanning the shore and walkways with his binos from just offshore.

"Copy that," I said. "Pete, how's the fishing?"

"Already hooked two snapper," he said in his pirate-like voice.

I smiled. The legendary seadog was drifting even farther offshore, standing by to play his part in the evening's activities.

I slid the small radio back into my cargo shorts pocket. Scanned the area around us once more in a full three-sixty.

"This place is beautiful," Jasmine said, her mouth open as she looked around. "I wish I were here under different circumstances."

She was right about that. The state park had my favorite beaches in the entire island chain. And the shallows off its southern shore in particular offered some of the clearest and most vibrantly turquoise waters I'd seen anywhere. There was also a campground and numerous scattered picnic areas among the lush landscape.

"You'll just have to come back someday," I said.

"Absolutely. I—"

She was interrupted by Jack's voice slipping through a quick mess of static.

"All right, I have a visual on the guy," he said. "He's heading up the walking path from the parking lot. Maybe two hundred yards from the base of the bridge."

Jasmine shot me a worried look.

Holding the radio up to my mouth, I said, "Is the boy with him?"

"Negative. It's just the guy."

"You sure?"

"Got a clear view, Logan. He's alone."

I shot Jasmine a look. Watched as the blood

drained from her face.

"All right, keep your eyes peeled for anyone else suspicious. And be ready, Jack. This thing might go south in a hurry."

"I got your back, brother."

I pocketed the radio, then patted my Sig secured at the back of my waistband right next to my sheathed dive knife.

"He told me they'd come alone, Logan," Jasmine said, her voice barely above a whisper.

"He also said he was bringing your son."

She frowned, kept her eyes forward. "He must be close by. Wyatt cares about Theo. That I know for sure."

She still wasn't grasping the extent of what was happening. Or maybe it was a defense mechanism internally protecting her from a truth she couldn't bear to fathom. But Theo not being there likely meant only one thing. And it wasn't good.

Jasmine sighed. "He's not perfect, but I know he cares about us."

"That's the second time you've told me that he isn't perfect," I said. There was something about her tone when the words had flowed out each time that caught my attention. "What do you mean by that?"

She froze like a deer in the headlights. Swallowed hard. "I mean, nobody's perfect, right?"

"Cut the crap, Jasmine. What did you mean by it?"

She paused again, then said, "He... has a short temper sometimes. But it's rare that he ever—"

"He's hurt you?" I said, raising my eyebrows at her. "Physically?"

She hesitated, biting her lip again. "A couple of

times. But it's not what you think."

"What the hell are you talking about? Did he hurt you or not?"

She nodded.

"Then I guess it's exactly what I think, isn't it? How can you trust this guy?"

As I pointed toward shore, a man appeared, walking along the winding path that poked out from the thick foliage. He was still a hundred yards off and quickly climbed over a gate installed to prevent foot traffic, continuing toward us. I glared as the man came into focus.

Jasmine cleared her throat. "We have a long history, Logan. And I... just promise me you won't beat him up."

"I can't do that," I said, shaking my head.

"Okay, well, at least let me talk to him first?"

I said nothing. Just stood there and watched as the guy came closer. He was dressed in tight faded jeans and a white-and-gold Gucci T-shirt with short sleeves that hugged his biceps. He was tan. Had straight dark hair that flapped in the wind. Wore big gold-rimmed sunglasses. And I could smell his musky cologne from a good thirty yards out.

He moved with a slow, arrogant gait. Shoulders back. Chest up. Wide swinging arms, like he owned the place. But there was something else in his mannerisms. A stiffness hinting that he was uncomfortable, maybe even borderline terrified out of his mind, but that he was doing his best to hide it by acting the part of the tough guy.

I stood motionless at Jasmine's side as he walked right up to her, shaking his head.

"Where's Theo?" Jasmine said, a hefty dose of motherly worry in her voice.

"You've really outdone yourself this time, Jazz," Wyatt said in a condescending voice. "You have any idea how much trouble you're in?"

"Yeah, I got a pretty good idea of it when Lucius's people tried to kill me. Twice. Now where's Theo?"

He fell silent a moment, a smug smirk on his face. His head swiveled back and forth between the two of us. When he looked at me, he threw his shoulders back even farther. Straightened his back and even leaned forward onto his toes to try and match my height. Like some kind of animalistic intimidation move seen in primates. All it confirmed for me was that this guy was scared shitless.

"He's safe for now," Wyatt said. "I've made sure he'll be fine, don't worry."

"What is that supposed to mean?"

He ignored the question, then jerked his head my way. "Who's he? Your new boy toy?"

"This is... Owen. He's the one who saved me."

He raised his eyebrows, pretending to be impressed. "Well, Owen, you're no longer needed. I'll take care of Jasmine from here."

"Where's Theo?" Jasmine asked a third time, her voice growing more frantic.

"Like I said, he's safe. But only if you come with me. *Alone.*"

He stared daggers at me.

"I'm not going anywhere with you," Jasmine snapped.

He chuckled and stepped forward. "Actually, you are."

He reached for her. The moment his hand touched hers, I snatched him by the wrist. A firm grip, but not enough to make him squeal. Not yet.

"Actually, she's not," I said.

Wyatt froze, turned his head, and gave me a cocky smile. "The strange, smelly man speaks."

Then he tried to yank his arm free of my grasp in what he surely thought was a brilliant fake-out maneuver.

His arm didn't budge.

"Like she said, she's not going anywhere with you." I squeezed tighter, just enough to provoke a wince. Then I lowered my voice a couple octaves. "And this is the part where you tell us where her son is."

Jasmine was staring at him, and I could practically hear her heart racing in her chest.

The guy faked a laugh. Like everything was all good and he had this under control. He was a terrible actor.

"All right, all right," he said. "I'll tell you. Just let me go."

"Tell me first."

His left hand tightened into a fist and he hurled it my way. Awkward and off-balance. I'd seen children with better form.

The punch missed me by a foot, and I swept a leg and sent him onto his butt. Still gripping his wrist, I twisted it behind him, then heaved him off the ground.

"What the hell, Jazz?" he spat. "Who the hell is this nobody?"

"Where's her son?" I said.

Wyatt looked frantically from Jasmine to me. She stayed silent.

I was getting tired of smelling his cologne. It reeked and burned my nostrils and was making me lightheaded.

I lifted the guy higher and dragged him to the side. Jerked him around and held his face over the top of the concrete railing.

"Tell me where her son is or I'm gonna slam your face into this," I said, threatening the thing I imagined he cared most about.

"Do you have any idea who I am?" he spat. "Do you have any clue how important I am?"

I said nothing.

"My nose is insured for half a million dollars."

I smiled at that, then manhandled him back a couple inches. "Perfect."

Then I shoved him forward, stopping him inches from the solid concrete barrier when he opened his mouth again.

"I'll sue!" he cried. "I'll sue you for everything you're worth and then some."

I yanked his arm back tighter and pressed his face hard against the thick slab. The last glows of sunlight were just slipping away to the west, firing off glistening rays over the water below us.

"Screw you," he grunted. "You won't do it. You don't have the—"

I reared him back again and bashed his face into the railing. His insured nose broke with a quick crunch. He shrieked and blood gushed out from his nostrils, staining his satin shirt and fancy jeans.

Letting out a high-pitched whine, he fell to his

knees, held both hands up to his bleeding nose, and tilted his head back. Quivered and whimpered like he'd just been dealt the most painful blow in the history of mankind. I'd never seen a more overly dramatic display in my life.

I grabbed hold of him again. A tight wad of his shirt with one hand and a fistful of his hair with the other. Then I lifted him off the road and hovered his face over the same devastating concrete surface once again.

"I'm going to ask you one more time," I said. "And if you don't answer me, I'm gonna break every bone in your face."

His sobbing cries somehow intensified. Then he calmed his breathing, fighting hard to muster something resembling composure.

"He's with Lucius, all right?" Wyatt gasped. "Theo's with Lucius."

Jasmine stomped over. "You left my son with that maniac?"

"I... I had no choice. He said he'd keep him safe. So long as I did what he told me to do."

"What did he tell you to do?" I said, tightening my grip even more on the guy.

"Just to bring Jasmine back with me. That's it."

My radio crackled to life. Jack's voice broke free of the static.

"We got a big SUV that's flying through the park," he said. "Heading your way."

I used my left hand to swipe the radio. "Copy. Let me know if anyone gets out when it stops."

"I don't think it's stopping, bro," Jack said, his voice filled with surprise. A distant crashing noise filled the air, then Jack said, "They just drove right through the barrier onto the footpath."

I pictured the area in my mind and knew that whoever they were, they'd reach us in under a minute.

"Copy that, Jack. Time to fire up the Baia."

"On my way."

I slipped the radio back into my pocket.

"Who is it, Wyatt?" Jasmine said, terror on her face. "Who else came with you?"

I shook my head at her. "He doesn't know. We're done with him."

Then I tightened my grip and pressed his face against the same spot on the concrete.

"How'd you hurt your face, punk?" I said.

He gritted his teeth and spat a gob of blood onto the road. "Some raging lunatic sucker punched me. My lawyer will—"

"Wrong answer," I said, tightening my grip and forcing his arm back to garner another squeal.

"How'd you hurt your face?"

He gasped. "I… I fell."

"Fell where?"

He paused, his eyes frantic, then swallowed and said, "In the shower."

"That's better. Now you're remembering it correctly." I leaned forward, my mouth just over his right ear. "Tell a different story, and I'll find you. Understood?"

He nodded frantically.

"And if you ever lay a finger on Miss Cruz again, there won't be a plastic surgeon in Los Angeles who'll be able to help you. You'll be a lost cause. Is that understood?"

He cried and shook and gasped a weak, "Yes."

"Good."

The sound of a distant roaring engine caught my attention. It was getting louder. Still holding tight to Wyatt, I slammed the punk temple first into the railing, knocking him unconscious.

I turned to see Jasmine with her mouth hung open as she stared at his motionless body.

"Is he…?" she gasped.

"Just taking a little nap. He'll be fine. That blood flow's already caking up. He'll wake up with a headache and a hundred mosquito bites, but that's all."

I gestured for her to follow me a couple strides to the end of the bridge. The Baia flew into view off our left shoulder, slicing through the calm waters.

I knelt and scooped up a coil of nylon rope stashed just out of view. One end was already secured to a curl of rebar protruding from the thick cement, and the other was looped through a harness that'd already been adjusted to fit Jasmine perfectly.

"Remember what I told you," I said, sliding the harness up around her waist and making sure it was snug.

"Slow and steady. Breathe."

"That's exactly right." Then I looked her in the eyes. "You can do this."

She nodded, then I tossed the line down as Jack piloted the Baia right under us, holding the vessel steady in the current between the old bridge piers. Once my friend had control of the rope, I helped Jasmine over the edge. She handled herself well, rappelling steadily and Jack helping her as she reached the padded sunbed.

She looked skyward and threw me a thumbs-up. I returned the gesture, then gave Jack a quick salute.

"You're not coming?" Jasmine said.

I gazed toward the shore and the sound of the rapidly approaching vehicle.

"Whoever these guys are, they've probably traveled a long way," I said. "They deserve a proper greeting."

TWENTY

I turned and hustled back toward shore, hurdling the metal gate. Ahead, the sounds of a big engine grew louder. The moment the Suburban came into view, blasting out from the encroaching branches flanking the dirt path, I threw myself over the guard rail and held on tight, watching from my hidden position as the SUV thundered across the bridge right past me.

I pulled myself up as it crashed through the metal gate, then continued at a confident walk, reaching the end of the bridge just as the big vehicle braked to a hard stop.

I turned and watched as doors flew open and men jumped out. They were far off, but there appeared to be four of them. I pulled out my little monocular and focused the lens. Counted four guys. They were all Hispanic and muscular. And they all carried firearms. Two gripped pistols, one a submachine gun, and the fourth a shotgun. They stepped to the edge of the bridge and gazed down, then split up and searched the immediate area, giving the unconscious Wyatt a quick look over before leaving him to continue his nap.

I pocketed my monocular and withdrew my Sig. Took aim. They were two hundred yards off, easy. Difficult shots, but I didn't need to hit them. Just rattle their cages a bit and give Jasmine and Jack more time to make their escape.

I let loose, firing a rapid succession of thundering pops. A round struck one of the guys as they all scrambled and took cover behind their vehicle. Then I emptied the rest of the fifteen-round magazine, peppering the rear door and bumper. Shooting up sparks and shattering the rear window.

I freed the spent mag and swiftly replaced it with a fresh one. Stood motionless and watched with the monocular as the four guys struggled back into their shot-up Suburban.

The engine roared, and the tires squealed and spat smoke as the driver turned the SUV around and floored them back toward the shore.

I stood facing them right in the middle of the road. Waited just long enough to be certain they'd spotted me through the windshield, then turned and took off into a sprint. I booked it off the pavement and onto the dirt path. Weaving past the encroaching bushes, I rounded a slight turn and veered off the path, disappearing into the brush.

I grabbed a backpack resting under a thick canopy of leaves. The second item I'd pre-staged. Unzipping the main compartment, I removed a spike strip, then strode back to the path and tossed it across. The metal links uncoiled like a snake and worked up a thin cloud of dust as they landed, the sharp spikes sticking up and extending clear across the walkway.

I retreated back off the path. The roaring Suburban appeared a second later, rumbling around the corner at well over fifty miles per hour. The driver spotted the spikes and tried to brake and turn, but he was too late. Both front tires exploded, and the vehicle lurched and flipped onto its side. The big SUV's frame crunched as it spun twice and crashed into the thick brush, eventually settling upside down against the base of a lignum vitae tree.

To my astonishment, three of the guys forced their way out of the damaged vehicle, their weapons raised. Still lurking in the shadows, I opened fire again, this time from just twenty yards away. I buried two rounds into the nearest guy and he fell facefirst onto the dirt.

The hitman with the submachine gun opened fire, shooting chaotically in my direction, and forcing me to drop back. I hit the ground and rolled, taking cover behind a tight cluster of trees. I slid down a steep slope, a layer of dirt coating my body, then crawled under a thick hive of cocoplum bushes.

I kept perfectly still. My eyes and ears alert.

Footsteps approached. Heavy boots. Then the two men still standing appeared above me, their weapons raised. One whispered something to the other, then they split up and moved steadily down the slope. I remained perfectly still. Waiting patiently.

Hunting.

I locked my attention onto the nearest gunman wielding a shotgun. He wore a bulletproof vest and a skintight black T-shirt, revealing big veiny muscles and tattooed arms. His face was hard. His eyes dark. He followed the faint trail of smooth dirt I'd left in the wake of my trip down part of the hillside. The other guy was covering him from ten yards farther away along the slope.

Moving slow and silent, I holstered my Sig and slid free my dive knife. I kept calm and alert. Ran through my upcoming actions in my head. Ready.

When the closest guy's left leg was less than five feet from my face, I sprang forward, reached, and slashed his Achilles. The tendon snapped and curled up. His leg went useless. He screamed as he fell, and I rose and caught him halfway, stabbing my knife into the base of his neck to finish him off.

I held my victim up as the second guy took aim with his MAC-10. Using him as a human shield, I charged as the guy opened fire, blasting a series of rounds into his comrade. I grunted and dove, throwing the dead guy into his buddy and tackling him hard. We all flew over the edge, rolling in a chaotic plunge down the steep slope. We crashed through bushes and trees, snapping branches and tumbling off trunks before breaking free of the brush and rolling onto a small sandy beach.

My body came to a stop beside a recently abandoned spread of beach chairs, an umbrella, and scattered toys. I groaned from the harsh fall, then reached for my pistol while coming to a knee. The final assassin spat sand and looked around frantically. He grabbed hold of a piece of driftwood and swung it toward me just as I took aim. I tried to avoid the sudden attack, but the heavy waterlogged plank crashed into my hands and knocked my weapon free.

I fell onto my back and he reared for an overhead strike. I rolled left at the last second, the wood striking the sand just inches from my face. I landed a solid kick to his breadbasket. His body curled and he heaved and released the driftwood. Then I spun and swung a kick across his face that gyrated his body, and he fell hard onto the sand.

I jumped to my feet and closed in to finish the guy off. He grabbed one of the beach chairs and whipped around, hurling it into my side. I stumbled and he charged like an angry bull, reaching me in a blink and throwing his shoulder into me. We flew backward, his powerful blow nearly knocking me unconscious, and we crashed onto the beach beside a moated sandcastle steps from the surf.

I threw a row of knuckles into his throat, then hooked my right leg around his upper body and rotated him off me. He collided into the hard-packed sand, and I rose onto his back. Now on top of him, I forced one of his arms back and shoved him facefirst into the shallow moat. He yelled out bubbles and kicked and thrashed with everything he had. Then his fight grew weaker, and his body eventually went limp beneath me.

TWENTY-ONE

In the silent aftermath of the brutal scuffle, I could hear my heart jackhammering, along with my quick breaths.

Letting go of the dead hitman beneath me, I forced myself to my feet. I fought to clear my mind and calm my breathing as I staggered across the sand and recovered my Sig. The moment the intensity of the fierce encounter began to subside, Jack's voice blared from the radio still in my pocket.

"Logan?" he said. "You all right?"

I let out a long breath. "Fine. What's your status?"

"We're back near the channel, and we've got more trouble incoming. It looks like there are more of them. They've stolen one of the ranger boats and they're flying our way out of the park's marina."

I turned and gazed to my right, focusing just beyond Calusa Beach. I spotted a white speedboat poking into my view from the opening into the marina and blasting southwest. The sky had grown dark, so I could barely make out more than a distant shadowy image as it blurred across the water.

How many assassins did this guy send? I thought, shaking my head as I watched the boat appear.

"We'll head your way and pick you up, bro," Jack said.

I stared at the distant boat, then the Baia as Jack motored it under the old bridge. A quick mental calculation convinced me that the ranger boat, and the hitmen aboard it, would intercept *Dodging Bullets* before it reached me.

"There's no time," I said, hustling across the beach. "I'll meet you there."

I threw myself into a sprint, pumping my arms and pounding my shoes into the sand before reaching a trail up the hill. I wound around, then cut back onto the dirt path, passing the upturned SUV and a small group of beachgoers gathered beside it.

I fought through the pain in my shoulder and legs from the violent fall, and raced onto the pavement of the bridge. Off my right shoulder, I could see the ranger boat in my peripherals. It was closing in, flying toward the opening where the Baia was idling.

I darted past the flattened gate and closed in on the end of the road. There was no time to use the rope and rappel down. Instead, I leapt onto the left guard rail and threw myself into open air.

Warm wind whipped past me and my stomach flew up into my chest as I picked up speed. I straightened my body, splashing into the water twenty yards from the Baia's bow. I sank deep into a white haze, and the moment my body slowed, I pulled at the water and kicked, breaking through a torrent of bubbles and out into the air.

I blinked and wiped the saltwater from my eyes and hair and then turned as Jack crept the Baia toward me. With a powerful kick, I forced myself up and grabbed hold of the bow rail.

"I'm up, Jack!" I called out, and my friend gunned the throttle.

The twin 600s roared and the bow rose up from the water, taking me with it. As the forward section of my boat tilted skyward, I used the momentary angle to hook a leg up onto the deck and roll up over the side. Holding tight to the rail, I managed to climb along the port edge and drop into the cockpit just as the Baia was getting up on plane.

"Nice of you to drop in," Jack shouted over the engines and wind.

I gazed west toward the bridge just as our pursuers continued their relentless approach, their vessel shooting back a powerful wake.

Water dripped from my soaked clothes as I balanced myself and focused over the stern. "It's a ranger boat all right."

"Fifty knots, max," Jack said.

They wouldn't catch the Baia so long as we kept full speed, but they'd stay neck and neck. And the silhouettes of their rifles told me that wasn't something we wanted.

"Keep her steady on this line, Jack," I said as he skirted us northeast along Bahia Honda.

Jack nodded and I helped Jasmine below deck. She stumbled off the bottom step, crashing into the couch. I pushed onward into the main cabin, then opened the closet door, punched in the code for my safe, and pressed my thumb to a biometric pad. The lock clicked, and I hinged the thick door open.

I went straight for my wife's collapsible Lapua sniper rifle, swiping it from a row of armaments, along with a little box of ammunition. I quickly jammed five rounds into the mag, then locked it in place and extended the stock and barrel. Less than a minute after I'd dipped below deck, I returned topside, reaching the cockpit just as a rattle of gunfire filled the air.

"Hold on!" Jack shouted, then cut hard to starboard.

We dropped low and their rounds missed, splashing into the water beside us and in our bubbly wake.

I gazed through the windscreen, carefully observing the landscape ahead of us. Off to the right was nothing but deep water for six miles until the outer reef line and drop-off. Ahead, just off the port bow, were sporadic shallows and winding cuts leading between the eastern shore of Bahia Honda and Ohio Key.

I thought back to a maneuver I'd used years earlier while being pursued by a Mexican cartel near Neptune's Table.

"I think we need to pull a Sierra," I said, eyeing our pursuers.

Jack gazed at the shallows far ahead, then gave a quick smile. "Like déjà vu all over again, brother. Tide's perfect for it."

I extended the bipod arms, then fought my way aft to the sunbed and sprawled out. Water flew past on both sides in a torrential blur right below me. It was like flying down a highway with your upper body angled over the back of the car.

I steadied myself as best I could. We were up on plane. Smooth riding, but still shaky and bouncing now and then with the occasional waves. My target was a hundred yards back and quivering as well.

I took aim, focusing intently through the scope, and fired. The stock jolted hard into my shoulder and the big round burst free. It struck the water just ahead of the boat, and I made a quick adjustment, then sent off another. This one struck and broke off part of the craft's radar assembly. The third hit the bow, but the fourth and fifth each struck the windscreen dead on, punching through and spiderwebbing the glass. The pilot was fine, but one of the other guys went down in a rapid jolt of movement and a mist of blood.

Then the third guy retaliated by opening fire again, this time holding down the trigger of his automatic rifle for a solid five seconds.

I scooted back and fell to the deck, hunkering down until the firing stopped, then inched my way back to the cockpit.

"Where we at, Jack?" I called out.

"Quarter mile from the nearest sandbar."

I poked up and scanned the water far out ahead of us. It was slightly white-capped in a long stretch, but no land was visible.

"Tide's perfect," Jack added. "Just as I'd hoped."

I set my rifle on the topside couch, then eyed my friend.

He nodded and shifted aside. "She's all yours."

Jack could pilot a boat with the best of them. But this was my baby. No one knew her better than me. And small-boat operations had been one of my primary specialties back in the Navy. I'd yet to meet anyone who could outmaneuver me on the water.

I made a rapid, careful assessment of the waters ahead of us. Waiting for the perfect moment, I kept the throttle pegged for thirty seconds, then let off slightly. Just enough for the boat behind us to gain some ground.

Taking intermittent glances over my shoulder, I let our pursuers get to within fifty yards of us, then thundered full speed again. It was a gamble, but one that was short-lived. A moment after throttling up, I brought us back down, then cut hard to starboard, turning as sharply as we could at that speed. Then I swiftly swooped up back to the left, held steady, then shoved the throttle forward once again.

My head snapped backward and I watched as the other boat continued straight, its hull striking a sandbar lurking just beneath the surface. Given their speed, and with their windscreen cracked, the pilot obviously hadn't seen it. The vessel skipped across the sand for a fraction of a second, then seesawed like mad before keeling over too far. The port bow struck the bottom, and the vessel flipped faster than a blink. A loud crash echoed across the water as the boat spun ferociously, breaking apart in a hazy, chaotic wreck.

TWENTY-TWO

The battered vessel splashed to a violent stop in a spray of water far behind us. We watched as the wreckage settled, then I eased back to a comfortable cruising speed and scanned the waters surrounding us. We were just past Bahia Honda, having covered over two miles in the short amount of time since we'd blasted away from the bridge.

I grabbed my radio. "Pete, what's your status?"

"Still floating offshore near Looe Key," he said a moment later. "You guys run into any trouble?"

"A little," I said. "Then they ran into a sandbar."

Pete chuckled. "That's what happens when you mess with the wrong conchs. Should I expect you guys anytime soon?"

"On our way there now. ETA fifteen minutes."

I set my radio on the dash, then shot a quick glance at the chart plotter and put us on a south by southeast heading away from the islands and into the dark Strait.

Jasmine, who hadn't spoken a word since she'd

rappelled from the bridge, sat beside me on the corner of the helm seat. She stared forward, lost in thought. After a solid minute of silence, she spoke clearly and confidently. "I'm not going to the safe house."

I nodded. "I know."

She turned to look at me, her face pale with dread. "I can't, Logan."

"You don't need to explain yourself. I understand."

She paused again, then buried her face in her hands and sobbed. "How did this happen? How could I have let this happen?"

I placed a hand on her shoulder, then let her sit there and work through everything in silence as we raced across the water.

It took a couple more minutes, the weight of everything that had happened, and the news regarding her son, a burden as heavy as any could be.

Once she was cognizant again, I said, "You remember what I told you yesterday after carrying you out of the water?" I looked her in the eyes. Hers were big and watery. "Everything's going to be okay. We're going to find your son, Jasmine. And we're going to deal with Lucius. I promise."

We continued on in silence for another five minutes. I kept my eyes forward on the dark horizon, listening to the growling engines, the water gushing past us, and the whipping wind.

"There's the old seadog," Jack said with a smile, rising and gripping the overhead and pointing ahead.

A stretch of silver moonlight bled down from above, sparkling over the dark silhouette of a small aircraft drifting on floats. As we motored closer, Pete came into focus. He was sitting barefoot on the port float. A fishing pole in his left hand and a beer bottle clutched in the hook of his right.

I couldn't help but smile as I laid eyes on the seventy-year-old, tanned, gray-haired conch. If there was ever an image that personified the Florida Keys, this was it.

"Who's that?" Jasmine said.

"Pete Jameson." Then I motioned toward my wife's Cessna 183 Skylane. "He was kind enough to bring over our ride."

She stared ahead for a moment, then said, "I already told you, Logan. I'm not going to the safe house."

"I know you're not." She looked at me, confused, and I added, "You should step down and pack up your things. And grab whatever food you want from the fridge. It's a long journey to the West Coast."

She cracked a faint smile. Bobbed her head and nearly teared up again while wrapping an arm around me. "Thank you, Logan."

I nodded, then gestured below deck. "We'll be reaching it soon."

Jack took over at the helm, and we both stepped down to gather up some supplies. I grabbed my go bag, which contained the usual necessities, and threw in changes of clothes. Then Jasmine and I opened the fridge and cleared out food I'd bought hours earlier while waiting for sundown and transferred them into a small cooler.

Jack was just easing us up to the Cessna when we returned topside. Setting everything on the sunbed, I threw over a couple of fenders.

"Thanks for meeting us, Pete," I said, throwing him a wave.

The islander smiled. "Happy to help. Had better luck off this bird than I've had all week on my boat." He lifted a line of half a dozen good-sized fish. Then he motioned to the calm, tranquil waters surrounding us. "Plus, you can't beat catching the evening bite on a day like this." He raised an eyebrow at Jasmine and added, "You know, you look very familiar."

Jack laughed. "Even Pete knows who she is, bro."

I laughed along with him. I guess I was the only one that far out of the loop.

"Jasmine Cruz," she said, introducing herself with a smile.

Pete pressed a hand to his chest. "I think I'm gonna have a heart attack. You're even prettier in person, Miss Cruz."

She blushed a little as we loaded our stuff into the back seat of the Cessna. Then Jack helped me heave additional gear I thought might come in handy during likely altercations on the Pacific coast. A set of rebreather gear, a sea scooter, dive fins, masks, and some extra firepower from the safe, including Ange's collapsible sniper rifle.

Once everything was loaded up, I thanked my friends for everything.

"After everything you've done for us over the years?" Pete said. "Your thanks are far from necessary."

Jack nodded and said, "Wish I could do more. You sure you don't need me to tag along?"

"I appreciate the offer, Jack. But Ange and I will handle it from here on out. Besides, I need you to look after Scarlett for me when she returns. Her flight gets in late this evening."

"I'll be there to pick her up."

Pete patted the Cessna, then climbed over to the Baia. "Main and aux tanks are topped off."

I thanked him again and told them to keep their wits sharp. I doubted there'd be any more hitmen in the Keys, but I wanted them to be on guard just in case.

Then Jasmine and I climbed aboard. We kept the windows down as I performed my preflight checks.

"You can fly a plane?" Jasmine said.

I shrugged. "How hard can it be?"

Her eyes widened, and I chuckled. "Just kidding. Yeah, I'm licensed." We each donned headsets and I fired up the engine. "We won't exactly be breaking any speed records with this thing," I said to her through the speaker. "It'll be a long first leg to an airstrip across the Gulf to refuel. Let's use that time wisely."

I threw a wave to Jack and Pete, then rolled up the windows and accelerated us over the calm Strait, lifting from the water and soaring west.

TWENTY-THREE

Angelina brushed back strands of her free-flowing blond hair and hit the gas, cruising a red Corvette convertible down Rodeo Drive. While hitting the streets of Tinseltown, she thought about her interaction with Scarlett back at LAX. It hadn't been easy to get her stubborn, adventurous sixteen-year-old to board her flight back to the East Coast. But her daughter had eventually relented. It was a necessary move as Ange was gearing up for a dangerously eventful evening.

She'd cooked up a fun plan and, after leaving Scarlett at the airport, she'd rented the most expensive sports car she could find at any of the lines of rental companies. Cruising the heart of Rodeo, she pulled her Corvette into a valet lot along the downtown Beverly Hills street.

Her first stop was a high-end salon for a haircut and coloring, along with a mani-pedi. Stepping out refreshed, she couldn't help but smile as she strolled the famous street known for being one of the most luxurious shopping destinations in the world. Ange glided along, gazing through big glass windows at the season's latest fashions.

She spotted an outfit she liked, then headed inside. After trying on the teal dress that showed off her figure and legs nicely, she took the whole mannequin, completing the look with a pair of black high heels. She finished up the outfit with a pair of gold hoop earrings at a jewelry shop the next door down and then iced the cake with a Louis Vuitton purse.

Ange was a head-turner no matter what she was wearing. But stepping out in the designer outfit, with the gold California sun hanging low in a blue sky, Beverly Hills at her back and the Hollywood sign off her left shoulder, she was like a movie star filming an eye-popping scene. In a sea of stars, she shone brightest. Dazzling and craning necks as she graced casually along.

She was engaged in serious business, but there was no reason she couldn't have a little fun with it in the process.

The valet stared at her as she strolled back to the lot entrance, his jaw hitting the pavement. She handed him her ticket, along with a twenty, and the Corvette roared up moments later. Then she punched in an address in her GPS app and gunned it out of the lot and south down to the I-10.

She didn't have far to go, twenty minutes later pulling into an underground lot beneath a sparkling skyscraper. She handed the valet her keys, along with another twenty.

"Take good care of her, Carlos," she said, reading his name tag. "For me."

She added the last bit with a wink and the guy nearly fainted.

Ange checked herself out in a big shiny mirror as she headed for the elevator. She was pretty sure she'd just spent more on clothes in a half an hour than she'd spent in her entire life, but they were a necessary expense. She didn't know a lot about Hollywood, but she did know that in Tinseltown, image was everything.

She stepped through the parting doors and pressed the button for the sixtieth floor. The one Officer Carter had mentioned. Not that she needed to remember the floor number. They were all marked, and the top was labeled with bold gold lettering.

It was one of the fastest and smoothest elevators she'd ever ridden, seeming to reach the top in a blink. When the doors parted open, an expansive reception area came into view. There were two huge oak desks spaced far apart and flanking big glass doors. Sparkling marble floors. Lush leather couches and antique tables. A glass dispenser filled with iced water and floating slices of cucumber. A line of crystal glasses beside it.

A petite young woman wearing glasses smiled as Ange stepped out of the elevator. She approached with a clipboard and welcomed her in with a friendly bow of her head.

"Good afternoon, miss. How can we help you?"

It was one of the most expensive-looking and sterile places Ange had ever been in. But the woman's expression had all the appearances of being warm and genuine.

"Hello, I'm Sofia Karlsson," Ange said,

exaggerating her Swedish accent, which had veered American over the years. "I was recently offered a modeling contract and I'm looking for the best representation in town. I was recommended to this office by Lucius Xavier."

The woman smiled and nodded. Made a quick note on her paper. "Congratulations, Miss Karlsson. And you've come to the right place. Here at Wessel we represent hundreds of the world's top models, actors, and musicians. Mr. Wessel is a busy man, but I'll see if he has time to fit you in."

Ange smiled, strode gracefully over to the nearest couch, and sat down.

She grabbed a magazine but kept her eyes on her surroundings, scanning the place over casually with her peripherals. It was all women working there. All young and pretty and skinny. In fact, she didn't notice any other lawyers at all. It seemed like the entire operation was just administrative staff and Wessel. That would've been a big red flag for her even without all the information she'd already obtained about the place and its connection to Lucius.

Sitting still and acting natural, Ange watched as the receptionist disappeared through the glass doors, clipboard in hand.

~ ~ ~

Ronald Wessel stood behind his huge mahogany desk, gazing out a floor-to-ceiling window offering a near-perfect view of the coast. In his mid-fifties, he was short and stocky. Had the bronze, orangish skin tone of a guy who spent a significant percentage of his week baking under high-powered tanning bulbs.

He wore a black Tom Ford suit worth more than the average American makes in a year, and handcrafted alligator skin dress shoes.

Everything was neat and tidy in his office. Bookshelves filled with thick volumes of case reports and various law books. They all appeared brand-new. Never opened.

He was talking on the phone when the receptionist entered. His voice was loud and powerful. Suave and cocky. While a voice blared from the speaker, he took a sip of scotch from a crystal glass, then set it down and gripped a putter and began sending golf balls across a narrow turf surface.

The receptionist waited there patiently, knowing not to interrupt. After a minute, Wessel finally acknowledged her with a curt nod. Then he continued the casual conversation for another minute before finally ending it.

He rested his putter over a shoulder and took another sip of scotch. Splashing the chilled beverage back, he eyed the woman. "What is it, Roxanne?"

"There's a woman here to see you," she said.

Wessel chuckled. "I see that," he said, then swiped a remote from his desk and eyed a security monitor angled toward him in the corner. It displayed a clear image of the waiting area.

"And what a woman," he said, looking the blond beauty up and down. "What's her problem?"

"She's a model. Foreign and upcoming, but has a contract offer apparently. She said she was recommended to you by Lucius."

Wessel stepped closer to the monitor. He used the remote to zoom in, focusing the clear image on the woman's upper body, then working slowly down to her legs. He smirked.

"What kind of car does she drive?" Wessel asked.

"A brand-new Corvette."

He laughed again. Beautiful, foreign, and with some money. "Not exactly a Ferrari, but I'll still see her."

He held his gaze on his new potential client. As the receptionist turned on her heel, he said, "Hold on. Where are you off to so fast?"

She paused, turned back, and looked at him, confused. "To get the wom—"

"Ah, that's right." He stepped closer, then made a vulgar show of checking her out as well. He moved close enough for her to smell his scotch-infused breath.

"I meant to ask," Wessel said slowly, "how's your husband, Roxanne?"

She swallowed, feigned a smile as best she could. "He's fine."

Wessel chuckled. Then suddenly sneered and slapped her on the butt.

She remained frozen, and he leaned closer and said, "Tell him I say hi."

She gave a barely perceptible nod, then turned for the door. As she grabbed the handle, Wessel downed the rest of his drink, then said, "Stop. Let me see your face." She froze and turned back to him slowly, and he added, "Great. Now let me see how much you love your job. How much you *need* your job."

She snapped out of it and resumed her friendly grin as best she could.

Wessel nodded. "That's a good girl. Now go and get her."

TWENTY-FOUR

The receptionist looked different when she returned. It was faint. But Ange noticed the disconcerting shift in her demeanor.

The woman glanced over at Ange, blinked, and then the look vanished, replaced by a cheery smile less than two steps back into the waiting area.

"Mr. Wessel will see you now," she said, stepping right over to the edge of the couch.

Ange smiled. Set the magazine aside, slid her phone into her purse, and rose. Followed the woman across the wide-open space and through the double glass doors. She led Ange down a short hallway to a pair of big, thick mahogany slabs. The receptionist opened the doors and ushered her in.

Ange stepped into the office. It was one of the biggest and most lavishly furnished rooms she'd ever seen. Classic, but modern. Bright and airy. The space oozed self-importance, and the cherry on top was a big portrait of the lawyer himself on the wall beside his desk.

"Miss Karlsson," Wessel said, standing from his leather desk chair and moving toward her. "Please, come on in."

They shook hands, and he smiled and admired her breasts. If he was trying to hide the glance, he was doing a terrible job.

"Please, have a seat. Can I offer you anything to drink? Coffee? Tea?"

"No, thank you," Ange said, trying her best to hide the fact that she wanted to slug the guy across his jaw. "And thank you so much for meeting me on such short notice."

He migrated smoothly back to his chair and sat down. "It's my pleasure. Really. I love what I do. And any friend of Lucius's is a friend of mine. I assure you, you're in friendly territory here. Like Lucius, I only want what's best for people. Now, how can I help you?"

"Like I mentioned to your assistant, I'm new to the industry. Lucius is helping me out. He's gotten me a series of modeling gigs lined up. He recommended that I contact you regarding legal protection."

The lawyer smiled. It may have passed for sincere, had Ange not already seen a glimpse behind the curtain. Knowing what she knew, the smile gave her the creeps.

"Lucius is a wise and generous man," Wessel said. "A true gentleman in the industry. Finding legal help early on is paramount in the fashion and entertainment world. Hollywood isn't all champagne and sparkling lights. It can get quite nasty if you don't cover all your bases." He leaned forward and lowered his voice. "Lots of people looking to take advantage of a beautiful woman like yourself. But fortunately for you, you've come to me. And I promise, I'll take good care of you."

He unlocked and slid open the bottom drawer of a metal cabinet at his back. Grabbed a small stack of papers and set them on the polished hardwood in front of him.

"These are standard representation forms," he said. "I'll have you sign them in a minute. But first, I like to begin by getting to know a little about my clients." He slid out a small packet from the folder along with a twenty-four-karat gold pen with his name engraved on it in silver letters.

"Usually, I charge a thousand dollars for an initial consultation like this. But since Lucius sent you, I'll do this one on the house."

He winked at her.

She tasted bile at the back of her throat.

The man's words were smooth and eloquent. Sounded memorized and well-rehearsed. Ange wondered how many women had sat in that very chair and heard that same speech. She guessed it was in the hundreds. It was nauseating to think about.

He opened the packet, pretending to scan over the top. "This part is just trivialities really. Basic things. Like where you're from, age, living family members. That sort of thing."

Ange had to fight hard to maintain her composure—to show only satisfaction and gratitude in her expression and not what she was really feeling.

These guys are even more disgusting than I imagined, she thought.

They covered all of their bases from the start.

Getting vulnerable, inexperienced, eager girls to sign all their rights away. Not only that, they had the women fill out a packet that was basically an extortionist's dream come true.

It was a level of wretchedness that rivaled anything she'd ever witnessed before, and it took all her strength to keep her from throwing herself over the desk and wringing the monster's miserable life away.

Wessel slid the packet across the desk and held out his pen. She grabbed the luxury writing utensil. It was heavy and well made. Thin and smooth, with a narrow tip. Maybe a quarter of a millimeter. A point capable of some serious damage. Capable of impaling deep through an eye, through the optic nerve and layers of soft tissue, and boring into the frontal lobe.

"Whenever you're ready, Miss Karlsson," Wessel said.

Ange eyed the page momentarily, then let out a breath and smiled and leaned back into her chair. She looked around the office. Looked out through the windows at the City of Angels.

She'd awoken that morning in a tent at the bottom of the Grand Canyon. Sweaty and dirty and smelly. Now there she was. In one of the most expensive offices in California, decked out from head to toe in designer clothes.

"This is a nice office," she said.

The man blushed. "Thank you. I've had a very fortunate career."

Ange nodded. Left the packet on the desk but kept the pen and stood up. She sauntered slowly toward the windows. "I mean, we're what, sixty floors up?"

Before Wessel could say anything, she turned and took a stroll about the space.

"And those doors are nice and thick and heavy," Ange said. "I bet you could do whatever you want in this office without anyone hearing. Not even your assistants."

The man shot her an arrogant smile, then glanced at his Rolex and gestured toward the packet. "Let's get back to the documents. I'm a very busy man, Miss Karlsson."

She waved a casual hand. "My apologies. Of course." As she stepped back to the desk, she added, "I think I will have that drink if the offer still stands."

He leaned forward and grabbed his phone. "Tea or coffee?"

"I was actually thinking something a little stronger," she said, eyeing his liquor cabinet.

He let go of the phone and was about to rise but stopped himself. "How about we drink in celebration of our new professional relationship? After you finish the paperwork."

She shrugged innocently, then ran her fingers over the brand-new books filling the shelves. She paused, then grabbed a Webster's dictionary and flipped through the pages.

"I'm doing one of those vocabulary word of the day things," she said while continuing to riffle through. "Trying to expand it, you know? Let me see if I can find it… there," she said, pointing her finger at the page. "This is my word of the day for today. You want to know what it is?"

Wessel sighed. "Miss Karlsson, with all due respect, I have dinner plans with some very important people. If you could—"

"Oh, of course," Ange said.

She used the pen to underline the word, then stealthily dog-eared the page and kept the dictionary in her hands as she closed back in on her chair. As she sat down, Wessel tapped the packet of papers and pushed them closer.

Ange eyed them again, then set the dictionary on the desk beside it. She leaned forward and was about to write something when she stopped again and looked up at Wessel.

"I actually just have one more quick question," she said in as innocent and naive a tone as she could muster. Then she fired him a seductive smile. "If you wouldn't mind, Mr. Wessel."

Wessel's face reddened. He smiled uncontrollably, then cleared his throat and gestured back to the packet. "We can discuss all your questions over drinks. After you fill these out. Business first, then play. That's the way it works."

"Please?" Ange said, batting her eyes.

The man sighed and pinched the bridge of his nose. "Fine. Fine. What is it?"

Ange grinned playfully, then leaned even farther across the desktop, staring at the man with her radiant blue eyes. "How many women have you helped Lucius abuse, rape, and murder over the years?"

It was like someone had shoved a flagpole up his butt. He turned stone rigid in a blink. Frozen solid. Then he coughed and narrowed his gaze. His expression going from friendly to pure evil in a blink.

"You're a reporter," he said, shooting her a cocky, evil smile.

"No," Ange replied calmly.

She stood.

He reached for his phone. "Get the hell out of my office."

The line was dead, and his eyes bulged when he realized it.

"No," she said again, then sauntered around his desk.

He reached for his cellphone. She snatched it on its way up and hurled it across the room, the device crashing into the waxed floor.

Sofia Karlsson was gone in a blink, Angelina Dodge taking her place.

He snarled and reached for her arm. Ange caught it, slammed his palm into the hardwood, then dropped her elbow into his wrist, putting all of her weight into it. The bone cracked and Wessel let out a sharp cry.

Ange grabbed him by his shirt collar and heaved him out of the chair. Hurled him to the floor against the window. He wailed and cursed. Ange stood over him, listening.

"Wow," she said casually, eyeing the doors. "Those babies are thick."

She glanced at the monitor displaying the security feed of the waiting area. "Your assistants don't hear a thing."

Wessel blared his teeth. "You lay another finger on me and I'll—"

Ange laid four fingers on him. Along with a thumb. Tightly packed in a fist. Base knuckles striking his abdomen and pounding the air from his lungs.

He cried out more and curled up, fighting to catch

his breath.

"If you're the police, you don't have a damn warrant," he hissed. "I'll have your neck for this."

She knelt down. "I'm not the police, Ronald."

Then she heaved him up again and dragged him to the corner of the desk. Slid the dictionary over to him.

"Check my word of the day," she said.

He snarled and cursed her out again. So she grabbed the gold pen and held it over his left eye.

"Read my word of the day, Ronald, or I'll stab this through your eyeball."

"You're insane!"

She chuckled. Began counting down from three. He frantically checked the dictionary, opening to the dog-eared page and scanning his shaky gaze down until he locked on to the underlined word.

His mouth dropped open.

"What's the word, Ronald?"

He swallowed and wheezed. "Vigilante."

"Read the definition."

"A… a self-appointed doer of justice."

Ange nodded. "That's right." She jerked him away from the desk, muscling him to the back of the office and slamming him facefirst into the glass.

"Sixty floors up," Ange said, pressing him against the window. "Eight hundred feet onto concrete. But that's letting you off too easy."

"What… what do you want?"

"Simple. I want everything you've got on Lucius Xavier."

Wessel's mouth fell open. "I can't do that."

"You're gonna have to do that. Or I'll break every bone in your body one at a time."

He began to cry. Then his sobbing grew mad and frantic, like a child having a tantrum.

"You can't do this," he whined. "I'll—"

"Do you need to read the definition of my word of the day again?" Ange said.

His head bowed. His face red and layered in sweat. His eyes big and terrified.

Ange snatched his broken wrist and yanked it back, sending a jolt of intense pain through the man's body. Then she shoved a knee into the back of his left leg and rotated his ankle with a strong jerk. The bone nearly cracked as well, and Wessel broke down, crying with his face against the glass. Completely losing it.

"Okay... okay," he gasped. "I'll do it."

TWENTY-FIVE

After nearly two hours in Wessel's office, Ange had everything she needed.

Statements, transcripts, paper trails from hush money transfers, and various other legal documents. Like Officer Carter had said, the place was a treasure trove of damning evidence against Lucius Xavier and his history of heinous activities.

Ange's bag was filled with documents, along with her zip drive and CDs containing audio recordings. She'd even transferred copies of everything on Wessel's computer to a secure cloud, just in case.

When every drop of intel had been obtained, Ange approached the injured, terror-struck lawyer a final time. He shook and flinched at the mere sight of her.

"Not so fun when the woman fights back, huh?" Ange said. Then she planted her hands on her hips. "This is a long time coming. But consider this your wake-up call."

She grabbed him by the hair and jerked him up. He winced and cried, tears and sweat coating his face.

Ange held the gold pen up to his eye.

"If you mention this interaction to anyone, you won't live long to regret it, understood?"

He sobbed again.

"Understood, Wessel?"

He nodded.

Then she leaned closer so her mouth was barely an inch over his ear and whispered, "You say a word and I'll find you. No matter where you try and hide. I'll find you and I'll end you. Slowly."

He nodded, then quivered, and she threw him to the floor again, his damaged, fatigued body sagging into a corner. Ange shouldered her purse, then headed for the door.

She stopped at a mirror on the way to fix her hair and to straighten her dress. When she noticed the liquor cabinet, she strode over and hinged the glass door open. She grabbed the fifty-year-old bottle of Glenlivet and held it up to the man as she exited.

"I'll be taking this. You have nothing to celebrate."

Ange slid the bottle into her purse and stepped out. The hallway was empty and quiet. So was the waiting area. An hour earlier, Ange had forced Wessel to text his staff to leave and take the rest of the afternoon off, telling them that he and Miss Karlsson were having a good ole time and didn't need anything more for the night.

We had a good ole time all right, Ange thought as her heels clapped across the space and she pressed the button for the elevator.

Eight hundred feet down, she exited, retrieved her Corvette from the young valet, and zipped out of the parking garage. She blended into evening traffic, heading for the interstate and LAX where she'd exchange her rental for something less inconspicuous.

While driving, she thought about her threat to Wessel. The spooked, spineless man was going to tell someone. Of that she was certain. But that was okay. In fact, if what she knew about their enemy was true, it would ultimately work in their favor.

Braking to a stop at a red light, she pulled out her phone and called Harper Ridley.

A close friend of her family, Harper had been a reporter for the *Keynoter* for most of her adult life. She was one of many islanders whose proficiency severely outranked her position. Though the local paper was held in high regard in South Florida, it wasn't exactly a major news agency. And Ridley had the investigative ability, intelligence, and sheer gut instinct to thrive in higher-paying positions in places like Atlanta, Chicago, DC, and New York. She'd been offered jobs in bigger cities many times, but like many conchs, Harper preferred sandy pockets to deep pockets.

"This is… incredible stuff, Ange," Harper said, having received copies of all the information Ange had obtained. "This is more than enough to completely destroy this guy. There's no getting out of this. No talking or finagling your way out of evidence like this."

"If it goes to trial, the prosecution will still need victims to testify, right?" Ange said. "I'm sure Miss Cruz's testimony will prove vital, but won't they need others?"

"Most likely. But after the article I'm going to

write goes viral, and it will, many of the victims will step forward. Trust me. I've seen this play out again and again."

Ange couldn't help but smile at that. But raining potent justice upon Lucius Xavier wasn't the primary objective at that moment. She'd recently been informed that there was a nine-year-old boy's life hanging in the balance, and he needed to be found and rescued as quickly as possible.

She'd discussed it with Logan, and they both agreed that the quickest way to get nationwide law enforcement agencies on their side was to post the incriminating information online as expeditiously as possible. And she expressed the fact to Harper yet again.

"Me and my team will be working on this non-stop until it's ready," Harper assured her. "We'll have something posted later this evening. This guy's cooked."

TWENTY-SIX

Ronald Wessel lay on the floor against the window, his body shriveled up. He remained in the fetal position for so long he lost track of time. His mind was a mess. His body broken and in intense pain. He sobbed and wondered what the hell had just happened—what nightmare of a storm had blown into his office and ripped him to pieces.

He'd built up a facade of confidence and authority over the years. A fortress with a steel-like appearance but the structural integrity of glass. And the mysterious woman had shattered his world to pieces in just a couple of hours, revealing the broken, terrified, cowardly weakling he was.

He lay there in the silence. Hearing only his muffled sobs and beating heart. After stewing in his misery for what felt like an eternity, he forced himself up onto his hands and knees, then raised his head. The sun was setting. Firing powerful streaks of golden rays across the Pacific and the sea of windows around him. He forced himself onto a knee, grunting from the pain to his face, ankle, and broken wrist.

Leaning against the desk, he checked the time via his ornate wall clock. It was just after seven. Though his mind was delirious and hazy and there were still stars circling around his peripherals, he fought to remember when the terrifying woman had first entered.

He could barely hold a thought, let along cycle back through time.

Two o'clock, maybe?

He'd hoped it'd all been a nightmare. But slowly snapping out of it only brought him right back into his horrifying reality. Into the aftermath.

His brain cells went to work. He was screwed. Beyond screwed. No matter what he did, he was done for. He had no doubt that the brutal mystery woman would follow through on her threat—that if he uttered a word about what had happened there, he'd be faced with a fate far worse than death or imprisonment.

But he couldn't tell Lucius either. No, he could never utter a word to the man ever again. Never face him or even think about revealing the truth.

It was all over.

Damned if he did, damned if he didn't. Nowhere to go. No choice to make.

He paused and thought hard. It wasn't easy. Then an idea reached him through the mental fog.

Maybe I could... yes. I do have a choice. One all-in, never-turning-back choice.

It was risky and callous. A coward's way out if there ever was one. But Wessel had been a coward all his life. Pointing fingers and shelling blame and letting others take the fall while he slipped through the cracks had been his MO for as long as he could remember. And it had served him well.

He grabbed the edge of the desk and heaved himself to his feet. Staggering to the painting of himself on the wall, he removed the portrait from its hooks, revealing a biometric safe.

The mystery woman had stolen so much from him, but fortunately for Wessel, there'd been one thing she'd had no interest in taking.

He opened the safe, revealing stacks of cash. Filling his briefcase, he shut everything back up, then limped for the door. He froze when he reached the handle, turned, and looked back.

It's been a good run, he thought, still unable to fully comprehend what was happening.

He pushed out to the hall and made for the stairs. They hurt like hell. Every brief moment of weight transfer shooting sharp pains all up his left leg.

In no condition to drive, he headed for the ground floor. Limped out and hailed a taxi. The driver shot him more than one hesitant, skeptical look, but the thousand bucks Wessel handed him squared everything away, and he floored it across town toward the lawyer's house along Benedict Canyon in Beverly Hills.

Fighting to calm his breath in the back seat, Wessel fumbled out his phone and made a desperate call to his assistant.

"I need a flight to Brunei," he said when she answered, the words rushing out. "Private. And as soon as you can secure one."

She gave a quick, confused reply, then Wessel added, "Money's no object. I'll pay three hundred grand. Just make it happen. And, Roxanne, you handle this for me quickly and I'll send you a bonus of fifty K."

He ended the call. The drive remained silent for the thirty-minute trip through vehicle-infested streets, out of the city and up into the hills. The taxi had barely come to a stop when Wessel threw open the door and scooted out without a word, wincing as he staggered through a security gate and up the steps to the front door of his mansion. A modern estate situated on one of the most exclusive promontories in the iconic neighborhood, his house offered sweeping views of the city and distant ocean.

He winced as he took on the marble steps of a grand staircase, heading straight for the master bedroom. Removing part of the headboard, he wriggled out a small section of the wall, revealing a safe identical to the one back in his office. He punched in the code and pressed his thumb to the scanner. Swung it open and pulled out more stacks of bills with shaky hands, along with a fake passport, driver's license, and birth certificate.

His heart beat fast and loud in the big, quiet house. Once finished, he closed everything back up and carried the briefcase and shoulder bag toward the door. There was no time to pack a suitcase with clothes. If his last-ditch plan was going to succeed, he needed to move.

Ignoring the pain, he forced himself back down the steps and slid out his phone when he reached the bottom. He placed a call to his assistant.

He hadn't heard back from her yet, which couldn't be a good sign. He waited impatiently, the clock ticking away in his mind as the call tried to connect and the rhythmic noise hummed through the tiny speaker.

A sound startled him. It came from behind him in the kitchen. He listened and realized it was a phone vibrating on a hard surface.

He trod slowly, keeping his ear pressed to his phone and hoping for Roxanne to pick up on the other end.

He stepped down through the grand entryway and into a spacious kitchen and distant shadowy living room. A smartphone vibrated on the granite countertop. He approached it slowly and saw his name on the caller ID.

It was Roxanne's phone.

The blood drained from his face. He gasped and looked around the dark room. Turned and stepped toward a nearby line of light switches but froze midstride when a familiar voice filled the air.

"Hello, Ronald," Lucius Xavier said.

Wessel's heart dropped. He gazed toward the voice that had come from his living room just as a leather recliner swiveled around. Streaks of moonlight reflected off his infinity pool and bled through the back windows, casting Lucius's face in a flickering ominous glow.

Wessel crept to the edge of the expansive living space. His heart trembling. His body aching.

"Where are you off to in such a hurry?" Lucius added.

He wore a dark gray suit. Slouched in the chair casually with one hand gripping a crystal rocks glass with barely a finger of remaining spirit.

Wessel fought hard for an explanation. Struggling to come up with anything.

"I... I was on my way to see you."

Lucius cackled. "Really? Then why did you tell Roxanne to get you onto a private flight to Brunei as quickly as possible?"

Wessel looked around frantically, then said, "Because we need to leave. Now!"

"We?" Lucius said, raising an eyebrow. "Of course, now it's we. But you were about to run away without me, Ronald." Lucius shook his head. Motioned around the house. "After everything I've done for you? Our partnership has made you rich beyond your wildest dreams. As I promised you years ago that it would. And this is how you repay me? Betrayal."

Wessel's mouth hung open. "You don't understand. I—"

Two big men dressed head to toe in black appeared seemingly out of nowhere behind Wessel. Before he could even turn around fully, they grabbed him by the arms and muscled him forward, forcing him to his knees right in front of Lucius.

"Then please, enlighten me, Ronald," Lucius said.

The man blinked like mad, trying to hold back the pain in his extremities and get his brain to work. But there was nothing there. No way out of this but maybe the truth.

"There was a woman," he muttered. "She attacked me and I... I gave her everything. Everything I had on our partnership."

Lucius's gaze tightened. Fire burned in his eyes. He squeezed so tight, the crystal shattered in his right hand. Shards breaking and tumbling to the floor. Cuts to his hand and the small streaks of blood that followed went unnoticed by the mogul.

"You did what?" he snarled, fury in his voice.

Wessel bowed his head. "I gave her everything. I'm sorry, Lucius. I'm so sorry."

The broken man cried out. He sagged all the way forward and buried his face into a white Persian rug, sobbing and trembling and begging for his life.

A powerful surge of rage took over Lucius, and he became a different man entirely. Like an uncaged beast or a deranged madman. Or the devil himself.

Lucius rose, grabbed hold of a heavy framed picture of the lawyer on a beach in Maui, and slammed it across the side of Wessel's face. Then he did it again. And again. A rapid series of fast, powerful strikes all across his body. Wessel wilted and squirmed. And nearly lost consciousness.

"It's not over yet," Wessel gasped, spitting out a spray of blood onto the carpet. "We can get out of this. We can escape if we go now."

"No," Lucius said, grabbing the corrupt lawyer by his shirt collar. "*I* can escape. You've done enough, Ronald. You've ruined everything, you pathetic weakling."

He threw him hard to the floor. Then one of the big silent men handed Lucius a .22-caliber suppressed pistol. Lucius took one more look into the man's miserable eyes, then ended his life, burying five rounds across his chest and face.

He stared at his dead partner, then stepped over the corpse and handed his head of security back his weapon.

"The private jet is ready, Lucius," the man said. "We can be out of American airspace within the hour. There are no charges against you yet. There's plenty of time to run and hide."

"Run and hide," Lucius said, thinking over the words. "No. I have other contingencies in place. But for them to work, we're going to need more chips in our favor. A little extra insurance."

He gave the experienced gun for hire quick instructions. One more important task that needed to be completed that night.

"Then we meet at the waterfront," Lucius said.

The man nodded and stepped away. Lucius took one more cold look at Wessel's corpse, then grabbed the lawyer's briefcase and shoulder bag and strode out of the mansion.

TWENTY-SEVEN

Officer Veronica Carter didn't finish her workday until well after ten o'clock. She'd had a lot of paperwork to do following her twelve-hour beachfront patrol. Heading out the doors of her division station in Culver City, she climbed into her Honda Civic and drove ten minutes across town to Lockhaven, the neighborhood in Inglewood where she'd grown up.

She pulled into the short driveway of a quaint two-bedroom house. She lived alone. Her family was all gone. Both her parents had been the victims of gang violence when she was still in high school. And her older sister had been an aspiring model years earlier when…

The tough police officer fought back a tear.

She sat in silence for a moment, then gritted her teeth and headed inside. Cleaned up and showered and settled into her living room sofa. She checked the fridge, but it was empty aside from old leftovers and a bottle of ketchup.

She grabbed her phone and called a nearby Chinese place. It wasn't her favorite, but it was open. And they delivered.

She ordered a meal of General Tso's, fried rice, and egg rolls. Settled in and watched *Cops* while waiting.

Ten minutes into the show, she muted the television and listened, thinking she'd heard something. Wondering if her neighbor's dog had gotten into her backyard again, she strode across the room and flicked on the back lights. A wave from two bulbs washed over an unkempt yard and porch. She surveyed the area, seeing nothing. No movement. Nothing out of the ordinary.

Being on alert in her house was nothing new. It was a tough part of a tough neighborhood in a town known for having much higher levels of gang activity than surrounding areas.

She sat back on the couch and continued watching the show. Wanting to escape the real world for a bit, she flicked the channel to a rerun of *Friends*. Then five minutes later, she heard a sound again.

This time louder.

She clicked off the TV, grabbed her service pistol from the nearby coffee table, and crept to the window, peering through the blinds. Then she stepped to the back door. It was thick metal, with a small frosted glass window on top. Unclicking the latch, she pulled it open and stepped out confidently, her weapon raised.

It was no secret around the neighborhood that she was a police officer. It'd caused trouble in the past. Vandalism twice. Her mailbox getting smashed, and a black pig spray-painted on her driveway. But nothing had ever happened while she'd been home.

Fortunately for whoever committed the vandalism, she thought as she scanned her weapon across the yard.

She blinked and shook her head. She needed to sleep. But not before—

There were footsteps at the front door, followed by the quick rapping of knuckles. She slid her pistol into the back of her waistband, then stepped to the door, unlatched the chain and slid over the deadbolt, and swung it open. A wide-shouldered guy wearing a ball cap and a bright red China Kitchen shirt that was too small for him stood on her doorstep. He held a plastic bag filled with Styrofoam containers and smiled at her as he held out the food.

As she dug a twenty from her pocket, she froze and turned around as a window shattered on the other side of her house. She reached for the weapon behind her as the shards rained onto her linoleum kitchen floor but stopped as the delivery guy pressed a pistol of his own into her back.

"Don't even think about it," he growled, his voice shifting from friendly to harsh in an instant.

He shoved the barrel harder, then grabbed her service pistol and tossed it to the carpet. Then he prodded her forward and shut the door behind him. The momentary glance away from her at the handle gave her just the opportunity she needed.

She spun, whipping a hand back and knocking the guy's suppressed pistol away. He pulled the trigger, firing a round through her television as she completed her turn, bashing her left fist across the guy's face, then redirecting and doubling back with an even more powerful elbow up into his jaw.

She forced his pistol around as the guy grunted and fell back hard onto the floor. Before he could reengage, she forced the barrel into his gut and pulled the trigger twice, blasting two rounds into his midsection.

Prying the weapon free, she turned as heavy stomps resounded behind her. But she wasn't fast enough to react to a metal Louisville Slugger that was hurled across the room by a massive brute of a man. She raised her left arm, and the bat struck her elbow, nearly breaking the bone as she cried and fell backward.

Carter turned and fought to take aim, but the guy was already upon her. He shoved the heel of his boot into her gun hand, breaking two of her fingers in an excruciating stomp. Then he kicked the weapon aside.

A third guy appeared behind the monster and they forced her up, then eyed the motionless guy lying on his back with two bullet holes across his chest.

"You're going to pay for that one," he said, then socked Carter in the gut.

She curled over and heaved. He reached back for another strike, and she struggled and grabbed the handle of the bat. Shoved it hard straight up and into the big guy's forehead. He snorted and fell back, out of it but still gripping her tight. She fought to strike another blow, but the third attacker swooped in, relieved her of the weapon, and restrained her from behind.

The big guy placed a hand to his bloodied forehead, then growled. He slapped Carter across the face.

"You'll pay for that as well."

Then he smacked her again before knocking her out with a blow to the temple.

TWENTY-EIGHT

We soared across the dark Gulf of Mexico, landing to refuel at an airstrip outside of Houston, before continuing our over-two-thousand-mile trip to the West Coast.

I managed to catch a few Z's, putting the craft on autopilot over the long stretches of nothingness in Texas. To keep alert between dozes, I nursed a big thermos of Colombian extra black.

We landed a second time in Las Cruces, catching the mesmerizing sunrise just before takeoff. We stared in awe as the blazing orb crept up over the Organ Mountains in a brilliant, colorful display. Rich pinks, vibrant oranges, and radiant purples. A sight that left us both speechless.

The early-morning sun continued to burn at our backs as we made the final jump across New Mexico, Arizona, and into California, heading for the coast.

During the first leg, I'd called some of my old contacts from the Navy. Scott Cooper kept tabs on everyone he'd served with, especially the guys under his command. He wanted to make sure they were all taken care of and doing well, even after they'd mustered out.

I'd only served three months in the same unit as Beck Ramirez. Back when I was a petty officer third class fresh out of the SEAL pipeline and he was a first class getting ready to transition to his shore tour. But when you face combat with someone, hunkering down from enemy gunfire and infiltrating hostile environments in the middle of the night, you form a bond quickly.

The brotherhood ran deep. Always had. So when I called him up and asked for a favor, he was happy to oblige.

His family had lived in California for three generations, his great-grandmother having moved to the Golden Coast from Mexico. And he owned a house on Alamitos Bay in Long Beach.

We soared over Greater Los Angeles, descending as we neared the coast. After a quick pass to make sure my intended stretch of water was clear, I splashed us down nice and easy in the calm waters of the bay, coming to a smooth three knots less than a football field from the docks extending out from Beck's house. I'd never been there, but his description made the place impossible to miss. The big United States Ensign and Navy flags flapping from a pair of tall poles in his backyard were a dead giveaway.

Beck appeared from his house as I motored us up toward the biggest of his two docks. It was easy to see why the man had been given the nickname "Battering Ram" back in the SEALs. At six foot four and two hundred and twenty pounds of solid muscle, he'd been one of the most intimidating men I'd ever met. Now he looked even bigger as he motioned me into a large boathouse.

I shut off the engine and slid out.

"It's good to see you, old friend," I said as he pulled the port float up against a row of fenders.

"You too, Dodge. It's been far too long."

We tied off the Cessna, then I stepped to the dock and we shook hands.

"How do you have more muscle every time I see you?" I said, gauging him to now be well north of two hundred and fifty pounds.

"Thankfully civvy life has no weight requirements," he said, referring to the Navy's strict physical standards. "It was hell keeping the pounds off back with the frogmen."

"Thanks for letting me drop in."

He waved me off, saying it was nothing. Then he stared behind me as Jasmine slid out the side door and climbed down.

Beck's mouth hung open. "Dude, do you know that Jasmine Cruz just stepped out of your plane?"

I offered her a hand and she stepped over to the dock. "You recognize her?"

Beck laughed. "Who the hell wouldn't?" I introduced them, then he added, "Your face is everywhere in this town, Miss Cruz. And on the internet. I'd have to be blind not to."

"It's good to meet you, Beck. And thanks for letting us use your dock."

"You're welcome here anytime, Jasmine. A friend of Logan's is a friend of mine." He paused a moment, then continued, "I heard through the grapevine that you'd gotten married, Dodge," he said, always one to say whatever was on his mind. If he had any kind of filter, it was long overdue for a replacement.

"It's not like that," I said. "I was lobster diving off Key West when... it's a long story. But I'm just helping Miss Cruz out with some trouble she's having."

"So Scottie mentioned. Going after a grade-A asshole, huh?"

"Even that's too kind a description," Jasmine said as we shouldered our stuff and headed out into the sun.

I left the dive gear in the cockpit, not needing it yet.

"I wish I could be of more help with whatever you're into," Beck said as we headed down the dock.

"You've done more than enough. Trust me." I eyed a custom blacked-out Zodiac tied off and floating on the other side of his dock. "Is that a raider?" I said with a smile, thinking out loud.

Beck nodded happily, then stepped over and grabbed the cover, pulling it free and revealing the interior. It was the same make and model we'd used in the Navy. A versatile, fast, and stealthy little craft whose super-buoyant nature allows it to operate in shallows and high seas. It was one of my favorite boats in the world, and his was identical to the ones back in the Navy, right down to its fifty-five-horsepower engine with a pump-jet propulsor.

"You bet, Dodge," Beck said. "Climb aboard."

I stepped aboard the small vessel I hadn't seen in years. My legs took me straight to the helm, and I grabbed the wheel and looked around. I'd spent hundreds of hours in that spot, and standing there took me back into the fray in a flash.

"Just like old times, right?" he said. "You at the helm. And me right here." He positioned himself on the starboard pontoon and held up an imaginary M4 carbine.

After the brief trip down memory lane, the three of us headed inside. We were greeted at the door by two German shepherds. They were lively at first, then Beck snapped his fingers and they both sat in unison.

"Don't worry about them," Beck said, petting the big, intimidating dogs as we entered. "Odin and Orion are harmless. To most people anyway."

He led us into a simple living room. The place was comfortable and spotless. Looked like what would happen if a man cave took over an entire house, with a katana mounted on the wall. A statue of Bruce Lee in a corner. A ceramic Aztec mask looming above a fireplace. And pictures on the walls depicting images of Beck over the years, mostly holding some form of firearm in a group of tough-looking guys. It'd been a while since I'd walked into a new space and instantly felt comfortable.

"I've got the den all set up for you, Jasmine," Beck said. "If you'd like a space with some privacy."

Jasmine looked at me curiously. "What's he talking about?"

"You need to stay here," I said.

Her nostrils flared. "Logan, he has my son."

"I know."

"My son, Logan!" she cried, sending the room into an eerie silence.

I placed a hand on her shoulder. "I know, Jasmine. And we'll find him. But you need to do what I say. You agreed to that, remember? We can't find your son and keep you safe unless you stay here. So if you come with, you have to make me and my wife choose: either we protect you or we find your son. Which is it?"

She hesitated. Looked away and placed a palm to her mouth. "I just feel so... helpless. I'm his mother. I never should have—"

"Now isn't the time for regrets or looking back or wishing you did things differently. That'll come later. Understand? After Theo's safe and sound and Lucius is behind bars or rotting in the ground."

TWENTY-NINE

Jasmine agreed to stay at Beck's place for the time being. Then I placed a quick call to Ange, running through the plan one more time.

We were confident that Ange didn't have a tail and that no one knew that Jasmine and I had recently splashed down in the coastal community. Neither of us were strangers to dealing with dangerous, powerful people. Or being hunted down and followed by hired guns. But caution was paramount. And the last thing we wanted was for Lucius and his cronies to have any chance at finding where Jasmine was hiding out.

I thanked my former brother in arms again, then gave a nod to Jasmine and headed out the front door. The lot was fenced and flanked with tall hedges. There were cars parked along the street, but none looked suspicious.

I walked a quarter mile under the late-morning sun to a sidewalk beside a shopping center. Sitting at the bus stop, I only had to wait five minutes for my bus to arrive.

The big vehicle groaned and grumbled and cruised along the coast. It was a city bus with a route spanning all around Long Beach.

I rode for ten minutes, getting off at the third stop at the South Bay Pavilion Mall. Then I cut across a big parking lot and waited. There was no one behind me. I walked through the width of the mall, relishing the momentary blasts of AC before stepping back out on the other side.

A new forest-green Subaru Outback idled in the second row of the packed lot. I went straight for the passenger door and slid inside onto the cool leather. My wife sat in the driver's seat. Wide awake and alert. Her blond hair tied back, her sapphire-blue eyes gazing at me, and her cherry-red lips forming an alluring smile.

She was wearing a black tank top and denim shorts, and she'd never looked better. A sight for sore eyes if there ever was one.

I leaned over and we locked lips for a long, passionate moment. My whole body ignited by the sensation. Her smell, her warmth, her taste.

"I missed you," she said.

"I missed you too."

Then the moment passed and it was down to business.

"Maddox is in town," I said.

She nodded. "He just met with local agents and officers. Apparently there was an emergency joint operation. Harper's sudden mass release of the damning evidence against Lucius did the trick."

"I'm guessing they've already paid a visit to Lucius's house?"

She nodded. "Maddox said he's gone." She sighed. "I debated with that one. We knew he'd disappear as soon as it was sent out. Maybe we should have waited until after we had him and the child was safe."

I shook my head. "He would've disappeared regardless. The moment he found out about the lawyer. At least now the gears are moving to bring charges against him and the truth is being brought to light."

Ange fell silent a moment, then said, "Jasmine doing okay?"

"As good as can be expected, given the circumstances. Beck and his dogs are watching her and no one knows she's there. Even if they did, God help any man who tries to break into that place."

Ange received a message from Maddox, and a moment later, she drove us out of the lot. She fought heavy northbound traffic for fifteen miles, then pulled into a business park a couple blocks down from the LAPD headquarters. There were people dressed in suits all over the place, coming and going in a blur for the lunchtime hour.

Darius Maddox seemed to materialize out of nowhere, the Homeland Security agent threading out from the mass and into the back seat of the Outback in a smooth, rapid motion.

"Tail?" I said, glancing at the imposing black man through the rearview.

"I don't think so," he said. "But just in case… your car's looking a little dirty. There's a wash two blocks up Main."

Ange roared us out of the lot and meshed back into the traffic.

"It's good to see you both," he said. "I guess you changed your mind about putting Miss Cruz in the Bahamian safe house."

"Things changed when her son wasn't flown down," I said. "And things changed again when we were attacked by a team of hitmen."

"She's safe?"

I nodded. "She's safe."

Maddox fell silent a moment, then said, "One way or another, Lucius is going down. It didn't take an extensive look at the intel Ange discovered to draw that conclusion. It's heavy stuff. He'll be behind bars for life, even if he cooperates."

Ange veered off Main Street and into a Shell station with a car wash. After paying, she pulled up to the lane and put the Outback in neutral. We just needed a place we could guarantee privacy while we spoke. Again, none of us expected anyone to be following us. But we all knew that Lucius had a powerful sphere of influence. And paid-off or coerced police officers and government agents weren't exactly unheard of.

I shifted in my seat so I could face both Ange and Maddox, then said, "The joint op make a move yet?"

Maddox nodded. "It took a little time to sift through all the details. We rushed the charges and warrant acquisition process as quickly as we could. His private jet was grounded this morning. We just got into his house an hour ago, and it was empty. And he wasn't at his offices on Hollywood Boulevard. No one we've called has seen or heard from him. No one knows where he is."

"He's running," I said.

"He must've found out about the intel leak," Ange said. "I knew I should've just offed the guy. You guys check his lawyer's house yet? Ronald Wessel?"

"That was another call LAPD received this morning," Maddox said. "A cleaner discovered him lying facedown in a pool of blood in his living room. Five gunshot wounds. Three to the chest and two to the face. All twenty-twos."

"Casings?" Ange said. "Not that it matters," she added. "We know who did it. Or at least who ordered it."

Maddox shook his head. "They policed their brass."

"How'd the burn marks look on the rounds?" I asked.

"They were subsonic," Maddox said, knowing where I was going. "No doubt fired from a pistol with a suppressor, which explains why no neighbors heard anything."

We reached the end of the car wash, the big dryers howling air into the vehicle. Drops breaking apart and scattering across the windshield. Just as the red light flickered green and Ange put the midsize SUV in gear and tapped the gas, Maddox received a message.

He went quiet, reading the screen as Ange pulled us around, then braked to wait for an opening back onto Main Street.

"I need to get back there," Maddox said, the words coming out stern and quick. "This thing just got a hell of a lot worse."

THIRTY

Maddox didn't explain himself as Ange blasted us back to LAPD headquarters, weaving in and out of traffic like a woman possessed. It was evident that something big had happened, but the DHS agent wanted to get back to the joint task group and hear everything from the horse's mouth before he fed us anything new.

"I'll be back," he said as Ange pulled up across the street from the building. "Thirty minutes max."

The man jumped out and hustled across the street, disappearing into the throng of businessmen and police officers. With nothing to do but wait, Ange pulled around until we found a hot dog stand. I picked us both up a Ball Park Frank resting in a warm bun and covered in caramelized onions, relish, ketchup, and mustard. I grabbed a couple bags of Rusty's Island Style potato chips and some bottles of water as well, then climbed back into the car.

We ate quickly, enjoying the meal but keeping our eyes peeled for Maddox's return. Just being in the presence of my wife felt incredible. Though we'd only been apart a couple of days, it felt much longer. There was so much that'd happened in that short amount of time. So much I wanted to ask her about, and so much I wanted to tell her.

But it would all have to wait for another time. We had pressing matters to attend to. And just as we finished up our food, Maddox appeared again. He fast walked all the way back to us and was breathing heavy by the time he sat and shut the door behind him.

"Let's go," he said, glancing over his shoulder. "I need to head straight to the Homeland office, so there isn't much time."

He gave Ange quick instructions. The Los Angeles DHS office was just three blocks away. Barely a quarter mile. A quick in and out of the car, regardless of the traffic.

"What happened?" I said as Ange peeled us away from the curb.

"We've got more big problems is what's happened. The chief of police just informed me that Lucius and his thugs have taken Officer Carter as well." He let out a heavy breath. "Apparently they broke into her house and took her last night. She was scheduled to be off today, so the department just recently found out."

"How do they know Lucius took her?" I asked.

It should've been a dumb question. But the fact that Maddox had been informed by the police that Lucius was the culprit so soon after the incident took place told me that the authorities had more information to go on.

"That's the worst part," Maddox said, gritting his teeth. "He's trying to make a deal."

"A deal?" I said, raising my eyebrows. "What kind of deal?"

"The secret, behind-closed-doors kind." He rubbed his chin in frustration, then said, "He's offering to return Theo and Officer Carter unharmed. And he's willing to give out names and details of worldwide accomplices in exchange for total amnesty, and for keeping his name clear of everything."

"But he's the head guy, right?" Ange said. "How the hell can he keep his hands clean of it all?"

Maddox threw his hands in the air. "I don't know, to be honest. But there's a lot of money and power here behind the scenes. And that's not all of his demands."

"What else could he possibly want?" Ange said.

"He wants safe passage to Vanuatu."

I shook my head. "Of course he does."

"He apparently owns an island and multiple mansions there," Maddox said. "And the Polynesian nation being a nonextradition country, he could live out the rest of his days there untouchable by the United States—covering himself in case we ever decide to change our minds and convict him of something."

The car fell silent. A light ahead flashed green, and Ange gassed us closer and closer to Maddox's destination.

"They still don't know where he is?" I said, thinking everything over.

Maddox shook his head. "That's the biggest problem here. They've checked all his properties on the West Coast. His private jet is grounded. So are his helicopters. Even his yacht was searched."

The tall white exterior of the federal building housing the local DHS offices loomed right in front of us. Ange pulled off, hugging the curb and coming to a stop.

"What sort of time frame are we looking at here, Maddox?" I said.

He shrugged. "Like I said, there are decisions here that will be made by people higher up the food chain than me." He grabbed the handle. "All we can do is keep searching for Lucius. Finding him, and fast, might be the only chance we have at ensuring he and his tribe of criminals face justice."

He told us he'd be in touch, then hopped out and strode toward the federal building.

THIRTY-ONE

"I just can't believe it," Scarlett sighed. "The most exciting thing to ever happen to us, and they won't let me be a part of it."

Isaac eyed her quizzically, then turned back to look at his computer monitor and resumed his game. "You're joking, right? You've literally done more exciting, crazy things in the past year than I've done in my whole life. And it's not even close."

Scarlett sat at the corner of Isaac's bed, petting her family's yellow Lab, Atticus, and letting out a long breath again as she peered out a window to the backyard where Jack and Lauren were grilling. After her flight across the country, Jack had picked her up at Key West International, and the adventurous teenager had felt caged up in their island home ever since.

"Okay, so I've certainly been a part of some excitement," she said, "but this is Jasmine Cruz we're talking about. She's like the most famous woman on the planet. And my parents know how much I'm dying to meet her. It's just not fair."

Isaac laughed and shook his head, keeping his eyes on his game.

"What?" she said, shooting him a chastising look.

He focused intently on his game, clicking and moving his mouse with one hand while swiftly tapping keys with the other. Then he grinned, shook his head and said, "You're just really sounding like a big baby right now."

She leaned over and gave a playful punch to his right shoulder.

"Hey, that's my mouse arm," he said, feigning pain as he rolled the joint around and continued clicking away.

"Okay. I'll admit it," she said, holding her palms out, then falling backward dramatically onto the bed. "Yeah, I'm acting like a baby. But I'm just so... this is Jasmine Cruz we're talking about."

"Why do you keep saying her name?"

"To help me wrap my head around the fact that it's actually her."

"She's just a person," Isaac shrugged. "Like you and me."

She rolled and propped onto her shoulder. "Oh, come on, Isaac. I know you're all about digital worlds and cartoons and whatnot. But—"

"They're called High Elves."

"Whatever. Even a techie like you has to admit that she looks like a goddess."

"I mean, yeah, she's beautiful. But so are you. So are lots of girls."

She beamed, and when he saw her face flush a little, he added, "And I mean that in a sibling sort of way. So don't let your head get too big."

She giggled, then paused a moment and looked out the back window again. It started raining. Thick drops cascading out of nowhere and pounding the roof and backyard. Jack, having already known the downpour was coming due to what he called his "conch instinct," had the grill set up under a wide covered area with an outdoor table.

"I just wish there was something I could do to help, you know?" Scarlett said. "Something we could do. She's in trouble. Big trouble. Like when we helped locate that underwater weapons arsenal. Or when we discovered those drug traffickers' unique method of moving drugs down the islands. Or when—"

"We don't have anything to go on. Not sure what we can do."

Atticus's ears perked up as a car pulled into the driveway. Scarlett leaned over the bed for a glimpse of the front, then scampered to the living room and opened the front door.

Cameron met her on the front porch, shielding himself from the rain with a thin coat. She jumped into his arms as he stepped from the deluge, and he lifted her up and they kissed a moment before he set her back down.

"Tell me all about how your spring break has been boring and miserable because I wasn't here," she said.

"Is that what you want to hear?"

She chuckled. "Just kidding. But really, how was your trip with your uncle?"

"Good," he said, wiping away wayward strands of his damp hair. "We kayaked to Carl Ross Key on the bay side and camped a night, then paddled to Little Rabbit Key for two more nights. He's been acting a little strange. Always wanting to hang out with me. He's always been present, but far more than usual lately."

"Well, you are leaving soon. Maybe he's trying to enjoy as much time as he can with you."

"Yeah, you're probably right."

"All right," she said, spinning around so her back faced the water splashing down from the eave. "Let's get inside, but first…"

She reached beside her with a cupped hand, catching the thickest part of the stream. Then in a flash, she chucked the little pool of water straight into Cameron, the water spreading and splashing right over his face before he could turn for cover.

He wiped his skin and hair aside, then laughed. "Oh, you've done it now, Dodge."

He held her playfully while catching water of his own, managing to hurl a tiny pool over her hair and back as she broke free and slipped inside.

They ran into the house, shutting the door behind them while grappling and tickling each other.

"All right, break it up," Jack called from the kitchen. He pointed a pair of tongs at Cameron. "And shoes off, superstar."

He did as the host said and stepped to the living room. Atticus met him there, his tail wagging like crazy and a slobber-coated tennis ball in his mouth.

"Smells good in here," Cameron said, while greeting the energetic Lab and inhaling a mouthwatering aroma of barbeque ribs, mac and cheese, cornbread, and fried pickles.

"Meat and three," Lauren said, the homegrown Tennessee woman getting the goods straight from her mama's old recipe book. "Grew up on this."

Jack eyed her proudly. "For this evening at least, the Rubio kitchen's the best soul food destination in Cayo Hueso."

Lauren stepped over and handed them each a fried pickle.

"Blow on it a little," she said.

They did so, then both took a bite that rapidly transitioned to the whole appetizer being thrown back. They smiled, their eyes big, while savoring the warm, crunchy, spicy delicacy lathered in ranch.

"This is amazing," Scarlett gasped.

"And it's just the tip of the iceberg when Sweetie's in the kitchen," Jack said, planting a kiss on her cheek.

Lauren tossed a handful of the little circles of goodness into a bowl and handed them to Scarlett. She thanked her, then said, "We're gonna be in the bedroom."

"Keep the door cracked," Jack said.

"No problemo, Uncle Jack," she said. "But Isaac's in there with us and he's basically a chaperone. He's an old soul. Not to mention a tattletale."

"I heard that," Isaac shouted from his bedroom.

Jack waved his spatula. "All right, all right. Dinner's in half an hour."

They glided into Isaac's room with Atticus on their heels and sat beside each other on a beanbag chair, downing more of the fried pickles while Isaac continued with his game. Cameron mostly listened as Scarlett spoke animatedly about all she'd seen while hiking the Grand Canyon, and how badly she wanted to go back someday.

"Then we had to fly to Los Angeles." She sat taller and raised her chin proudly. "'Cause my parents are helping none other than…" She paused, playing fake drums, and letting the suspense build, then proclaimed, "Jasmine Cruz. You believe that?"

"Yeah, I kinda met her," Cameron said with a nod.

Her proud look turned sour on a dime. "Wait, you met her? Okay, now this is officially really unfair. When did you meet her?"

"I was just going for a run. Ran into her and your dad. It wasn't exactly a deep, life-changing interaction if it makes you feel any better."

"I'm not sure it will," Isaac said. "She's been going on and on about her for the past hour. Good thing this headset has a noise-canceling button so I can drown her out when needed."

He and Cameron laughed, and she grabbed a pillow and tossed it across the bedroom, striking Isaac in the back of the head and nearly knocking the headphones off.

"You're lucky I grace you with my presence and entertaining ramblings," she said, perking up exaggeratingly. "And you secretly like them. Admit it."

Isaac held his smile but didn't reply, keeping his focus on the game.

"Your parents aren't back yet?" Cameron said.

"No. They're still in LA. Having all the fun."

"Scarlett was trying to find a way to help," Isaac said. "I just don't know what we can do from all the way over here in Key West."

"I'm sure your parents can handle it," Cameron said.

Scarlett sighed again. "I know they can." She leaned back and stared at the ceiling. "I just wish there was something I could do. I mean, this is—"

"Jasmine Cruz, we know," Isaac said.

She glared at him, then turned to face Cameron. "Like I was telling Isaac earlier, she's amazing. I mean, you've seen her Facebook, right?"

Cameron paused, eyeing her suspiciously. "Is this some kind of trap?"

A significant percentage of the photos posted on Jasmine's profile featured the celebrity wearing barely enough clothing to comply with the social network's terms of service.

"It's okay," she said with a chuckle. "You can answer truthfully."

Cameron cleared his throat. "I mean, yeah, I'm sure everyone has. But it's been a while."

"So, you know she's beautiful."

"Yeah, but so are you."

Isaac tilted his head. "That's what I said."

She blushed. "Okay. I'm dealing with two people who don't—"

She froze as she brought up Jasmine's page and eyed the socialite's most recent post. Hovering her thumb over the screen, she tapped on a pair of pictures and corresponding text that had been uploaded less than an hour earlier. The first image was of her nine-year-old son, Theo. The second was a picture of a gray-haired man with a heavy tan and dark eyes.

She read the caption in stunned silence.

This evil, wicked man, Lucius Xavier, has taken my son. If anyone has any info regarding his or my son's whereabouts, please contact LAPD immediately. —A frantic mother who's terrified for her child.

THIRTY-TWO

Intrigued by a mother's desperate plea for help, Isaac needed no convincing to log out of his game and help Scarlett dive into the task at hand as best they could.

He quickly opened up new internet tabs. One was for listening to live LAPD scanner feeds, which he put on speaker while cycling through the different channels. He also pulled up live news feeds from the area, the hordes of eager newsmen already publishing responses to Cruz's Facebook post.

"Apparently they've checked all of Lucius's properties," Isaac said, reading through a news report that'd just been posted. "Along with his offices. They can't find the guy anywhere."

Scarlett and Cameron hovered over him, poring over the information as well.

"I've never seen anything like this," Isaac said, rubbing his eyes as he gazed at his screen. "It's like the whole world is coming together, looking for this guy. Trying to help her track down her son." He held out an arm, his skin bumpy. "I'm getting goosebumps just thinking about it."

But while the mass group effort was doing a very good job at identifying where Lucius wasn't, there'd yet to be anyone pinpointing the mogul's location.

"Okay, so every property this guy owns has been accounted for," Scarlett said, thinking hard. "What about properties owned by his friends? Let's search his name online and bring up related names. Then let's scroll through their social media feeds, looking for any sort of clue."

"That's smart," Cameron said. "But what exactly are we supposed to be looking for?"

Scarlett shrugged. "I don't know. Somewhere secluded, maybe? Like a mountain cabin or someplace remote within a day's drive from LA."

Scarlett pulled out her phone and brought up social media accounts of Lucius's known acquaintances. Supposed members of his inner circle and people who'd worked with him. She tried a couple big names and scrolled down, coming up empty.

"Dinner's ready," Jack shouted from the kitchen. "Get it while it's hot."

The three teenagers had never eaten a meal so fast in their lives. Despite the incredible food, Scarlett barely ate, wanting to get back to her search. As soon as she could, the go-getter peeled away from the dining table and was back in Isaac's bedroom. The boys quickly followed, and the trio was back at it, browsing through pages and pages of pictures and posts. Not sure what they were looking for, but hoping they'd realize it when they found it.

An hour passed. Seemingly fruitless and with little chatter amongst the group.

To break up the monotony, Cameron stepped out back and played fetch with Atticus, hurling the tennis ball again and again across the yard. When he toweled off the dog and returned to Isaac's bedroom and saw there'd still been no progress, he let out a heavy sigh, blinked, and sat down.

"I'm not seeing anything that could act as a good hideout," Isaac said. "A couple of mountain houses, but they're all close to other houses or too far away for them to have already reached them by car. Maybe we should change up our strat—"

"Wait a minute!" Scarlett exclaimed, cutting him off. She sprang forward, then tilted her head to examine her screen closer and zoomed in. "Look at this," she said, scooting toward Cameron and motioning Isaac over.

The two young men leaned over her shoulders and gazed at an image of four people lounging on the deck of what appeared to be a yacht. She zoomed in on each of the people pictured in turn.

"This is Lily Cohen," Scarlett said, pointing at a beautiful blond woman. "She's an actress who died just three weeks ago. And this is Lucius." She zoomed in on the guy. He was wearing an unbuttoned shirt and sunglasses and had a cigar in his left hand and his right wrapped around Lily. "I don't recognize the other two. But this picture has me thinking. What if he's not in a house. What if he's—"

"On a yacht?" Cameron said.

"His yacht was searched," Isaac said. "It's mentioned in the latest news reports."

Scarlett bit her lip. "Maybe he's on a friend's yacht. Or a charter."

"Are there any other pictures of it?" Isaac said.

She swiped through the photos. The only two other pictures in the post were a selfie of Lily in a bikini on the bow and one of deep blue water and a distant sunset. She clicked back, but there were no other posts with the yacht pictured.

Scarlett thought a moment, then said, "Okay. I've got another idea."

She clicked back to the picture of the four people, then scrolled down to the comments. Sifting through them, she found one that mentioned how it'd been a hell of a day. She clicked on the profile. It was another woman. A young Brazilian model. She scrolled way back to the same date range as the picture on the yacht, freezing when she saw a post the woman had uploaded.

"All right," Scarlett beamed, clicking and zooming in on one of the pictures. "I think we have something here."

It was a low-angled shot of the woman posing on the swim platform next to a pair of fins and snorkel gear. Right beside her was the name of the boat in elegant gold letters.

"It's called *Fortuna*, and she even tagged the location," Scarlett said, then she slouched and let out a big sigh. "Great. I guess that dead-ends that lead."

"What is it?" Cameron said, craning his neck.

"The picture was taken off some island called Santa Catalina. That's Spanish, right? It's probably someplace off Spain or South America. So it can't be—"

"It's not off either of those," Isaac said, stepping back to his computer. "I recognize that building in the background from the movie *Step Brothers*." He typed ferociously, then slid his chair away so the others could see his screen. "It's in California. Just off the coast of Los Angeles."

"That doesn't look like California," Scarlett said, scanning the thumbnail-sized pictures of a stunning jagged island surrounded by rich blue waters.

"Trust me," Isaac said, clicking on one of the pictures. "It is. Look at this picture and look in the background of the one the woman posted."

Just beyond her along the arid, tropical shoreline was a tall, round white structure rising up from the breakwater. Beside it was the opening into a cove filled with moored boats and clusters of houses rising up from a beach and set amongst flat green hillsides.

The background of the picture matched perfectly with an image Isaac had up of Avalon, the only incorporated city on the island.

"You see?" Isaac said.

They both patted him on the back.

Then the trio fell silent, and Scarlett bit her lip. "Okay, this is good. But now we need to see if there's some kind of ongoing connection between Lucius and this yacht. You know, make sure this wasn't a onetime occurrence or something."

"Way ahead of you," Isaac said, typing ferociously.

He performed a quick Google search of the yacht along with Lucius Xavier, then clicked over to image results. A handful of paparazzi photos popped up, showing pictures taken from far away of Lucius lounging and walking about the yacht. And the dates indicated the mogul had been aboard the vessel at different times over the years.

"The connection definitely isn't random," Isaac said. He typed again, then scanned through lines of text. "It looks like it's owned by a company based out of the Cayman Islands."

"Could be a shell corporation," Cameron said as he pried a slobbery tennis ball from Atticus's mouth. "My uncle was watching this documentary once about a big time criminal who hid most of his assets through shell corporations."

Isaac rubbed his chin. "So, maybe the police never searched this yacht or looked for it because it's not officially linked to Lucius. Heck, if the guy's so rich and powerful, he could have multiple secret yachts for all anyone knows. Maybe people think they belong to associates of his or something."

Scarlett fell silent, taking their thoughts into account. "Okay, we're making progress," she said. "Let's say the *Fortuna* does secretly belong to Lucius. How do we figure out if he's currently hiding out aboard it?"

Cameron leaned back, bounced the tennis ball off the door and caught it, then said, "We could contact marinas along the coast. Big yacht like that, I can't imagine there are more than a dozen places that could accommodate it in the immediate area. Even in a populous place like Los Angeles."

Isaac nodded and smiled. "Good idea. But we just call them up one at a time inquiring about the *Fortuna*? How do we get them to talk? This Lucius guy seems pretty private. Wherever this yacht's moored, I highly doubt the marina staff will just openly spill the beans on where it is and who's aboard."

Scarlett though a moment, then perked up. "*I'll* call them up," she said. "Some things require a woman's touch."

It took a half hour of phoning various marinas along the City of Angels' coastline, but Scarlett eventually got a hit. She reached a young marina worker and the sharp-witted teenager pretended to be a young actress and asked whether the Fortuna had set sail yet.

"I was supposed to come aboard today," she explained in a flirty voice. "I spoke to Lucius about it yesterday."

She listened to the young man's reply, then chuckled and said, "That sly devil. Who was he with?"

She nodded as she listened to an even lengthier reply, and wore a broad smile when she ended the call.

"The *Fortuna* apparently set sail late yesterday evening," Scarlett said. "He said he was too far away to recognize anyone in the group as they boarded, but that there was a boy with them."

Cameron rubbed his hands together, tightening his gaze. "I think it's time to call your parents, Scar."

THIRTY-THREE

It was just after five o'clock when my phone buzzed, indicating a call from our daughter. Ange and I were both feeling drained and disheartened. Since dropping off Maddox at the Los Angeles Homeland offices, we'd both run into one dead end after another. Lucius, Theo, and Officer Carter had all just disappeared. And even with Jasmine's Facebook post, and millions of people searching, no one had been able to find them. Or even offer up any clues.

Then, barely half an hour earlier, we'd received word from Maddox that the deal was being accepted—the fine details being ironed out behind closed doors. It was nothing short of depressing feeling like Lucius was going to win, so I handed Ange my phone, not in the mood to talk to anyone.

We were back at Beck's place by then, having made sure we weren't being tailed, then parking two blocks away and approaching from the waterfront side. I stood beside the kitchen counter, my hands planted on the tiles as I gazed out over the bay.

Beck was standing across from me, and Jasmine was pacing back and forth beside the biggest window, checking and swiping through her new phone multiple times a minute. It was an encrypted smartphone I'd purchased for her earlier that day. The same phone Ange and I used, the advanced device was untraceable, and offered privacy protection from third parties.

I observed Jasmine as she really began to worry, a look of barely subdued panic on her face. Despite the common stereotype surrounding supermodel celebrities, she was anything but brainless. Posting the pictures and message on social media had been a great idea. And she'd been a huge help in trying to locate Lucius. But the pressures and worry were amping up with every passing second.

Ange took my vibrating phone and plopped onto the living room couch. My wife was weary when she answered. Mentally and physically drained. But she livened up and leaned forward mere seconds into the call.

"Wait, Scarlett, slow down," she said. Her words and the tone she gave them reeled all of us toward her in an instant. "I appreciate the help, Scar, but police have already checked his yachts."

"Have they checked the *Fortuna*?" my daughter exclaimed, her voice loud enough to hear through the tiny speaker.

Ange shook her head. "The what?"

Jasmine let out a breath. Her eyes went big and she said, "Of course. The *Fortuna*. Why didn't I think of that?"

Seeing Jasmine's reaction, Ange put my phone on

speaker.

"What's the *Fortuna*?" I said.

"It's a yacht owned by Lucius," Jasmine said. "Well, it's owned by a shell corporation of his. For tax evasion and whatnot. I can't believe I didn't think of it. It's been years since I went out on it. It's usually abroad in Polynesia. Lucius has a couple yachts in the area, but this one is more private."

"We figured it out from a picture on Lily Cohen's feed from a couple months ago, Miss Cruz," Scarlett said. "The yacht was just off the coast of Avalon, a city on Santa Catalina."

"Please, call me Jasmine," the socialite said, her voice laced with emotion. "That's remarkably clever of you, Scarlett. Did you happen to figure out if it's moored anywhere nearby?"

"It left Peninsula Yacht Marina late last night," Scarlett said, the speaker on full volume. "A group of people boarded." She paused a moment, then added. "One of them was a boy."

Jasmine threw a hand over her mouth. She shook, her knees wobbly, and nearly collapsed. Ange rose and wrapped an arm around her.

"That's great stuff, kiddo," I said. "You may have just saved this whole thing. None of the marina workers knew where it was heading?"

"The one I spoke to didn't, and he seemed pretty in the know, so I doubt any of the others do. But Isaac just checked, and the *Fortuna* has a cruising speed of twenty knots, so he's likely not more than a hundred miles from the coast."

I listened, stunned that I was hearing on-the-fly intelligence gathering conducted by a group of teenagers.

"My guess would be Catalina," Jasmine said. "He knows the island well."

"I agree," Scarlett said. "And I wish I was there to help you guys look for it."

We thanked our daughter for everything. Jasmine especially expressed her emotional gratitude. Then we ended the call.

"It sounds like we have the perfect place to start," I said, then turned to Ange. "I think it's high time we took a scenic flight off the coast."

We wasted no time loading into the Cessna, chugging away from Beck's dock, and taking off out of Alamitos Bay. With the sun arcing steadily toward the Pacific, we had maybe two hours of sunlight to complete a search of Catalina's coastline. After dark, the task of locating a specific yacht would prove significantly harder. Especially one whose passengers didn't want to be found.

It took fifteen minutes for Ange to fly us the twenty-seven miles west. Seeing the island grow bigger on the horizon brought back a flood of memories. I flashed back to years earlier when I'd received the worst news of my life: that my father had died in a tragic accident off Curaçao in the Dutch Caribbean.

Living on a sailboat in Fiddler's Cove Marina in San Diego at the time, I'd stepped away from my work schedule and, after handling his burial, I'd spent two weeks sailing around Catalina. Just getting away from it all. Silence and solitude. Time to think and let go, and heal.

A different cove every night. Living mostly off the

sea. Thinking about my dad and all the memories we'd shared over the years.

That was six years ago, and the island has always held a special place in my heart. Even before those two weeks, I'd spent most of my time off sailing to Catalina with a buddy or lady friend. It offers the closest vibes I've ever found to the Keys on the West Coast.

Twenty-two miles long and with a peak elevation of two thousand feet, the popular California island looked beautiful on approach, basking in the late-afternoon glow.

We cut straight across its heart, flying over the dry, mountainous landscape, and reaching the cliff lined coast of its west side. Though Catalina is popular, the western and northern edges are mostly devoid of people, so we started there. We agreed that if we were corrupt moguls looking to stay under the radar, that was where we'd drop anchor.

The rocky shore stretched along a white surf in rippling contours, offering one secluded inlet after another. But that side of the island was harsher, facing the massive expanse of the Pacific and its long brewing waves in full force. So we only spotted one vessel moored along the windward side, and it wasn't a yacht.

We spotted two more boats after rounding West End and the northwestern side of the island, but they were both far too small to be the *Fortuna*.

After soaring just over a mile over the northern coast, we spotted a large yacht tucked into one of the many coves. I zoomed in with my monocular. The vessel appeared to be the right size, shape, and color.

It was quiet, with no visible people on deck, the nearby shore, or in the clear waters surrounding it. The landscape appeared untouched, the only footpaths far up the hills or east along the beach a ways.

Ange descended a little and looped around, trying to fly casual while offering me a clear shot of the yacht's stern. A nation's flag I didn't recognize flapped from a pole sticking out of the transom. I focused the optics on the stern, giving myself as good of an angle on the vessel's name as I could. Then I adjusted the words into focus.

Dreamboat.

I shifted my gaze and saw that it was also the wrong make and model.

"False alarm, I guess," Ange said, banking back to the east and ascending back to two hundred feet. "Let's keep at it. There's still a lot of coastline left."

We continued east, then cut southeast, flying over campgrounds and summer camps before reaching Two Harbors. I gazed down at the two ports right beside each other, and the slit of land barely half a mile wide separating them. There were dozens of boats anchored there, and a couple of them were big enough to be Lucius's, but they didn't match up. One was the wrong color, and the other was surprisingly too big.

"This island sure makes this side of the country look appealing," Ange said through the headset. "Did you ever think of settling down here?"

I nodded. "Better not tell Jack that," I said. "I love it here. But for me, there's nowhere better than the Keys."

"He ever been here?"

I shook my head. "Not that I know of. But then again the guy isn't exactly vocal about the places he's visited. I'm sure he'd fit right in here."

"Yeah, did you see the pictures of the lobster Beck caught?"

My old comrade had a couple pictures of himself holding up monster California spiny lobsters. Twenty-pounders he'd caught barehanded out in Newport Harbor.

"We might have to return for a real visit," I said.

We continued along for another seven miles before Long Point, then eventually closed in on Avalon. We'd spotted many more anchored boats along the way, but none met the description we were looking for.

The harbor in front of the island's largest town was packed with boats of all shapes and sizes. A dense array of houses, condos, shops, and restaurants hugged the shore and a nice sandy beach.

We made two passes over the harbor so I could inspect each of the larger boats. One was beyond promising. It was the right size and color, and as we swooped around for a better view, I saw that its name was covered up.

"Could be him," Ange said. "I didn't expect him to be here in Avalon, but we both read that this guy's cocky. Maybe he still thinks he's untouchable, or he's showing off by mooring in the island's busiest body of water."

I nodded. "I'll call up Maddox and see if he can clear the air a bit. In the meantime let's keep at it."

I phoned the Homeland agent, seeing if he could

get in touch with the Avalon Bay harbormaster for some info on the hundred-and-fifty-foot yacht.

Ange piloted us back along the southeasterly line, passing more jagged coves as we pushed toward the southern tip of the island. While we were circling back to where we'd begun our search ten minutes later, Maddox got back to me.

"Looks like a swing and a miss, Logan," he said. "The harbormaster said that yacht's been there three days. And that there's been no activity aboard her except for the crew ever since." He paused, then added, "And like Scarlett said, the *Fortuna* left the marina late last night."

I thanked him, then ended the call and stared back out the window.

We fell silent as we finished our loop around the island, spotting a couple sailboats and a sport fishing boat, but nothing resembling our prospective vessel.

I shielded my eyes, gazing west toward the sun that was sinking closer and closer to the ocean.

"We've got maybe twenty minutes of light left," Ange said. She let out a loud sigh, then added, "I guess it's back to the drawing board."

I fell silent. It'd been a long shot, we'd all known that. But as Ange shifted our course east, piercing through the glowing sky and soaring us across the island, something inside me felt off. I couldn't place it, though. But a gut instinct deep within me was trying to tell me something.

"Hey," Ange said. "We'll find him, all right? I just hope we do before the government makes a deal. After everything this guy's done? The thought of him slipping through our fingers and finding refuge in some distant country makes me sick."

My eyes bulged as everything clicked in my head. I rolled it around a moment, then turned to my wife.

"Ange, that's it," I gasped through the headset.

"What's it?"

I rubbed my chin and looked out through the windshield just as we popped over the hills to the other side of the island. Then I whispered to myself, "I can't believe I missed it."

"What?" Ange said, leaning over and eyeing me like a crazy person.

"How's our fuel?" I asked, craning my neck for a glimpse of the gauge.

"Hair over a third. What's going on?"

"We need to fly back to the north side of the island."

"Why?"

"I think we've got him, Ange."

THIRTY-FOUR

I called Maddox again. I needed clarification on something, just to be sure. Ten seconds after the call connected, we ended it, and I brought up Google on my phone and rapidly thumbed in a search. Pressed image results. Then leaned back and lowered the device.

Ange was about to ask me yet again what was going on when I showed her the screen. She leaned over and squinted at it a moment, then gave a surprised smile.

"You've got to be kidding me," was all she said.

"I know."

We flew back to the northern coast, over Two Harbors and sporadic waterfront campgrounds, Land's End ahead of us in the distance.

"There she is," Ange said, pointing through the glass at the first yacht we'd seen.

She descended a little and turned. I focused on its stern again, paying less attention to the name and more attention to the fiberglass surface around it.

Then my mouth dropped open and I shot Ange a knowing look.

"The name's recently been painted. There's a slight discoloration of the white background, indicating a name change."

"I can't believe he's waving a Vanuatu flag."

"Like you mentioned earlier," I said, "it's not against this guy's character to be cocky and showboat. Maybe for when the deal is struck. I don't know. The guy's got a twisted mind. Plays a lot of power games."

"Well, it's about to be game over. He's messed with the wrong people. You see anyone aboard?"

I stared through the magnifying lenses, running my eye over every inch of the vessel's sleek, expensive exterior.

"Nothing. And the windows are all tinted." I zoomed in near the stern and added, "The guy even had the yacht's make and model names changed. Unbelievable."

With daylight fading away by the second, we made mental and physical notes of the yacht's position and orientation, then Ange piloted us back to the mainland.

The sky was dark, moonlight bleeding through the clouds and washing over Alamitos Bay as we snugged back up to the dock in front of Beck's place. Jasmine was standing there, her arms folded across her and a thin blanket draped over her shoulder. Beck was right beside her, along with his two German shepherds, the well-trained canines heeling at either side of him.

Ange killed the engine, and I tied us off and

offered her a hand down. Jasmine stepped forward, her face wracked with worry.

I locked eyes with her, then gave a slight nod. "We found it."

"Where?" Beck said.

"Northwestern side of the island. Near Parson's Landing."

He nodded. "A logical hiding place."

"We have no way of knowing for certain if he's aboard though," Ange said,

"Or how much longer the yacht will be there," I added. "If he is there, my guess is he's—"

Odin and Orion's ears shot up. They turned and gazed toward the front of the house and growled softly. I froze when I saw movement near the driveway. My right hand hovered momentarily over my holstered Sig at the back of my waistband, then I saw a familiar figure stepping out of the shadows.

"It's Maddox," I said.

With one quick sound, Beck silenced both his dogs, and they returned calmly to his side.

The Homeland agent held his hands up a moment, then strode over to us. Quick introductions were made, then we gave him an update on what'd happened.

"What's going on with the negotiation?" I said. "Have the details been finalized yet?"

He swallowed hard, then motioned to the house. "Can we talk inside?"

We all entered through the back door, then headed down a set of old wooden stairs into the den. It was cozy down there. The windows were curtained, and Beck switched on his security system, giving us surveillance camera views all around the house from a monitor. Not that we'd really need it. There was nearly forty years of Special Forces experience in that small space. And with Ange and the two German shepherds, it would take a small army to engage us.

"They're going to make the deal," Maddox said, never one to beat around the bush. "But there's a catch. Lucius won't release Officer Carter and your son until he reaches his destination."

"What?" Jasmine said, her face turning pale. "What if he doesn't follow through on his promise?"

Maddox sighed. "It's a gamble. And I disagreed with the decision. But they're trying to be as cautious and diplomatic as possible."

"Diplomatic?" Jasmine said. "Every second Theo's with that maniac might be his last."

"I know, Miss Cruz. And I'm sorry."

"It doesn't matter," I said.

Jasmine and Maddox both went quiet and eyed me curiously.

"First off," Ange said, stepping up to explain, "Theo's your son. And if you want to let the powers that be handle it, make the deal, and hope that Lucius follows through and releases him and Carter, we'll respect that."

"That's right," I said. "There's risk involved either way. That needs to be understood. If we make a move tonight, we'll do everything in our power to find them and get them both out safe. But there're no guarantees. There never are in situations like this. Think about it. But we'll need your answer soon, one way or another."

"I don't need to think about it," Jasmine said. "Not

for a second. I don't trust Lucius. He's a lying, conniving murderer. Please make your move tonight."

I nodded. "All right, then." Then I turned to Maddox.

"I wish I could help," he said. "You know that. But I'm already compromising my position enough just by talking to you guys. Angelina, Logan, good luck," he said, placing a hand on both our shoulders. Then he headed upstairs, then back out into the evening.

"I owe you so much," Jasmine said in the silence that followed. "I owe you both so much already and I know I'm in no position to ask more favors of you, but please… please bring my baby home to me."

"You don't need to ask," I said. "We're going to do everything in our power to get your son out of there." Then I turned to Ange and said something I'd been itching to say ever since I'd first heard about Lucius Xavier and he'd sent men to kill Jasmine and me. "I think it's high time I introduced myself to this guy."

THIRTY-FIVE

You're in big trouble. You're in really, really big trouble.

Theo Cruz sat on a cold floor in a dark cramped space. His little arms were bound behind him at the wrists by duct tape.

The past thirty-six hours of his life was a blur. A long, confusing, painful, and frightening blur, ever since Wyatt had dropped him off at the strange mansion. He'd been grabbed forcefully, a gag put around his mouth, a sack thrown over his head. Tied up and hauled into a car and driven for miles before being carried again. Hauled around like a rag doll for what felt like an eternity before eventually being chained to a big eye bolt sticking out of the floor in the dark space.

He'd screamed at the top of his lungs the moment they'd removed his gag. Shouted like crazy. Then they'd struck him. Twice. Heaving blows to his chest that had made him wheeze and cough and keel over.

They'd told him if he made another sound, they'd

hit him twice more, and he'd gone silent. Hadn't uttered a noise since, and that had been so long ago he couldn't remember. There was no way for him to know what time it was in there. There were no windows—no lights of any kind. And he didn't have a watch.

No one had said anything to him. He hadn't even seen anyone aside from the four times big men had entered, blindfolded him, and practically dragged him out so he could use the bathroom. They'd given him food and drink, but that seemed like forever ago. His stomach growled, and his throat was parched. But he didn't care. Other more powerful internal sensations had completely hijacked his mind. He was utterly terrified. He wanted to get out of there. And above all, he wanted his mom.

He tried his best to keep calm as he looked around in the darkness. Thought as hard as his weary brain could about his predicament and how he'd gotten there. He was on a boat. That much was obvious. The gentle, rhythmic sway. Then the growling of engines. Even the occasional squawk of a seagull. The engines had stopped long ago, but the floor still swayed.

He tried to think about what a nine-year-old kid could've done to deserve being grabbed and held prisoner. He was right in the middle of it when he heard footsteps through the heavy door in front of him. A big lock clicked aside, and the door creaked open.

Theo closed his eyes as a wave of brilliant light blasted into him. Through slits, he saw blurred glimpses of two figures. A colossal brute of a man and a bound woman. The guy knelt down and secured the woman to an eye bolt across from Theo. Then he suddenly smacked her across her face, leaving her lying there on her side, gasping for air.

The brute grunted and turned back toward the door, then a second man stepped into the room. A man Theo recognized.

"Whatever you're doing, it'll never work," the brave boy snapped. "My mommy will come for me."

Lucius stepped closer, eyeing Theo pitifully. "I own your mommy, kid. She's mine and believe me she's not coming for you, Theo. Nobody's coming for you." The vile criminal turned and eyed the woman. "And you, Officer Carter," he said, looking her up and down. "That's just the first of many beatings you can expect to receive over the course of the next week. We've got a long voyage ahead, and you've done a good job of pissing me off these past couple years."

She met his gaze, then smirked and said, "Nice to see I got under that scaly skin of yours, you snake."

Lucius's eyes turned fiery, then he snickered. "Sad to see that you still don't understand. Well, I'll get through to that puny brain of yours. You can be assured of that. And long before I'm through with you, you'll wish you'd never crossed me. You'll beg me for mercy... but you won't receive it. You will receive only pain."

She growled, then shifted and threw herself forward, reaching to wring the mogul's throat. But the chain stopped her. Jerked her back tight, and she fell onto the cold floor. Lucius laughed again, then leaned over her body, staring intensely into her eyes.

"Yet another failed attempt on your part," he said.

Then he laughed harder as he stepped out, the door slamming shut and locking behind him. The room went pitch black again.

~ ~ ~

There was a brief moment of silence, then Carter adjusted herself into a seated position as she caught her breath.

"I'm glad you're okay, Theo," she said.

Theo hesitated, then said, "You know who I am?"

"Yeah. I know who you are."

She'd recognized him upon entering the cramped space. A good chunk of the world was interested in Jasmine Cruz and every little detail of her life. Paparazzi hounded her, especially in LA, more than just about any other celebrity. So Carter had seen plenty of pictures of Theo on magazine covers and on the internet over the years.

"Were you here trying to rescue me?" he said innocently. "If you were, I'm sorry. I don't want anyone getting hurt because of me."

"I'm not here to rescue you. They grabbed me in my house, they… I don't remember much after that."

"Same here. Just darkness and confusion after that."

Carter adjusted her hands, her shackles clanking in the quiet stillness.

"How long have you been here?" she asked.

"I don't know."

"Best guess. How many times have you slept?"

Half his face squinted in thought. "Once. But barely."

"Did they knock you unconscious when they took you?"

He shook his head. "No. Wyatt Cash, my mom's boyfriend, led me into someone's house. Then I was grabbed and blindfolded."

He told her about the various stages that had led to him being locked away there in the bowels of a mysterious ship. And how he'd heard engines and splashing water for a time.

"Okay," Carter said, "that means we can't be far from LA. We're not moving now."

She fell silent a moment, thinking through everything.

"I didn't come here to save you, Theo. I was taken. Just like you. But maybe we can work together to get out of this." She paused, then added, "I'm Veronica. Veronica Carter."

"Theo Cruz," the boy said.

"It's good to meet you, Theo." She looked around the dark room, then jerked her wrists and the thick layers of duct tape securing them. "We need to find a way to help each other get free of these.".

"I don't need any help getting free," Theo said. "It's that door that's the problem. Do you see that thing? It looks like a blast door from Star Wars. It'd take a real lightsaber to get through it. But if we can find a way, we're home free. I take karate, you know. I'm already a purple belt."

"Wait, what do you mean?"

"I mean, I'm pretty good at martial arts."

"No, I meant what do you mean you don't need

any help getting free?"

He gave a slight smile, then shimmied his left hand, wriggling it free of the tape and holding up his bare wrist to her. "I worked at it for hours and was able to slide them free. I just keep my wrists there so they don't come in and realize it."

"You're a smart kid."

He slid his tiny wrist back into the thick loop of tape with the other, then sighed. "Yeah, but like I said, that door is a big fat problem. We still can't get out of here even if our arms are free."

She thought again. Took a solid minute. Then an idea came and she did her best to think of an analogy he'd understand to explain it.

Star Wars, she thought. *He likes Star Wars.*

"Maybe we don't need to open it," Carter said. "If you can help me get free as well, maybe we don't need to worry about figuring out the door."

"I'm listening."

She pressed her knuckles to her lips a moment, then said, "Remember that scene in *A New Hope* when Luke, Han, and Chewbacca needed to find Leia? How did they get to the prison block without being stopped in order to catch their enemies in a surprise attack?"

He fell silent, then smiled broadly. "That could work. But how do we get you free?"

THIRTY-SIX

We spent just thirty minutes cooking up the rough framework of a plan, then loaded gear from the Cessna into Beck's blacked-out RHIB. Less than two hours after verifying Lucius's yacht from the air, we were motoring along Catalina's northern coast with Beck at the helm.

He'd kept the throttle full for most of the trip, zipping us across the open water at over forty knots. Being on that small, powerful, versatile boat and flying over open seas at night took me back. A blink and I'd flash to a jungle in Africa or South America. A shoreline with monkeys howling, surrounded by my brothers. All of us venturing courageously into hostile territory.

Beck eased back on the throttle for the first time as we rounded Stony Point, a nice tucked-away beach coming into view. The rocky shore glowing with the moon. A passive surf lapping against it.

Beck piloted right up to the beach, its hull piercing the sand and scraping up to a stop. He kept the engines at a steady idle as Ange grabbed her gear. Tightening the straps of her pack, we performed a quick mic check of our radios, verifying yet again that we'd all be able to communicate.

Once she was ready to roll, I gave her a good luck kiss, then she shot me a serious look and said, "Be careful."

I nodded, then her face turned stern and focused. Flipping the switch, Ange became a different person entirely as she climbed over the side, her tactical boots crushing into the sand. She gave us a shove, then turned and disappeared into the shadows. The former mercenary and one of the deadliest women in the world was in battle mode. Wearing all black with camo face paint, and hustling across an unforgiving landscape at night.

On the hunt.

I stared across the dark shoreline, sweeping my eyes over the foliage and steep hillside, hoping to catch just another glance of her. But she was gone. In her element. And the only way someone was going to spot her now was if she wanted them to.

Beck switched over to an electric motor, clamping the small engine to the transom right beside the beast that had rocketed us to the island. Though providing the equivalent of just three horsepower, the little device was nearly silent as Beck eased us around, pointing the bow to the west and motoring us the rest of the way.

We chugged along at barely five knots for a couple more minutes, then spotted a distant, towering rock that sprouted up three hundred feet from the surf.

"That's the point right at the gateway to Emerald

Cove," Beck said.

I nodded. I recognized it from my earlier trips to the island. There was excellent lobster diving nearby, I remembered. But that would have to wait for another time.

I'd already donned most of my gear by the time he slowed, keeping us steady with the current.

My eyes met Jasmine's for the first time since we'd reached the island.

"I wish I could do something," she said, her eyes watery. She was wearing a black hoodie and sweatpants. Sat curled up across from me just up from the console. "I'm so sorry again that I dragged you all into this."

I shot her a stern look. "I'm not a victim, Jasmine. Never considered myself one even for a moment in my entire life. You've made your decisions, and I've made mine, and that's that. Like I said, I'm finding your son."

And just as importantly, I was going to find and deal with Lucius Xavier. The man's evil, murderous reign had lasted far too long already. And I was eager to bring about its end.

Beck performed a buddy check, making sure everything was operating correctly. Rebreather gear is far more complex than scuba. The extra intricacies are worth it as rebreathers don't vent bubbles, offering me a much stealthier approach.

"You're all set, Dodge," Beck said.

In addition to my dive knife strapped to my ankle, I had my Sig and a .22-caliber pistol and suppressor stashed securely in a watertight bag, along with two full magazines for each. Though I was partial to my

Sig, the bread-and-butter sidearm of Navy SEALs for years, I needed something quieter. At least to start out with. And the subsonic .22 rounds and suppressor fit the bill.

I triggered the internal mic of my full-face mask just to make sure yet again that it was working. After receiving verbal confirmation from Ange and Beck, I sat on the starboard pontoon with my back to the water and donned my fins.

Jasmine gave me a quick, emotional nod. Then Beck said, "Give 'em hell, Dodge."

I flipped backward, splashing into the cool waters of the Pacific, clusters of tiny bubbles appearing and fluttering to the surface around me. I sank the twenty feet to the bottom, then clicked my dive light on to its dimmest setting. The seafloor was rocky, and I used it to stabilize myself as I took a quick look around. Then I performed another check of my gear before hailing Beck.

"All set, Rammer," I said.

"Copy that. We'll keep close. Just a call away, brother."

He fired up the boat's electric motor and turned, gliding back in the direction they'd come.

The viz was perfect as I clicked on the high-powered beam of my dive light. Crystal clear for over a hundred feet in all directions. The sea lapped lazily against the shore to my left, the bottom dropping off rapidly to my right into deep, dark water. There was a thick patch of kelp beside me—an underwater forest that danced with the waves and current. At sixty degrees, it was much cooler than the seawater I was accustomed to back in Key West, so I was thankful for the 7mm wetsuit.

Getting my bearings, I flattened my body and pushed off the bottom, kicking with big, smooth cycles of my fins and skirting west. The waters off the beautiful island were exactly how I remembered them, and I thought back to the hours I'd spent freediving and spearfishing and searching for lobster in the abundant nooks and crannies.

Being back in the waters of the Pacific off Southern California also brought back memories of swimming the shores of Coronado just eighty miles to the south during the first and most notorious phase of SEAL training.

I kept my eyes forward, the glow of my flashlight revealing the way ahead of me. The going was slow against the current, but I soon reached the edge of the towering point.

I clicked off my light, casting myself into darkness. Then I kicked harder until I was sure I was beyond the corner of rock and turned into the cove. There was a little light bleeding down from the moon. Just enough for me to make out part of a massive, solid black object gently bobbing at the surface.

I finned onward, piercing through the dark underwater world and closing in on the yacht. I cut beneath the shadow of the monstrous vessel, into blackness so thick I could barely notice my hand moving right in front of my face.

I steadied myself and triggered the internal mic.

"I'm under the stern," I said. "What've we got, Ange?"

"A guy right above you," she said. "Standing on the afterdeck and puffing on a cigarette. Other than that it's all quiet on the northern front."

"No sign of Lucius?"

"Negative. There's no one else on deck. And with these tinted windows, I won't see anything unless they step out." A moment later, she said, "You could do a surface and snatch of the guy at the stern. The huge decks are tiered, and he's near the bottom. There shouldn't be a good view of him, even if people are looking out from the nearby interior. The rear bulkhead covers him nicely."

"Copy that," I said after thinking her words over briefly and adjusting my position. "Time to give myself the private tour. Give me a play-by-play of smoke break guy."

I kicked to the tip of the stern as Ange relayed the guy's every movement. He was along the starboard side. One hand on the rail, the other clasping his cigarette. Looking out over the water. Maybe a yard from the swim platform.

Once in position, I said, "Going dark for a bit, Ange."

"Copy that. I've got your six."

I removed my gear, then held a breath while letting the rebreather sink to the bottom. Then I slowly surfaced, my head steadily and silently rising out of the water. I took a quiet breath, then looked up just as an exhale of smoke appeared overhead, gusting out over the gunwale before being carried off with the breeze.

I slid out my knife, then gripped it tight with the handle facing outward in a forward grip with the edge in. Stealthily, I turned around to face the side of the yacht. Then I took a breath and narrowed my gaze.

Here we go.

Descending a couple feet, I pushed with my arms, then kicked my fins with everything I had, forcing myself up out of the water. Reaching high overhead, I grabbed a fistful of the guy's shirt and yanked him forward while arcing my right hand around. Before he knew what was happening, the butt of the handle bashed into the crown of his head, and he grunted and went limp.

I slid down, letting go of his shirt and letting him collapse in a daze against the gunwale while I caught the bottom rail. I reseated my knife, slipped off my fins, and hauled myself up over the side and onto the deck. Opening my drybag, I positioned an earpiece, then closed in on the guy I'd struck.

Ange had been right. The spot was well shielded from the interior and upper decks by the natural contours of the vessel.

I grabbed the guy, who was treading on the verge of unconsciousness. Dragging him across the deck, I shoved him into the base of a long couch built into the deck. Everything was sparkly clean and new. The couch soft white leather.

I slapped and shook the guy until he came to.

"Where's the woman and boy?" I said, keeping my voice low.

The man's eyes danced around. He struggled to make a sound, let alone speak.

I shook him again and slapped his face, trying to snap him out of it.

When I asked him a second time, voices emanated from forward of me, just out of my view.

"You've got more company," Ange's voice came

through the earpiece.

"Santana, boss wants us inside," a rough, low-pitched voice said.

As quietly as I could, I lowered the dazed guy to the deck at the foot of the couch. I crouched and crawled right, trying to cut the approaching man off just as he rounded the corner. But he arrived faster than I'd anticipated, popping out five feet in front of me. I jumped into a roll, then swiped a leg, knocking him to the deck.

As I sprang to finish him off, he landed a hard elbow to my gut, then reached for his holstered pistol. I dove and forced it free, the handgun rattling to the base of the transom. He landed one more solid punch before I muscled him hard into the rail, then grabbed and buried my knife into the base of his neck.

Keeping a hand over his mouth, I lowered him slowly, then heard footsteps approach from overhead. Another guard appeared out of nowhere, gripping a submachine gun. He aimed it straight at me, managing to catch me completely off guard.

I bent my knees, preparing to jump and roll out of his view. Before I made the move, a high-caliber round burst through his head. He jolted and tumbled over the side, crashing into the edge of the lower deck before flailing and splashing into the cove.

THIRTY-SEVEN

Angelina crept along the beach, blending perfectly into the dark, arid, and sparsely vegetated environment. With her backpack strapped tight, she took on the steep shoreline, trekking up a series of switchbacks before venturing off the trail.

Being off the beaten path in total darkness and zeroing in on an enemy target, she was in her element. She was no stranger to it. One of the best snipers in the world, she'd gunned down high-value targets on five continents. Over the years, she'd spent thousands of hours at the range or in the field, looking at the world through the lens of a rifle scope.

The landscape was rough, and unforgiving. Littered with short trees and bushes that attempted to block her way. Dropping off completely at places. Stones breaking free.

But with every step, her eyes adjusted, and her night vision improved. And though the way was tough, she had no trouble navigating to the base of the slope, passing through a steep gully and up the other side to a steep ridge.

She trekked along the apex, following the natural contours of the cliffs before eventually getting her first glimpse of the yacht. It was anchored with its bow facing west. The same place it'd been a couple hours earlier. Though it looked much larger from the ground. The hundred-and-fifty-foot luxury vessel catching the light from the glowing moon.

She followed the edge for a couple hundred yards, scoping the area as best she could and using her night vision, before settling into her chosen perch. She was concealed by a thick bush, and one of the bigger branches provided a nice natural bipod. The spot offered a near-perfect view of the yacht that was barely three hundred yards away and down from her.

"Three hundred and twelve," she said as she measured the distance with a range finder.

She unzipped the main compartment of her backpack, then removed and assembled her rifle. It was her trusty collapsible Lapua. One of her favorite midrange sniper rifles.

Then she rested the barrel on the branch and scanned over every inch of the yacht's exterior.

"In position," she said into her radio.

"Copy that," Logan replied. "About to enter the cove."

Scanning through her scope over the decks of the yacht, she reached the aft section and caught a brief glimpse of blurry, shadowy movement beneath the surface. There one moment. Gone the next. Her husband moving into position.

As she continued to observe the quiet vessel, she spotted her first sign of movement. A guy wearing jeans and a black T-shirt stepped out and onto the main deck at the stern. He quickly lit up a Marlboro, taking puffs as he stepped toward the starboard railing.

Logan's voice cut through brief static in her earpiece. She told him about the guy, and an idea she had for taking him down, then watched and waited. She continued to scan over the yacht's exterior, wishing that Lucius would make a sudden appearance so she could put an end to the vile man with one flex of her turquoise-painted finger.

She swept back to the guy at the stern intermittently, looking him up and down as he puffed on the burning tobacco and stared at his phone. She checked her watch. From her angle, she could see the starboard side of the vessel. But she figured her husband would make his move at any second.

Suddenly, a hand reached up and yanked the guy back. He jerked backward, jolted, then collapsed to the deck. Logan appeared a moment later, heaving himself over the side and rolling to the deck.

While her husband questioned the guy, she heard a voice, then spotted movement.

"You've got more company," she said, then the guy dropped out of her line of sight.

She watched as her husband dove and rolled and engaged the second attacker. Ange put them both in her crosshairs as they went at it, but she didn't have a shot. They were too close to each other, and jerking each other wildly.

As Logan shoved the guy into the rail and finished his adversary off, she noticed more movement in the corner of her eye. She turned and focused on a guy racing along an upper deck, wielding a submachine gun. The moment he took aim at her husband, she opened fire, blasting a round right through the upper part of his skull. It caught him on a downward angle, the bullet bursting out through the guy's upper vertebrae and killing him instantly.

He tumbled over the edge, flipping and smacking into a lower railing before splashing into the cove.

"Safe to say they know you're there now," Ange said.

She scanned the deck as Logan headed forward toward the closest doors, and said, "Time to put an end to this."

THIRTY-EIGHT

Lucius Xavier sat in a bubbling Jacuzzi in an enclosed upper deck near the bow of the yacht. His head was back and his eyes closed. His arms out, draped over the two bikini-clad beauties in their early twenties beside him.

The middle-aged mogul stretched his neck, then tilted forward and gazed out through the tinted windows spread out ahead of him, offering a view of the northern corner of the cove and the dark, flat Pacific.

He smiled arrogantly. Inhaled the strong scents of organic bath salts and eucalyptus. Relished the powerful jets blasting into the muscles of his back.

A man in his forties with slicked-back blond hair approached with a phone pressed into his chest.

"They've agreed to your new demands," the man said. "The deal has been struck."

Lucius grinned. "Of course they have." He leaned over and sniffed a trail of cocaine from the edge of the hot tub, then shivered and gave a cocky smirk and pulled the two women in closer. "Because life is full of winners and losers. And I… am a winner." He planted a kiss on one of the young women, then glanced back at his business manager. "Tell the captain to make ready. And make sure that authorities see to it that we receive our safe passage west."

He did as ordered, stepping out of the room.

Lucius chuckled to himself, blown away by his own genius. The deal had been made without him even having to give up his bargaining chips. He leaned back, sinking deeper into the bubbling heat. The taste of victory was sweet indeed.

A moment later, a radio barked to life. It belonged to Lucius's head of security, and a rushed, booming voice on the other end informed them that they were under attack.

"What?" the muscular man grunted. "Where? How many?"

"At the stern," the voice said through frantic breaths. "Three of our men are already down."

"How many attackers are there?" the man said, motioning for his men to move for the rear door.

"One," the voice replied. "One man. But he—"

The guy on the other end grunted and cried. Then the radio went silent.

"Shit," the guard said, then pulled out his .45-caliber pistol.

Lucius climbed out of the pool, then grabbed a towel from a nearby rack.

"Stay here, boss," the man said. "We'll take care of this."

Lucius nodded, not saying a word as the head of his detail and two other guards pushed through the rear door. Lucius threw on a robe, then stepped barefoot into an adjacent room, water dripping onto the teak hardwood. The two women followed him into a lounge, then he eyed security feeds displayed on a monitor. He rapidly clicked through them until he found a brief image of their attacker pushing into the interior from the aft deck. He rewound the footage. Paused it and zoomed in.

Then he cursed as his business manager stormed into the room and eyed the image.

"Who is it?" he said.

Lucius gritted his teeth. "Get the hostages. Meet me at the escape boat."

The man nodded, then turned on his heel and raced toward the nearest stairwell.

"What are we supposed to do?" one of the women cried.

Lucius ignored them, then ran down a passageway and into his master suite. He opened a safe and grabbed a leather bag. Then he got dressed as fast as he could. Shouldered the bag and gripped his pistol as he rushed back out.

THIRTY-NINE

"It's no use," Theo said, digging his fingers into the loops of duct tape restraining Carter's wrists. "There's way too much. I can't even get part of it to pry free."

He'd been at it for nearly half an hour, the nine-year-old's body sprawled out and his arms extending as far as he could just to reach Carter's back.

"It looks like they used something to melt edges of the tape," the boy added. "A lighter or something."

Carter shook her head. Lucius and his cronies sure were good at kidnapping people. She eyed the chain and bolt securing her ankle to the deck—the handiwork of a sick man who'd been kidnapping women for decades.

"Just keep trying," Carter said.

"My fingers keep slipping," he said, wiping them routinely on his shirt. It was hot in there and they were getting sweaty. "And my arm muscles are burning."

"You can do it, Theo," Carter said. "I know you

can do this."

He tried again, tugging and forcing his fingernails in and prying and twisting. All to no avail.

He gave a big sigh, his arms falling to the metal.

"I can't do it. It's no use."

"You have to, Theo. It's the only way we're getting out of this."

He heaved and tried again, using every ounce of strength and energy. Still the tape didn't give and he failed to rip even a tiny crack. Despite all his efforts, along with Carter's twisting and pulling, the thick layers of tape were steadfast.

Theo dropped again, wiping moisture from his brow, and catching his breath once more.

"I can't feel my arms," he said.

While the boy massaged his hand and arm muscles behind her, Carter looked around the dark space for what felt like the thousandth time. There was nothing there. Just empty, sleek walls, and even they were too far off for her to reach. She scanned the corners and the floor, hoping to find something—anything—that had been overlooked by their captors. A loose screw or fallen bolt. A bobby pin. Anything.

But the place was spotless and sterile.

Then she shifted her legs again. Her pockets were inside out, Theo having pulled the fabric free while looking for something they could use to help remove the tape. But they were all empty. The men had searched her head to toe, and all she had was her clothes.

"Check your pockets again," Carter said.

Theo sighed. "I've checked them ten thousand times. They're empty."

They were both barefoot, their captors not even letting them keep their shoes. The laces would've come in handy. They'd know that, of course. It'd be common knowledge for experienced kidnappers.

Carter bowed her head and closed her eyes. She tried her best to combat the hopelessness of their predicament—to push through the bleak dark clouds swirling and see some light through it all.

"You need to keep trying, Theo," she said, raising her voice. "It's the only way. You have to dig deep."

Theo forced himself off the floor once again. He reached and grabbed at the tape, and yanked and twisted. Clawed and heaved until he was completely exhausted again, then fell back to the cold deck. This time even his neck muscles gave out, and his head angled awkwardly into the metal. And in the darkness, a sudden, quiet tap filled the air as a tiny object made contact with the hull.

Carter's eyes sprang wide. "What was that?"

Theo gasped, then patted the area in front of his face before he touched the object.

"My necklace," he said. "My…"

He sprang up, energized with newfound vigor like a surge of electricity had coursed through him.

"You have a necklace?" Carter said.

"Yes," he said, his voice filling with enthusiasm. "I'm not sure how they missed it. It must've been hidden under my shirt and the hood they put over me. My mom gave it to me for my birthday last year. She had it made using a shark tooth I found at El Matador Beach."

"A shark tooth?" Carter said, smiling as well.

Theo reached his hands back and unclasped the

necklace. Ran his fingers over the smooth, sharp bone. It was small, barely the size of a dime, but the tip was nice and pointy.

"Pull the tape tight," he said. "And hold still."

He reached over, feeling the tape with his left hand while gripping the tooth with his right. He angled the cutting edge down, then stabbed it into the tape and clawed. Again and again he scratched at the tape, the top layer finally breaking free.

He gasped with excitement, and continued, putting all his strength into it. The next layer cut free, then a third one—each ripping apart easier and easier. The rapid progress fueled him, and they were both struck with eager excitement as he clawed relentlessly at the duct tape.

He was halfway through the layers when heavy footsteps resounded from the other side of the door.

Theo froze.

They both stared forward as the thick locking mechanism slid aside.

The boy dropped and rolled into a seated position and threw his arms behind him in a flash, stopping himself just as the bulky door hinged outward.

Their hearts pounded as a wave of intense light flooded into the small space, forcing them both to close their eyes.

Two men stomped inside, their movements rushed. One was huge and wore a T-shirt. The other had blond hair slicked back, a blue button-up, and cargo shorts.

"Wakey-wakey," the blond guy said as he dropped down and worked at the locks securing them to the deck.

Carter squinted as she eyed the two men, then shot a look toward Theo. The boy struggled to gaze back at her, fear and confusion filling his face as he kept his untaped hands behind him.

The bigger guy held two hoods, and he reached for Carter first.

He shook it out, then gestured for her to rise.

"On your feet," he barked.

She did as he said, keeping her hands hidden behind her back.

She fought to keep her face calm as she forced her arms apart with all her strength. Her limbs shook, and her wrists burned, the remaining tape biting into her flesh. She gave everything she had as the big guy angled the hood toward the crown of her head.

Pushing through the pain, she couldn't help but wince, then the tape cracked and ripped free. Her arms flew apart, and she gasped from the intense relief.

Ignoring the tingling and numbing pain, she lunged forward and threw her hands in front of her, clapping her palms into the big guy's ears before he could react. Snatching his pistol, she shoved the barrel into the man's gut as he yelled and fought to get her off him.

He landed a punch to her side just as she pulled the trigger, blasting two quick rounds into his chest. He shook and fell hard.

Reacting as fast as he could, the blond guy reached for his weapon. With Carter's attention still on the bigger guy, Theo threw his already freed arms apart and pounced. Planting his left leg, he struck the man with a side kick to the chest. He heaved but recovered and grabbed the boy, hurling him across the room in a fit of rage.

Carter took aim at the well-dressed guy as he reached for his waistband a second time.

"Hands in the air!" she shouted, but the guy grabbed and revealed a handgun, ignoring her order.

She pulled the trigger, firing a round into his chest. He let go of his weapon and slammed to the deck, wailing and crying out as blood flowed from the wound. Then she finished him off with a second bullet before racing over to help Theo.

The boy was on the floor in a daze.

"Are you all right?" she said, inspecting a cut to his forehead.

Theo gave a shaky nod, his eyes circling a moment. He placed a hand to his head.

"That was amazing how you broke free like that," he said, stumbling over his words.

"I was amazing? Look who's talking. You saved my life taking on that guy."

His face reddened again, and he fought back a wince.

"Come on," Carter said, helping Theo to his feet. "We need to get out of here. Now!"

FORTY

As the crew were alerted to my presence, I threw stealth to the wind. No longer needing to be sneaky, I stormed forward across the deck, my all-consuming objective center stage: get to the hostages and deal with Lucius as quickly as possible.

And take down everyone who stood in my way.

I withdrew my Sig and gripped it with two hands as I headed up the right set of steps to the second level. Another guard appeared just as I rounded a corner. I opened fire, sending a round that struck him center mass and sent him curling forward. I slid beside him, then hooked an arm around his back and hurled him toward the gunwale. His lower body struck the fiberglass hard, and he cartwheeled over the edge in a blink.

A splash resounded at my back as I focused forward, shouldering through the door and into the rear saloon. The space was massive and lavishly furnished. The moment I entered, two more guards appeared, letting loose sporadic shots in my direction the moment they stepped out of a forward door.

I had no choice but to drop down, crouching for cover behind a bar counter.

They were firing automatics, spraying a storm of bullets across the space and into everything. Shards of fabric and glass rained down around me. And the sounds of the constant exploding gunpowder were deafening.

"I'm pinned down, Ange!" I said into the radio, raising my voice over the incessant gunfire.

"I have no shot, Logan," she replied through my earpiece. "I can't see a thing inside."

In the chaos of the moment, I ran my eyes over the port side of the vessel, then got an idea.

"Second level," I said. "Three panes forward of the stern. Light it up."

My wife said nothing, needing no further explanation. Her focused, analytical mind no doubt firing on all cylinders.

She opened fire moments later, blasting high-caliber rounds into the glass on the far side of the room. The bullets shattered through the port window, whizzed across the room, and crashed out the other side. She might not have been able to see her targets, but the two guys had no choice but to cease firing and drop for cover as her rounds soared across the room.

I rolled right, jumped out of my crouch, and took off, cutting the distance to a couch before dropping for cover again. When the maddening, thunderous blasts of Ange's rifle shots ceased, I popped up and sent a bullet of my own into the farthest guy's head. Then I dove across the table into the closest one before he could level his weapon at me.

We rolled violently into the bulkhead. Forcing his legs up, the guy managed to kick me off him, then staggered to his feet. I jumped up as well, and just as he turned to engage me again, I reared back and struck my dazed adversary with a sudden front kick to his chest. He whipped backward, whirling into a one-eighty before smashing headfirst through the glass table.

Shards burst free and rattled in all directions as he crunched to the deck. As he fought to recover again, I grabbed a nearby gold clock from a shelf beside me and chucked it, the heavy object striking his forehead.

My relentless adversary finally went motionless on the carpet of shards, and I stepped across the loose glass and retrieved my fallen weapon.

FORTY-ONE

Lucius returned to the bridge, his pulse quickened, and a thin layer of sweat formed on his forehead and dampened the corners of his recently donned polo shirt. The room was empty, and eerily quiet. Broken up only by muffled gunshots coming from the aft section of the luxury vessel.

Growing frantic, he turned to the security monitors and cycled through different cameras. He scanned the aft deck cameras, eyeing dead members of his security detail strung out across the white fiberglass. Then he worked forward and spotted another near the aft starboard doorway on the second level. He clicked to the second-level aft saloon and saw two more men sprawled out and bloodied on the teak floor.

His pulse quickened even more.

His eyes narrowed.

He jolted as the door slammed open at his back. Spinning around shakily with his right hand gripping his pistol, he gasped as he saw his head of security burst inside.

"He's got help," the man said. "Snipers up on the cliffs."

Lucius's mouth dropped. He turned to look out the window beside him that offered a partial view of the shoreline off the port bow, the towering rock a black silhouette against the silver-tinted night sky.

"My men are all dead," the guard said through gritted teeth. "We need to get out of here. This is our last chance."

Lucius's face scrunched up and turned red. He snarled and said, "No. *I* need to get out of here." He stomped toward the soldier and waved his pistol at him. "You need to do your damn job."

"It's over, Lucius. We need to run. We—"

"I'm not paying you to run. I'm paying you to protect me. And if you kill him, I'll give you a cool two million." He held up his bag, then opened it, revealing stacks of cash. "Now get your ass back there and protect me."

The man's nostrils flared. He checked his weapon, then shot Lucius an evil look and turned on his heel. Lucius followed behind the soldier out into a corridor, then stopped as the man reached the end and rounded a corner.

Cutting into the forward saloon, Lucius slipped behind a bar counter and opened a cabinet. Grabbing bottles of tequila and vodka, he tossed them to the floor, the glass shattering and the contents splashing all over.

After destroying ten bottles and splattering the spirits all over the rug and nearby corridor, Lucius stepped back and pulled out a Zippo. He didn't give a damn about his men. Or his business manager.

Sneaking out the back door when all hell breaks loose was no new concept for him. He was good at it. Efficient at getting away and clearing things up. Shirking blame, coming out unscathed, and starting anew. If he played his cards right, he could pin the whole operation on Wessel and his business manager. Strike a deal. Buy off the right people. Whatever he needed to do.

He clicked a flame to life, then smiled as he stared at the little flicker of bright heat. With the flick of a wrist, he tossed the lighter to the deck, the metal clanking and the flame lighting the pools of alcohol. A roar of scorching fire swelled up, the blaze rapidly spreading and forming a wall in front of him before climbing up the furniture to the overhead.

Lucius's smile broadened as he watched the flames increase, then he turned and headed for the nearest stairs, racing to the lower levels to make his escape.

Not only would the fire help slow his adversaries, but it would also deter his head guard from turning and running for the getaway boat. He didn't care what he had to do. He didn't care how many people died in the process. Or how many people he hurt or screwed over. He'd make his escape and live to thrive another day.

He always did.

Lucius froze as he heard soft voices while heading down the stairs. He tilted and poked his head down for a view of a lower level hallway just as Officer Carter and Theo came into view. They were moving quickly, the young boy sticking to the officer's side as she led them toward the base of the steps with a pistol clutched in her hands.

Lucius's eyes widened, and he cursed under his breath before getting an idea and turning and hustling as quickly and quietly as he could back up the stairs. He rounded a corner at the top, then looked around. Spotted a fire extinguisher secured in a case twenty feet away.

He stowed his pistol at the back of his waistband, then rushed over and grabbed hold of the ten-pound red canister. Then he crept back to the corner and waited.

The sounds of his escaped hostages' approaching steps grew louder. They soon reached the top, and the moment Carter's gun appeared around the edge, Lucius heaved, rotating and hurling the extinguisher as hard as he could. Carter raised her arms to protect herself from the rapid, unexpected attack, but it was no use.

The extinguisher bashed into her arms and face, knocking her back in a violent strike and sending her tumbling back down the stairs. Her body flailed wildly, colliding hard with the corners as she picked up speed, rotating uncontrollably before striking the bottom and coming to a violent stop along the passageway.

Theo screamed as he watched the woman fall, his eyes big and terror-struck. He stared at her motionless body for a brief moment, then lunged toward the stairs. A strong arm stopped him, grabbing him from behind by his shirt and jerking him backward. He fell, his back slamming hard onto the deck.

Theo squirmed and cried out, fighting to break free. But he was no match for a grown man. Lucius kicked the boy in the side, then forced him to his feet.

Pressing the barrel of his pistol into the kid's back, he snarled, "You keep fighting, punk, and I'll end you, you hear me?"

Theo ignored the threat and struggled some more. "You won't do it. You need me alive. That's why you kidnapped me. So you can—"

Lucius silenced him with a vicious slap across the side of his face. Theo spun and nearly lost consciousness. Lucius maintained his steady hold on the boy and looked him dead in the eyes.

"That was a big mistake, you little twerp."

He wrapped an arm around Theo's neck, then forced him down the steps. The boy cried as they passed Carter's motionless body. Lucius dragged him toward another staircase, and the last thing Theo saw was the police officer lying battered and bruised on the passageway above.

FORTY-TWO

"Thanks for the distraction, Ange," I said, catching my breath as I pushed to the far side of the saloon. "Any activity outside?"

"Nothing, Logan. But we've got a problem."

"What is it?"

"There's smoke seeping out from the forward section. A lot of it, and it's growing thicker."

I cursed under my breath, continuing my push across the massive space.

"Let me know if you see anyone," I said. "I'm heading forward."

"Roger that."

Gripping my Sig with both hands, I closed in on the far door. I pushed it open and ran my eyes over the length of a long hallway. There were doors on one side, leading into rooms with faded glass partitions. Doors led to the left as well, these walls normal. Cabins, I guessed.

I pressed forward. Halfway down the hall, I caught a whiff of pungent smoke. Then I spotted fumes creeping out from the door far ahead. I took two more steps, then saw a barely perceptible faint blur of movement in my peripherals. It came from over my right shoulder, and I turned and focused as a distorted dark figure moved slightly on the other side.

I hit the deck.

Instinctively throwing my legs back and falling to my stomach as a shotgun blasted a mass of pellets through the glass, raining tiny bits of metal and glass onto me as I kept low.

A second shot thundered across the tight space, blasting more pellets and pieces of fiberglass. I crawled forward and reached for the handle of the first door I came to, forcing it down and throwing the slab open with a strong shoulder check. Then I doubled back, turning around and crawling back in the direction I'd come. A third shot filled the air, the door I'd flung open splintered to pieces by a wave of projectiles.

I rose and dove through the shattered windowpane and into the dark room. With my attacker's aim directed toward the door, I caught him off guard just enough to tackle him from the side without being blown to pieces by his fourth shot.

We crashed and rolled, and I smacked his gun hand to send his weapon bouncing to the deck. He retaliated with a quick, strong attack of his own, pounding his knuckles into my body in rapid succession, and ripping my weapon free as well.

The smoke grew stronger and more pungent, the toxic haze flowing into the space and making it difficult to see.

I managed to throw the guy off me, then land a

front kick that sent him back and flipping into the hallway. But he landed well and was fully recovered with a knife gripped in his hands by the time I jumped over to reengage him.

The smoke grew even thicker. The sounds of monstrous flames crackling from adjacent rooms.

"You don't have to do this," I said to the guy. "I just want Lucius and the hostages."

My big, formidable opponent spat, then cracked his neck. "You can beg better than that."

I reached back and slid my knife free as well. Then gave him a quick nod. He smirked arrogantly, then came at me with two quick strikes, slicing his sharpened blade toward my flesh. I evaded them, then struck his instep with a heel pound and slashed him across the forearm. I took a step back as he grunted, swiftly regained his composure, then charged.

Reaching right, I threw a nearby door open, slamming the wood into his upper body. His punch broke right through the door, splintering the wood and nearly colliding into me. I grabbed his fist, pulled it hard against the jagged pieces of hardwood, then turned and kneed him in the gut. He heaved and fell back for barely a split second before going into a frenzy, throwing one powerful slash of his knife my way after another.

The ever-thickening smoke was becoming a problem. Stinging my eyes and making it difficult to see. The flames peeked through the cracks of the doors opposite us, hungry and hot and intense.

I blocked a strong overhead strike, then my attacker landed a solid kick of his own. As I curled forward and whipped around to bury my blade into his neck, he beat me by a hair, slashing his knife across my right arm. It cut deep and my muscles gave way, releasing my knife as I fell back against the window.

He didn't give me a moment to recover. Charging, he grabbed me and slammed me into the glass, spiderwebbing it as he held the knife.

"I said... you can beg better than that."

I yanked my arms free and muscled him up over me with everything I had. His upper body struck the window, punching a big hole through the glass and letting a gust of cool ocean air sweep inside.

He turned, enraged, and struck me with a powerful backhand. Then, with the shattered window at his back, he reached high overhead to skewer me with his knife.

A round punched through his midsection, bursting out his flesh and causing him to shake and then collapse to the floor right beside me.

I coughed and fought back the pain. Felt around in the confusion and found my knife and radio before sucking in a breath of fresh air through the hole in the window, and heading back into the hall.

"Okay, now you really owe me for that one," Ange's voice said through the tiny speaker.

But I barely heard it, let alone comprehended her words as the smoke consumed me and the roaring flames closed in. With the fire spreading like mad, I had no choice but to turn right and backtrack. The smoke was too thick to see anything, so I didn't bother searching for my Sig as I hustled out of the madness and back into the aft saloon.

"Logan, are you all right?" Ange said.

I coughed, and winced, blood flowing from my shoulder, my eyes burning, and the fumes choking my lungs.

"Never better, Ange."

Her tone shifted dramatically. "I'm hailing Beck. We're coming in there."

I coughed again, fighting to catch the fresher air as I migrated toward an aft door. Using my dive knife, I tore away part of a curtain and tied it tight over the cut to my shoulder. It was far from ideal but would slow the bleeding.

"You hear me, Logan?" Ange exclaimed as I pushed back outside. "I'm coming. You need to get the hell out of there."

I wheezed and blinked, stepping all the way to the starboard rail to stabilize myself and clear the toxic gas from my lungs. I forced myself to snap out of it, then gazed forward toward an outside set of stairs leading forward.

"They're still here, Ange," I gasped, then pushed away from the rail. "I need to find them."

FORTY-THREE

Lucius practically dragged Theo down the hall, then forced him into a side room running along the yacht's starboard side. He slammed the door shut behind them and locked it. The space was wide and open, a speedboat resting on a platform and strapped down in the middle.

The criminal tossed Theo to the deck, then swiftly removed the straps and pressed a series of buttons on a nearby control panel. The entire wall hinged open, revealing a dark sky and a calm sea. When he pressed more buttons, a deck extended out over the water and a series of motors kicked in, carrying the small vessel out toward the edge. The speedboat was then mechanically lowered by a pair of small cranes, splashing gently into the Pacific.

"Get on the boat," Lucius said, aiming his weapon at the boy.

"I'm not going!" Theo snapped, planting his hands on his hips. Then he yelled, "I'm not going anywhere with you."

Lucius closed in and reached for him. Theo stepped back, then spun, sending a whipping roundhouse kick right across Lucius's jaw. His head snapped sideways, then he turned back to look at the boy, rage taking over. The blow had been solid, but not nearly enough to take down a full-grown man.

Lucius rubbed his jaw then stomped toward the boy. "You'll pay for that one, you little punk."

Theo darted away from him, racing for the door. He unlocked and threw it open just as Lucius grabbed hold of him from behind. Theo screamed as the man wrestled him back and threw him hard to the deck once again.

Lucius aimed at the boy's head, shifting the barrel down until it was pointed at his leg.

"I don't need you in one piece, kid," he snarled. "I just need you alive."

The boy's eyes widened and his mouth dropped open. As Lucius tightened his trigger finger, a sound caught both their attention, coming from the doorway. Theo saw her first—Officer Carter stumbling out from a thin haze of smoke, struggling to stay on her feet.

Lucius laughed. "You're pitiful, you know that?"

He turned and shifted his aim. Theo gasped, then threw himself forward, grabbing at Lucius's back ankle and pulling on it with all his strength. The criminal's foot slipped back, and he fell hard, collapsing onto his left arm and chest and blasting a round into the bulkhead.

Carter stumbled over and kicked the pistol free. Then Lucius turned, mad with rage, and jumped to his feet, grabbing hold of the dazed police officer and throwing her to the deck as well. When he hovered over her to finish her off, Carter twisted and threw her right foot forward, springing her heel right into Lucius's crotch.

The man's eyes bulged and he cried in intense pain. His knees buckled and he keeled over, nearly toppling to the floor beside them. Carter struggled to come to her feet, but Lucius fought through the pain and grabbed her and threw her back down. Then he staggered toward his fallen weapon, squealing and wincing with every step.

"You'll pay for that one, bitch!" he yelled, then dropped and scooped up his weapon.

With his back to the open door and the smoke billowing out of it, he turned and put Carter right in his sights.

FORTY-FOUR

The task felt nearly impossible.

The yacht was huge—an intricate hive of hallways and lounges and staterooms and galleys. I had no way of knowing where any of them were, and with every passing second, the yacht went further up in flames. I had minutes at most to find them. If that. And I knew that the fire could spread to the tanks and blow the whole vessel to pieces at any moment.

But I had no choice. I'd come this far. With innocent lives at stake, I reached a lower-level passageway, covered my face, and pressed into the smoke. Fighting my way onward and hoping to spot any sign of Lucius or the hostages.

The smoke swirled around me as I kept low and fought for every breath. With my eyes burning and my lungs trembling, I was just about to turn around and attack the search from a different angle when a sound filled the air.

A faint, distant scream that sounded like it'd come from a young boy.

Theo.

I picked up my pace, still shielding my mouth and keeping as low as I could to combat the rapidly intensifying smoke. The thick gases deviated up ahead, pouring out to my right through an open doorway.

More sounds filled the air. Cries and grunts. Then voices.

My mind in a haze, and with thick swirls of toxic fumes completely surrounding me, I forced my legs to move. I reached the corner of the doorway, practically stumbling through with the river of smoke. The image ahead of me cleared. Through burning, blurred eyes, I saw a large bright room. Theo and Carter were on the deck. And a man with his back to me was aiming a pistol at them.

Lucius Xavier.

I dove and rolled as he turned to look my way. He cut around, swinging his weapon to aim at me and pulling the trigger twice before I reached him. The bullets smacked into the deck beside me as I swung my knife, slashing at his lower right leg. The razor-sharp edge of my blade severed his Achilles tendon, and the cord of tissue sprang up under his skin.

He shrieked as his leg completely gave out, and he collapsed to the deck, writhing in pain. I rolled on top of him. Grabbed his own pistol and smacked him in the face with it, fracturing the fragile bones under his left eye.

I socked him twice more. A solid blow to his solar plexus, followed by a punch to his throat, feeling his trachea crunch beneath my knuckles.

The mogul grunted and wailed in pain. He was

barely able to move when I struggled to my feet.

I glanced at my shoulder and saw that blood had completely soaked my makeshift tourniquet. I was exhausted, and pain nagged at me from all over my body. My gaze was blurry, my eyes still stinging from the trip through the clouds of dense smoke.

With Lucius's pistol in my right hand, I staggered across the room toward Theo. The boy stared at me with a heightened level of uncertainty. After everything he'd had been through, it was amazing he was still holding it together.

"I'm friends with your mother, Theo," I said, dropping to a knee beside him. "I'm here to get you both out of here."

The kid stared at me a moment, then swallowed hard and nodded.

The smoke parted as outstretched flames flickered through the doorway. I helped Officer Carter to her feet, then partly carried her toward the bobbing speedboat. Once she and Theo were aboard, I untied the lines and climbed aboard myself, wincing as I took position at the helm and fired up its big inboard engines.

An intense, primal shriek filled the air, coming from the space we'd just stepped out of. As if we were witnessing the devil himself force himself from the clutches of Hell, we watched as Lucius willed himself to his feet and staggered toward us. His eyes big and fiery. His mouth fuming.

In a smooth, rapid act, Carter swiped my pistol, took aim, and blasted three rounds into the evil, possessed criminal. I blocked Theo's view as the rounds struck flesh, blasting through the man's chest and sending him back down right at the edge of the black smoke.

I took one more look inside at Lucius's motionless body sprawled out and bloodied on the sparkling deck. The flames already reaching him and singeing his clothes.

Then I hit the throttle, rocketing us away from the burning yacht.

FORTY-FIVE

I shot us forward, taking a wide turn around the bow to avoid the blazing yacht before heading toward the shore. The yacht spewed out flames beside us, the scorching tendrils breaking through windows and smoke billowing in a colossal tower of blackness.

"You have no idea how long I've wanted to do that," Carter said, still gripping the pistol as she sprawled out on the deck and let out a heavy sigh.

She was banged up bad. Her clothes tattered, exposed flesh bruised and cut. Her voice raspy. But it was clear her faculties were slowly returning.

I tapped the woman on the shoulder and gave her a proud, satisfied look.

"I don't know who the hell you are," she said, staring at me. "But thank God you showed up."

I smiled softly and extended a hand. "Logan Dodge."

She shook it. "Angelina's husband? Of course you are." She closed her eyes, concentrating on her breathing, then added, "I don't know how I'll ever be able to repay you. Thank you."

I nodded to her, and we both noticed as Theo stared at the inferno beside us with wide eyes, then blinked and looked my way. "Where's my mom?" he said in a soft, innocent voice.

"You'll be with her in a few minutes," I said.

I eased back our speed as we approached the beach, cutting to an idle and letting the bow gently kiss the rocky shore. Ange appeared moments later, materializing from the shadows and gliding across the beach. She shoved us off and jumped up and onto the bow in a fluid motion. Setting her bag on the deck, she cut across the boat and threw her arms around me.

We embraced for a few silent seconds, then I kissed her forehead.

She gave me a quick look over, then examined my bloody shoulder.

"I'll be all right," I said. "We need to get out of here."

Ange pointed behind me and said, "We should help them first."

I turned and gazed toward two young women as they paddled a life raft toward the shore.

"I'm on it," I said.

I turned us around and motored toward them. Ange scanned the deck a moment, then rummaged through gear lockers and retrieved a life ring and a coil of rope. She stepped to the transom and told me to get close to them.

I did as she said, aiming the bow toward the raft then skirting slowly right beside the women.

Ange held up the life ring. "Grab this. We'll pull you to the nearest beach."

She tossed it over and into the raft. One of the

women grabbed hold of it, then Ange tied a line to a stern cleat. The girls gave me a thumbs-up, and I throttled up to an easy five knots, not wanting their emergency boat to capsize.

I hailed Beck as we cruised along the jagged island, letting him know we were on our way and that Theo and Carter were aboard. We rounded a point, then passed a series of coves and beaches until eventually Parson's Landing came into view.

Ange untied the rope, letting the nylon slither free and into the water, then pointed to shore. "There's a campground there."

A couple of hikers were standing beside their tents just up from the beachfront, staring toward the distant smoke and having no doubt heard the distant gunfire.

"We'll call for help," Ange added.

Without another word, I turned sharply, then shoved the throttle all the way forward, rocketing us away from the cove.

A sudden booming explosion tore across the air from behind us. It thundered and sent a shockwave through the night. The yacht's fuel tanks bursting into flames.

"That was cutting it pretty close," Ange said.

I only nodded, feeling out of it. My head dizzy as the adrenaline wore off.

We flew along the coast for five more minutes, then slowed and ducked into a small, dark inlet. The blacked-out RHIB appeared, Beck piloting it out of the shadows.

Jasmine stood at the bow. Her eyes searched our boat as Ange threw two fenders over our port side, and we eased against each other. Jasmine leapt over to us, unable to control herself. She fell to her knees and threw her arms around Theo, her son burying himself against her. She held him tight, her body shaking and tears of sheer joy streaking down her cheeks.

We all just watched them for a moment. It was an emotional sight. After everything Jasmine and her nine-year-old son had been through, I couldn't imagine the emotions taking hold of them.

Beck gave a quick, low whistle that snapped me out of it. I blinked and looked toward him as he tapped a finger to his watch.

I nodded, then approached the mother and son. "We need to get moving," I said, kneeling beside them and speaking softly. I gestured to the speedboat's bow. "You can both be here for now."

They shuffled forward, then resumed their embrace.

We helped Officer Carter over to Beck's RHIB. Then we fired up the engines and rocketed east full speed, blasting away from the tropical island.

While slicing through the Pacific at forty knots, Ange found a first aid kit in the locker and went to work on my shoulder. She was no stranger to stitching me up after a scuffle, having fixed me up so many times I've lost count.

My warrior woman managed to clean it and thread a line of stitches just as we reached the halfway point to the mainland. She wrapped a bandage as Beck and I brought our vessels to an idle in the quiet open ocean.

"I'm reading just over five hundred feet here, Logan," Beck said. "This is as good a place as any."

I nodded, then we brought our boats together once more. With the water and skies around us clear of police boat or Coast Guard traffic, we helped Jasmine and Theo over to the RHIB, then Ange and I scuttled the speedboat. The luxury craft quickly took on water, air bubbling out from its lower compartments. Ange and I joined the others on the RHIB, then watched as the sea overtook the speedboat and it vanished into the depths right before our eyes.

"Such a shame," Ange said. "She was a beautiful boat. And that yacht wasn't too bad either."

I gave a quick smile. "At least this one will make a nice artificial reef."

With all of us aboard the RHIB, I nestled on the deck, my head resting on the port pontoon and Ange nestled up against me as Beck motored us the rest of the way back to the mainland.

Jasmine and Theo were still locked in a tight embrace as we navigated into Alamitos Bay, then pulled up into his boathouse. He tied us off and killed the engines.

Beck offered me and Ange a hand, and we rose beside him.

"Thanks for everything," I said. "We sure as hell couldn't have done this without you."

He waved a hand. "You'd do the same for me."

As Jasmine and her son peeled apart for the first time since we'd left Catalina.

"Mom, this is Veronica," Theo said, smiling at Officer Carter. "She saved my life."

Jasmine's tears intensified again, and she hugged the officer tight.

"In fairness, he saved mine as well," she said.

"Your son has an uncanny ability for getting out of restraints. And he remained calm, despite the gravity of the situation. Not to mention his karate paid off and he landed more than one strong kick. Truly impressive."

I maintained a heightened level of focus as we hauled our stuff out of the craft. We weren't out of the woods yet. Not completely.

Too many times I've been part of missions that appeared successful, the team right at the end, about to reach an extraction point. Then everything goes haywire. It got to the point where I never relaxed until I was back on a military installation, or aircraft carrier.

Now we needed to get the story straight. Theo had been kidnapped. That had been verified by authorities and made public. And so had Carter. And Lucius had disappeared, and the damning revelations about him were already circulating the internet.

The story we agreed on was that Carter and Theo had managed to escape, and then the officer had engaged the guards. A fire broke out. And the place blew up right after they managed to escape. A hero of the LAPD and a brave young boy taking down a vile criminal mogul. It was a slight deviation from the truth, but it wasn't completely untrue.

Then Beck had been out scouring for lobster off Catalina's coast when he'd seen everything and picked them up and taken them to a hospital on the mainland.

Carter bit her lip after we ran through the story. "I can't take the credit for this. It wouldn't be right."

"You said earlier that you had no idea how you'd

ever repay us," I said. "Well, this is it."

"It's much better this way," Ange added. "For everyone."

Carter thought a moment, then said, "All right."

"It's not that big of a stretch," I said. "You guys did escape and you did save each other. And *you* killed Lucius."

Carter sighed. "Yeah, but you and your wife took down everyone else. And we both would've been done for if you hadn't shown up."

With that settled, I reached down and grabbed the last order of business, lifting up Lucius's leather bag. The criminal had hauled it into the speedboat before I'd made my entrance on the burning yacht, and we'd noticed it on our trip to the mainland.

"There's gotta be five million dollars cash in here," I said. Then I held it out to Beck. "It's yours and Carter's to do whatever you want with."

"You sure?" Beck said.

Ange and I both nodded, then my wife said, "How about donating our share to a good women's abuse program around here? Put some of Lucius's money to good use for a change."

My old friend smiled. "I'll just donate all of it. Life's been good to me. How much money do you need anyway?"

Carter didn't want her half either. "There's a great shelter near my home."

Jasmine looked around at us in awe. "You people amaze me."

"Like I said before, Jasmine," I said, "it might be time for you to look into getting a new circle of friends and acquaintances. Though I'm sure that's far from easy given your status. But not impossible."

Once everyone was on the same page, Ange and I turned our attention to Jasmine.

"You know, if you ever get the chance," I said, "Key West is a much nicer place when you're not being hunted down by assassins."

"You're welcome to visit anytime and we'll give you a proper Conch Republic experience," Ange said. "Once you've both recuperated, of course."

I nodded. "Take your time with that. You've been through an unbelievably trying ordeal. Both of you," I added, eyeing her son. "So you'll need time and healing to grow from this. I'd recommend taking a lot of time off work. Hell, from all unnecessary responsibilities. At least for the time being."

She eyed us gravely, bowing her head slightly as she squeezed her arms even tighter around Theo. "I think we're both due for a long trip. An escape from the madness."

I smiled at that, remembering when, just earlier that year, I'd needed to escape my own madness. Sometimes you just need to step away from it all. See things from a different, faraway perspective. And I hoped the two of them managed to escape theirs for as much time as they needed.

"I wish you could stay a little longer, brother," Beck said. "So I could remind you what a real lobster looks like."

I smiled. "We'll have to come back for a real visit sometime. I forgot how much I love it here. Though there's only one Key West."

The Golden Coast had been my home for years, after all. But there's a different vibe to the Keys. Not necessarily better or worse, just different. And it's the little idiosyncrasies that've made the beautiful, crazy little slab of ancient coral feel more like home than anywhere else I've ever hung my hat.

We stepped out through the back door, stopping at the base of the dock.

Jasmine eyed Ange and me with powerful admiration as we said our goodbyes. She stayed silent a moment, seemingly overwhelmed by her emotions.

After hugging and thanking Ange, she turned to face me. "Logan I… I don't know what to say. What can I say? This is… I'm just completely in awe right now."

"I think you were right," I said, shooting her a friendly smile. "Back in Key West when you said that it was fate our searching for lobster, and my spotting you while you were attacked." I bobbed my chin while replaying the memory that'd set the whole ordeal in motion. "I'm glad we were there," I added, wrapping my arms around her. "I'm glad I was able to lend a hand."

"Lend a hand?" she said through sniffles. "You and your wife…" She bowed her head. "Thank you, Logan. You've saved my life." She pulled Theo into the fray. "You've saved us both."

After goodbyes, Ange and I climbed into the Cessna. She performed the preflight checks, then we eased the floats away from the dock, motored out into the bay, and took off. She soon had us up to two hundred feet and soaring east.

Heading home. I let out a deep breath and relaxed my body for what felt like the first time in ages.

We'd done it. It was over.

FORTY-SIX

We landed outside of Tucson to refuel, touching down at a small airstrip in Oro Valley. Raiding a vending machine at the tiny office, we ate a gourmet breakfast consisting of peanuts, Clif Bars, and Sun Chips while catching a glorious desert sunrise over the Catalina Mountains.

The second leg of the trip took us just outside of Houston, where we stopped to refuel again and for a proper meal before the final jump across the Gulf.

We splashed down in Tarpon Cove in the evening, wrapping up the long trip across the country. We'd both managed to get some shut-eye but were still utterly exhausted by the time we pulled up to her slip.

We both got a jolt of energy when we saw some happy faces heading toward us down the dock, a furry canine leading the charge with his slobbery tongue hanging out.

My feet had barely touched the planks when Atticus dove into me, knocking me to my butt and nearly sending us both into the drink. He covered my face with licks as I scratched him, paying special attention to his favorite spot behind the ears.

"It's good to see you too, boy."

I looked up as our daughter arrived next, nearly tripping over her flip-flops.

"Hey, there's the genius now," I said, then threw my arms around her.

I stood and offered a hand to Ange, then she and Scarlett embraced. It seemed tighter and longer than usual, Ange having been deeply moved by Jasmine's emotional reunion with her kidnapped son.

"We were only apart a day," Scarlett said. When Ange eventually loosened her grip, she smiled and added, "I see you two managed to make it out without my particular set of skills."

"Barely," I said. "But we never would've found the yacht were it not for you."

She gave a quick, overly dramatic bow. "Happy to be of service. But from what I've seen from online news reports, you did a whole lot more than just find it. What the heck happened?"

Ange and I exchanged glances, then she said, "We'll tell you all about it. Well, mostly all about it. But first we're in dire need of a shower. And a long nap. And some good food."

"And you've still got to tell us all about your adventures in the Grand Canyon," I said. "Your mother mentioned on the flight here that you were quite the hero yourself. Something about a waterfall?"

The Dodge clan loaded into Scarlett's baby-blue Ford Bronco, and we cruised across town with the top down. Though I'd only been gone a short while, it felt good to be back in the capital of the Conch Republic.

It always did.

We made a quick stop at the marina to say hi to Jack and Lauren.

With our new house still little more than a skeleton, and with the Baia's galley barren of food, we decided to book a night at a hotel. Fortunately, it was the back end of spring break, and nearly all of the school-aged tourists had returned north. Sunburned, likely dehydrated, and loaded with exciting stories to tell and memories to savor.

After a quick search, we found a two-night vacancy at Ocean Key Resort right along the waterfront. We were able to get an early check-in, then followed Ange's previously mentioned itinerary. After showering, Ange and I power-napped in the bedroom. Then we woke and ordered room service. Lobster bisque and crab tostadas to start, followed by plates of blackened shrimp and tuna tacos. Then Key lime pie and Cuban bread pudding for dessert.

We ate it all right on the balcony, which had a nice view of Wisteria Island and Sunset Key from three floors up. We also had a peekaboo glimpse of the nearby Mallory Square. It was a great perch to observe boats coming and going, people watch, and take in all the sights and sounds that the heartbeat of Key West has to offer.

We spent the entire next day in the unit. Relaxing and eating and only venturing out to enjoy the waterfront swimming pool.

We had dinner delivered again, this time just before sunset, and watched the famous evening spectacle unfold right in front of our unit.

In Key West, watching a sunset at Mallory Square

is possibly the most touted experience. A real bucket list item. And despite how many times I've seen it, the experience never gets old because it's never quite the same.

In addition to the variances in the colors and luminosity of the sun's rays through the shifting skies, new batches of street performers and visitors inhabit the square every day.

We ran our eyes over the scene, searching for the most interesting and unusual of the bunch. Scarlett spotted a big remote control car with a toy Pomeranian riding around, the little fluffball of a dog sporting purple sunglasses and a tiny cowboy hat. There was also a guy dressed up as a Transformer, one second looking like a robot, then he'd quickly collapse and look like a car the next.

Then, the moment everyone was waiting for arrived. The sun gave in and melted into the sea, shining big and bright over Sunset Key. Shooting rays through the sails of passing boats. Sparkling their rippling wakes to life. A collective moment of awe, followed by the final flicker of brilliant orange. And then it vanished to a familiar soundtrack of cheers and claps and an orchestra of conch shell horns.

It was a sight that demanded reverence. A sight that had mesmerized writers and actors, presidents and popes.

The look and landscape and populace of Key West shifted with every passing year. But the heartbeat, the soul, of Cayo Hueso was one that continued to beat on and live and thrive in the eyes and hearts of all those who visited.

When the evening display was finished, we made

popcorn and settled into the couch to watch a movie. Ever since adopting Scarlett, Ange and I had made a list of our favorite movies she hadn't seen and we'd been working our way through them. That night it was *12 Angry Men*, one of my favorites.

As the classic film began with the courtroom scene, I leaned back with my arms draped over the women of my life while Atticus curled up at our feet. It'd been a fun couple of days while they'd been away. Hanging out with Jack and pretending we were rambunctious kids again. But I'd missed my family.

And it was good to have them back, and to be granted yet another day in paradise.

FORTY-SEVEN

A couple days later, after I'd mostly recuperated from the trying ordeal, we met up with the gang at Salty Pete's. It was a Wednesday night, but the place was packed. We barely managed to squeeze the Tacoma into a space between a telephone pole and the curb, the front right tire up on the concrete edge.

"Good thing you drive a four-by-four," Ange said.

"Isn't needed too often in a county whose highest elevation is twenty feet, but sometimes it comes in handy."

We climbed out and headed across the crammed lot.

"I haven't seen Pete's this packed since Buffett himself showed up," Scarlett said.

Atticus settled into his favorite spot under low-hanging gumbo-limbo branches right by the entrance. The happy Lab enjoyed watching the people come and go, and getting some islander love.

"I'll have Mia bring you out some fish," I said, using a nearby spigot to fill a water bowl laid out for dogs.

We headed inside, greeted by the familiar chime of a bell, the sound of live music emanating from upstairs, and a wave of mouthwatering aromas. Though I'd done what I could to help renovate the place when I'd first moved back to the islands, Pete's felt like a blast from the past. A real island relic, with faded black-and-white pictures on the walls along with various mariner memorabilia and stuffed fish.

Every table was filled as I ran my eyes over the wide-open space.

"Ah, the man of the hour," Mia, the head waitress, said as we filed in.

"What was that?" I said with a confused, friendly smile.

She covered her mouth, then waved me off. "Oh, never mind. Forget I said anything. Pete's got your table reserved upstairs."

She turned on her heel before I could ask her anything more.

Apparently, in addition to Sunny Jim playing, Pete was also running a special on beer. Half off on all island brews.

We headed for the stairs up to the second level of the unique establishment. The second floor was a museum, with rows of glass cases housing artifacts and coins that'd been recovered over the years from Biscayne Bay to the Tortugas. Some of which were even items that I'd played a part in locating, including artifacts from the *Intrepid* wreck, a pirate treasure we'd found on Lignum Vitae Key, and a German U-boat that had run aground off Key Largo.

A big sliding glass door led out to the expansive

balcony. On the left side was a small bar. On the right a stage. And in between was a sea of tables and chairs, all filled save for the one in the far back corner.

We stepped out and threaded our way through the throng of patrons, enjoying a smooth island melody by Sunny Jim, one of my favorite island musicians.

Pete, who I'd last seen fishing barefoot from our Cessna as it had drifted along the Strait at night, rose and bounded our way. The happy islander greeted the three of us with a big hug, then ushered us over to the table.

Jack, Lauren, and Isaac were already there, along with Harper Ridley. And Calihan and his wife, Maggie, were in town, having made the drive down from Marathon.

As we ordered appetizers and drinks, I eyed Pete skeptically. "Half off all island brews?" I said. "You really think that's a good idea?"

The man gave a big belly laugh. "In Key West? It's a terrible idea. Unless you're looking to turn your working restaurant into a zoo. But today is a special night."

"Why's that?" Scarlett said.

The proprietor winked. "You'll all just have to wait and see. But let's just say that Jim is going to be joined by a special pair of islanders later on this evening. I don't want to spoil the surprise, but I think their performance will be the talk of Key West for many weeks to come."

"I wonder who it is?" I whispered to Ange.

The last time Pete had surprised us all with a musical guest, Bubba himself had graced the balcony with his presence and legendary lyrics. Pete's list of friends and acquaintances ran deeper than anyone I'd ever met, and I pondered who he could've possibly gotten next.

Ange grinned and opened her mouth to say something. But as the first word left her lips, a man whose face I unfortunately recognized approached the table.

"Good to see you, Logan," Mayor Nix said with a big smile. "Good to see all of you."

He had his politician voice booming full blast, and he held out his hands as he spoke. Like we were all close friends.

No one at the table replied.

We just stared in awe and utter bafflement at the man.

"Doesn't he know that dogs are supposed to be outside?" Ange whispered into my ear.

I made a face at that. It was an insult to Atticus.

Then Nix patted me on the back and said, "Hey, first round of drinks is on me tonight. I'll see you guys around."

I didn't know what else to do, so I just thanked him, then he sauntered off.

For a brief moment, I thought that maybe I'd misjudged him. That maybe we'd both made bad first impressions on each other and that our butting of heads was just a big misunderstanding.

My mind strove for diplomacy, but my facial expression apparently hadn't gotten the memo.

"You all right, Logan?" Pete said.

I shook my head, snapping myself out of a trance. Then I squeezed the loose skin of forearm. "I'm just checking to make sure I haven't stumbled into an alternate dimension or something."

Scarlett stared bug-eyed at the mayor as he headed inside. "Yeah, what the heck was that about? He's never nice to you, Dad."

"What does he want is the real question," Ange said, folding her arms.

Jack and Pete exchanged glances, then the table fell silent a moment.

I held out my palms, eyebrows raised to the max. "Something we're missing here?"

Jack said, "You guys really don't know?"

We all shook our heads.

"Know what?" Scarlett said.

"The election's coming up," Pete said, then cleared his throat. "For mayor. And there's word on the coconut telegraph that Logan Dodge might run."

I nearly spat Key limeade all over the table.

"What?" Ange said, shaking her head.

"You've got to be kidding me," I added. "Just months ago I was public enemy number one. My name tarnished and trampled by most of the news outlets from here to Bar Harbor."

Pete rubbed his silver beard. "I think I recall reading a quote somewhere about crowds being fickle. Could just be this foggy brain talking, though."

I fell silent, utterly baffled by the idea and wondered who could've possibly spread such a rumor.

"Nix is wasting his brownnosing," Jack said. Then my best friend turned to me. "Logan, what are the chances you'd ever run for mayor?"

"Zero," I said without giving the idea a moment's

thought. "Not in a million years."

Jack chuckled. "That's what I thought."

"Though it would be nice to see Nix lose," Ange said.

"I think Pete should run," Scarlett said between bites of conch fritter.

"Yeah," Isaac chimed in. "If anyone should be mayor, it should be you."

Pete leaned back and laughed. "Well, you two have just earned bottomless fritters for life."

"You've never thought about it?" Ange said.

"When I'm not thinking about fishing or diving or running this place?"

"So never," Jack said, causing everyone to laugh.

The entrées showed up, and we all ate while listening to the music and enjoying each other's company.

While eating dessert, Pete leaned over to me. "Jack told me about your lobster duel this year."

"Yeah, too bad," I said. "I guess neither of us will be gracing your establishment with our vocal talents this year."

Pete grinned as he shrugged. "Maybe. Maybe not."

"Neither of us lost, Pete," Jack said. "I guess we'll have to wait and see until next year's duel."

Pete took a slow sip of his margarita. "Neither of you lost, but neither of you won, either." He paused, looking back and forth between us. "Isn't your deal that the winner avoids the stage?"

My laid-back expression turned serious in a blink as my slightly intoxicated mind realized where he was going with this. And one look at Jack told me it'd just clicked for him as well.

"Don't you boys worry," Pete said before either of us could say anything. "I've got a healthy collection of duets."

He motioned toward the stage. Jack and I gazed forward, and for the first time I noticed that Pete's ancient karaoke machine was set up at the corner with two microphones already plugged into the unit. Everything ready to go.

Pete's smile broadened. "Only question is, however will I pick just one?"

Before Jack or I could utter a sound, Pete turned to my daughter. "Scarlett, do you think you could do me a favor and help me pick one out?"

She pushed her chair back in a flash and rose, a huge grin on her face as she looked at Jack and me. "It'd be my honor, Pete."

My mouth went slack as they pranced away, heading over to the edge of the stage and sifting through an old case of CDs. Unable to believe the unexpected and unfortunate rapid turn of events, I sat speechless. Then I turned to Ange, and my wife just giggled, so I shot Jack a look.

"Can he do this?" I said.

Jack turned pale, then chuckled.

"Hey," Ange said, patting me on the back. "A deal's a deal. Pete's right. Neither of you won." She slipped her smartphone out and patted my knee. "Don't worry, babe. I'll be sure to get nice footage of it so we can cherish this moment for years to come."

I stared at my wife. She and Lauren had been cracking up uncontrollably since Pete had revealed the night's surprise.

"You knew about this, didn't you?" I said,

narrowing my gaze at Ange.

She laughed again. "Of course. Who do you think gave Pete the idea to do half-off beer to ensure this place would be packed to the brim on a Wednesday evening?"

"Wow," I said, rubbing my chin. "You never expect your own family to betray you."

She playfully hit my arm. "Oh, come on. It won't be so bad."

"We're gonna need another drink," Jack said, motioning for the attention of the nearest waitress.

Scarlett jumped over by the stage, beaming as she held up a CD. The look on her face as she scampered back to our table told me everything. Jack and I were in big trouble.

"We picked it!" she exclaimed loud enough for half the balcony to hear her. "Oh, you're both going to love it."

She told us, and when the waitress came over, I corrected Jack. We were going to need another pitcher.

Jack and I downed drinks and were far gone by the time Pete called us up to the stage. We stumbled our way through a crowd that hollered and cheered us on and patted us on the back.

"I've got the volume cranked up," Pete said with another wink as he handed us each a microphone. "They'll hear you two all the way over on Stock Island."

We stepped on stage and the music started. Fortunately, I don't remember much, having downed more alcohol in the time leading up to the performance than I have in years. We belted out "It's

Raining Men" in a blur of slurred words and loud, off-pitch notes. But the claps and cheers were off the charts. We kept singing even after the music finished, adding our own special finishing touches by throwing off our shirts and spinning them over our heads.

The next thing I remember, I was sprawled out on the back seat of Scarlett's Bronco with Atticus on my lap. Ange helped me down the dock to the Baia, and I passed out on the sunbed with my wife in my arms.

"Best night ever," she said with a sly grin, then kissed me on the cheek.

EPILOGUE

News of Lucius Xavier's evil little empire and his years of abuse and murder spread like wildfire. Two more big names were caught up in the scandal that had sent shockwaves through Tinseltown. Fortunately, the story we'd cooked up for what'd gone down on the yacht had been bought and circulated, thanks partially to help offered by Maddox from the inside, so our involvement was never discovered.

Scarlett returned to school following her event-filled spring break, the sociable, easygoing teenager enjoying her sophomore year. Ange and I passed our time in the usual fashion. Days out on the water, spearfishing, and diving and exploring. Helping Jack and Lauren at the marina. And lending a hand with our new house. Though neither of us were craftsmen, Ange and I had fun helping out, and kept particularly busy with the bathroom tiling, wood floors, and new wraparound porch. The house was shaping up nicely, and the Dodge family was eager to move back into a larger space.

A couple weeks after the incident in California, we had a nice group of friends able to get away for an afternoon out on the water. We dropped anchor near the Eastern Dry Rocks, a cluster of bank reefs just seven miles southeast from the marina.

Jack had the *Calypso*, his forty-five-foot Sea Ray he'd used for fishing and dive charters for years, anchored down thirty yards from *Dodging Bullets II*. He, Lauren, and Isaac were all able to get out for an entire afternoon. And the whole Dodge clan was there, along with Pete and Cameron.

Jack had been talking my ear off about some new water toys he'd acquired from a watersports company that'd upgraded its equipment for quite some time, and was eager to try them out on the open water. We used a compressor to pump up a twelve-foot tall climbing tower with a slide, along with a floating trampoline.

We spent hours climbing, sliding, bouncing, and splashing in the tropical paradise. Then we dipped beneath the surface, freediving the colorful reef laid out beneath us. Given that we'd picked a weekday and were anchored to a lesser known section of the reef, we had the area completely to ourselves. And with a crisp blue sky overhead and barely a breath of wind, we had all the ingredients for a perfect day.

The kind of day you live for.

When our stomachs began to rumble, we gathered up on the bridge of Jack's Sea Ray and enjoyed a lunch of grilled grouper, shrimp kabobs, and garlic potato wedges. To drink, Ange brought out the fifty-year-old bottle of Glenlivet she'd taken from Wessel's office. And we filled glasses and toasted to family and friends.

When the savory meal was finished, Pete carried up a Key Lime pie from below deck.

"Fresh from Blue Heaven this morning," he proclaimed.

We sliced it up and we savored the artistic, otherworldly combination of citrus, sweet, and tart resting on a foundation of graham cracker crust and covered in mountains of baked meringue topping. The signature dessert of the Keys has always been a favorite of mine, and I've never tasted any better than Blue Heaven's. The fabled dish was a true work of art.

While we all ate and relished the creamy blend of sweetness, Scarlett glanced at her phone, then perked up. She angled the screen closer to her face and shielded her eyes from the sun reflecting off the turquoise waters around us.

"Something you want to share with the group there, Scar?" Ange said.

Her eyes ran over the screen a couple silent seconds more, then she beamed and chuckled.

"Dad, you're gonna want to see this," she said, handing the device over to me.

I swallowed a big bite of nirvana incarnate, then angled the screen. Ange leaned over my left shoulder, Jack over my right. All of us eyeing a recent post Jasmine Cruz had made on Facebook.

There were three pictures, one of herself in a bikini wearing a snorkel mask. One of her feet dangling over a boat's bow. And the third was her standing in front of the southernmost marker, wearing a big hoodie and leaning against the concrete buoy. It was the picture I'd snapped of her during our morning run.

My eyes drifted down to the caption.

Despite recent unfortunate events, my trip to the Florida Keys had silver linings. I fell in love with the enchanting tropical paradise, and hope to be back someday. And though he's never sought recognition, I'd like to thank a guardian angel for saving my life. You're a true hero. Thank you, Owen.

Then she wrapped up the post with a wink and a heart.

After I read the message twice, Scarlett said, "You know, Dad, if I didn't know any better, I'd say that Jasmine Cruz likes you."

"Oh she definitely likes him," Jack chimed in.

"You were never nervous?" Scarlett said, turning to Ange. "Even when you found out she'd spent the night on the Baia with Dad?"

My wife savored her final bite of pie, then shook her head. "No. I trust your father."

Scarlett turned to me, and I cleared my throat and said, "You don't step off the mound when you're throwing a perfect game. You don't fold a winning hand."

Ange chuckled and held me tighter. "Ooh, keep going."

I smiled confidently at my beautiful wife. "Nothing against Jasmine, but I think Paul Newman said it better than I ever could. 'Why would I go out for a hamburger when I've got steak at home?'"

Ange tilted her head back and smiled. "There's that silver tongue of yours. Don't open your mouth too wide or we're all gonna go blind from the glare."

I laughed and added, "Besides, Ange gets flirted with far more than I do. We all know that I'm the reacher and she's the settler here." I glanced back and forth at my little family. "I'm just lucky you two let me stick around."

Ange and I kissed, and I noticed a thin layer of moisture in her eyes.

"Well," Scarlett said, "before you go flattering us too much, maybe you should hear my new ringtone."

She held it up, then played "It's Raining Men" full blast, a huge smile on her face.

"I've set it for you so I'll hear it every time you call me."

I pinched my bottom lip, then turned to my wife. "Ange, we're new to this whole parenting thing, but can we ground her until she's eighteen?"

She chuckled, then slid out her phone. Tapped the screen, then played the same tune. "I set it as my ringtone too."

"Me three," Lauren said, holding out her phone and playing the song I could live the rest of my life without hearing again and be just fine.

Everyone got a nice kick out of their new ringtones, and Pete nearly fell out of his chair.

I let them wrap up, then leaned back and eyed my best friend who sat across from me with Lauren in his lap. "Hey, Jack, weren't there more toys you got from the watersports place?" I said, shooting him a sly look.

He smiled, then nodded and we both rose.

"There are more?" Scarlett exclaimed.

"Oh yeah," I said, patting her on the shoulder.

I followed Jack down the steps and into the saloon, then reached up to a storage locker and pulled out two toys we'd both been itching to test out. After a quick stop at the sink, we marched barefoot back out into the sun and up the steps, our super soakers fully loaded and held at the ready.

"No, Logan," my wife gasped as we returned to the bridge. "We have our clothes on!"

That wasn't going to save them.

Jack and I opened fire, blasting two thick streams toward the women. They ducked for cover and scrambled out from behind the table, and were all drenched and dripping by the time they came to their feet.

Jack and I sprang down and aft in retreat, maintaining steady cover fire on the three as they closed in. My liquid ammunition ran dry as I reached the swim platform, and I turned to see my wife charging toward me. With nothing more to lose, Ange dove into me, sending us both flying over the edge and into the translucent sea.

THE END

Note to Reader

I hope you enjoyed this latest adventure. If you'd like to continue the sea stories of Logan, Ange, Jack, and company, you can find more installments in the Florida Keys Adventure Series on my Amazon page.

In recent novels I've been featuring some of my favorite island musicians—artists who capture the soul and rhythm of the tropics. Sunny Jim has been one of my favorites for quite some time. If you'd like to learn about him and check out his music you can visit his website at: sunnyjim.com

I'd like to offer a special thanks to you, my loyal readers. I'm constantly blown away by your support, whether it be reviews, comments, messages, or recommendations of my stories.

Cheers to the next adventure,
Matthew

LOGAN DODGE ADVENTURES

Gold in the Keys
Hunted in the Keys
Revenge in the Keys
Betrayed in the Keys
Redemption in the Keys
Corruption in the Keys
Predator in the Keys
Legend in the Keys
Abducted in the Keys
Showdown in the Keys
Avenged in the Keys
Broken in the Keys
Payback in the Keys
Condemned in the Keys
Voyage in the Keys
Guardian in the Keys
Menace in the Keys

JASON WAKE NOVELS

Caribbean Wake
Surging Wake
Relentless Wake
Turbulent Wake
Furious Wake
Perilous Wake

Join the Adventure!
Sign up for my newsletter to receive updates on upcoming books on my website:

matthewrief.com

About the Author

Matthew has a deep-rooted love for adventure and the ocean. He loves traveling, diving, and writing adventure novels. Though he grew up in the Pacific Northwest, he currently lives in Virginia Beach with his wife, Jenny.

Made in the USA
Columbia, SC
26 October 2022